GW01018242

PUBLISH AND BE DEAD

TONY SAUNDERS

APS BOOKS
Yorkshire

APS Books,
The Stables Field Lane,
Aberford,
West Yorkshire,
LS25 3AE

APS Books is a subsidiary of the APS Publications imprint

www.andrewsparke.com

Copyright ©2022 Tony Saunders
All rights reserved.

Tony Saunders has asserted his right to be identified as the author of this work in accordance with the Copyright Designs and Patents Act 1988

First published worldwide by APS Books in 2022

This is a work of fiction. Names, characters, places and incidents either are products of the author's imagination or are used fictitiously. Any resemblance to actual events or locales or persons, living or dead, is entirely coincidental.

No part of this publication may be reproduced, stored in or introduced into a retrieval system, or transmitted, in any form, or by any means (electronic, mechanical, photocopying, recording or otherwise) without the written permission of the publisher except that brief selections may be quoted or copied without permission, provided that full credit is given.

A catalogue record for this book is available from the British Library

PUBLISH AND BE DEAD

1

All this will disappear if that bloody man Burtonlee gets his way, muttered Sophie to herself as she gazed at the open farmland at the end of her garden. *There must be a way to stop him.* She ground her teeth in frustration at the mere thought of his name.

Standing in front of the kitchen window of her isolated cottage, washing up after her solitary lunch, her thoughts were interrupted by her mobile phone sitting on the worktop next to the sink. The phone began to slide across the unit as it vibrated. Sophie grabbed a tea towel, quickly dried her hands and picked up the phone, glancing at the screen. She didn't recognise the number. She touched the green icon to answer it.

'Hullo…Hullo? Hullo?'

There was no one at the other end. The screen went dark again as the caller rang off.

Puzzled, she put it down, wondering whether it was just a wrong number or another whistle blower who had changed his mind at the last minute. Resuming the washing up, she thought about the acres of farmland stretching into the distance beyond her small garden. The whole area was steeped in history with its ancient hedgerows and drover tracks, and rich in both flora and fauna. Now, Burtonlee Homes, a Kent based private developer, planned to fill the land with several thousand houses, shops and schools, turning a peaceful hamlet into a small town.

Nobody wanted it. Sophie, after twenty years as an investigative journalist with a leading Fleet Street newspaper, *The Daily Enquirer,* now had her own national television programme, *Ask Sophie,* and had been looking into Burtonlee Homes for a while. She had received a mountain of consumer complaints from people who had bought houses from the company. Now she had joined the local action group to oppose the scheme.

The company knew that she was part of this local pressure group. With her national television profile, she represented a tangible threat to the project, and possibly even to their long term business. A whistle blower had told her that the developer was in serious financial trouble. Terry Burtonlee, the owner, had just gone through an expensive and messy divorce, so he needed to build this huge estate to rescue his personal finances. She had also been tipped off, anonymously, by someone alleging that brown envelopes had been passed around to bribe certain local councillors. Burtonlee wanted to ensure planning permission would be tacitly agreed before the formal application was made. If this did not go through then his business might fail.

To add to her problems, Sophie now had complications in her private life. Her husband, Richard, a partner in a prominent City insurance broking firm, had walked out five weeks ago.

Her emotions were still raw as she recalled the evening he'd arrived home from his office and calmly announced he was leaving her for another woman. It was just like one of his business deals. Dispassionate. Finished. Next…

Even worse, he had packed his clothes into those two expensive designer suitcases she had given him recently as an anniversary present, put them in his car and just driven out of her life. She certainly hadn't seen it coming – she had always believed their lives together were perfect - although in retrospect, maybe the clues were there when they had bought that isolated cottage.

It was supposed to be a haven of peace and quiet for Sophie to concentrate on her work as a journalist and somewhere for Richard to return to unwind after a pressured day in the City. Richard had been unimpressed at first by a cottage called The Piggery. *Damned stupid name,* he had protested when they had bought it, but Sophie thought it gave the cottage a certain cachet and rustic charm. His partners had pulled his leg when he and Sophie had first moved there until, thankfully, the joke had worn off.

He had also complained bitterly when he had been persuaded to sell his beloved Porsche 911. He had bowed, reluctantly, to Sophie's suggestion that a 4 x 4 was a more sensible vehicle for the narrow rutted lanes around the cottage and had replaced it with a Range Rover. It was more practical but not as much fun as the Porsche.

The shock of his departure had proved too much for her. Her lip had quivered, but she had managed to keep her composure until he had driven off, when all self-control had gone. She had collapsed, sobbing uncontrollably, on the bed they had shared, and eventually cried herself to sleep. When she woke up next morning, the reflection that greeted her in the mirror was bad news – red, tear stained cheeks and very puffy eyes. She knew even the most skilled make-up artist at the television studio would have been unable to make her presentable for the cameras that day.

She had considered removing her wedding and engagement rings permanently and putting them in a drawer out of sight. On a whim, she transferred them to the third finger of her right hand. Surprisingly, they were a good fit. Maybe it was a sign. She twisted them absentmindedly whilst she contemplated a future without Richard. She had been independent before she met him, so she'd just have to get used to it again.

Now, she was trying to get on with her life. Too many people depended on her, particularly the producer and team behind her television programme. With a new series about to start, she had to face the world and put her personal problems behind her. Then there was *The Daily Enquirer,* the national newspaper where she had started her career and made her reputation. She was still contracted to provide articles for the paper on a regular basis.

She stared out of the kitchen window, taking in the view, trying to clear her head and concentrate. There was a small wood a couple of hundred yards away and she thought she saw a flash or reflection.

The birdwatchers are out again with their binoculars, she thought. *Plenty for them to see round here. Fields and hedges are full of birds. Burtonlee will ruin it all if he gets his way. The wood pigeons had better watch out, too. A peregrine falcon dived on one in flight last week, hitting it in a cloud of feathers before carrying it off. Absolutely incredible.*

Finishing the washing up, she put the plates and cutlery on the rack to drain, and reached for the tea towel. Her mind was still elsewhere as she picked up a large soapy metal serving spoon. Distracted, she allowed it to slip from her hand and it landed with a resounding clang on the quarry tiled floor and bounced under the dresser.

'Damn,' she muttered in exasperation.

She dropped to one knee to pick it up.

There was a sudden explosion of breaking glass, and she was aware of a movement in the air above her, followed by a thud on the lime plastered stone wall behind. All this in a split second, but it seemed longer, almost in slow motion.

She looked up at the window in front of the sink, exactly where she had been standing a moment before. Shocked, she saw a hole punched through the double glazing, with ragged edges and cracks spreading, spiderlike, in all directions. The wall behind her was chipped. Horrified, she realised the damage must have been done by a bullet.

This was no accident. Someone had tried to kill her...

2

Her heart racing, Sophie tried to collect her thoughts. *Who could have fired the shot? Journalists weren't killed in England, were they?* She knew she had upset quite a few seriously influential people in the past, but had never thought it would come to this. Even the police hadn't been very interested in all those threats against her posted anonymously on line.

Irrationally, thoughts of the peregrine falcon flashed into her mind.

Exactly what happened to that unfortunate pigeon? One moment, it was flying across the field looking for food - the next moment…dead.

Her experience in pursuing and exposing high profile wrongdoers had given her inner strength, and a sense of self-preservation took over. She reasoned it wouldn't be smart to stand up. Her mobile was still on the kitchen worktop and she couldn't risk reaching for it. Instead, she crawled out of the kitchen along the passageway into the small front living room to reach for the house phone on a side table. Picking it up from its base, she tapped in 999.

'Emergency. Which service do you require?'

'The police. Quickly, please.'

'I'm putting you through.'

'Police. How can I assist?'

'I need help here immediately. Someone's just tried to kill me.' She was trying to appear calm, but her voice was rising as the adrenalin kicked in and her pulse rate had gone into overdrive. 'They may come back.'

'Try to stay calm. Can we start with your name?'

'Sophie Blaxstone.'

'Address?'

'The Piggery. It's a cottage in Blackthorn Lane, near Foggenden.' She gave the postcode.

'What exactly happened?'

'Someone's just tried to shoot me. There's a bullet hole in the window, exactly where I was standing a moment before. I dropped something on the floor and as I bent down to pick it up, I heard the glass break. If I'd been standing there it would have killed me. I'm terrified. Whoever was responsible may come here any minute to try again. I need protection. I've been threatened in the past but…'

'We'll get an armed response unit there as soon as possible. In the meantime, stay away from the windows, out of sight and don't answer the door. You'll hear the siren when they arrive.

Time just dragged. Minutes passed and seemed like hours. Sophie felt vulnerable, crouched on the floor. What if whoever had fired the shot came to the house to check and finish the job? She was concerned that she might be visible through the window. Crawling behind the settee, taking the cordless phone with her, she tried to make herself as small as possible, almost burrowing into the fabric and wondering whether help really was on the way. She tried to calm down, to rationalise. It was a good job her viewers couldn't see her now. The smart and attractive host of a national television series had been reduced to a frightened figure hiding behind the sofa, in her scruffy tee shirt, old jeans, hair all over the place and no makeup. That wouldn't help her public image at all.

Despite threats in the past, she'd never really felt vulnerable until now.

Worse still, Richard was no longer there to protect her. She started thinking about past cases, stories she'd written in the national press for *The Daily Enquirer*, some of which had resulted in dire outcomes for the people who were the subjects of those articles. Then there were the television exposures. She certainly hadn't gone out of her way to make friends. Richard had commented on it a number of times, expressing his concern for her welfare. It was a good job she still had the files. The police would want to look at them, of course.

3

At last, Sophie heard the welcome sound of a police siren.

She crawled to the front of the room, stood up and cautiously peered out at the lane from behind the curtain.

A marked police car had arrived outside the cottage. Two uniformed policemen carefully got out They were wearing anti-stab vests and were armed with Tasers, personal radios and holstered Glock 9mm pistols. More significantly they were carrying Heckler and Koch G36 carbines as they surveyed the house from behind the car.

Sophie tried to attract their attention from the corner of the window. Spotting her they moved cautiously up the path, looking carefully around them.

She opened the front door.

'Thank goodness you've come. Someone tried to kill me. If I hadn't bent down to pick up the spoon I dropped, the bullet would have hit me.'

'Where did this happen?'

She pointed to the kitchen.

'Out there. It's the window. That's where the bullet came through. It hit the wall behind.'

The first officer, satisfied there was no one around, pointed to a flattened piece of metal on the floor.

'That's where the bullet finished up. Crime Scene Investigation will need to look at this.'

Meanwhile, his colleague was swiftly searching the rest of the house, and re-joined them, shaking his head. 'No sign of forced entry. The other rooms are all secure. I'll just check to make sure there's no one around outside.'

He spoke into his personal radio.

'No further problems here. There's definitely been a shooting. Whoever was responsible has gone. You can send CID in now. You'll need uniformed as well to secure the place until the Crime Scene Investigators have had a look.' He turned to Sophie and said, 'We'll wait until the CID gets here, and if they're happy, then we'll leave them to it.'

4

A knock at the door.

A man and a younger woman stood there.

The man was probably in his early forties, clean shaven, above average height with neatly styled dark brown hair, wearing a mid-grey suit, white shirt and a striped tie. *Someone who takes a pride in his appearance,* thought Sophie. *Not bad looking.* He also had a serious air about him. Was it this situation, or was he preoccupied with something else?

The woman with him was about five feet six inches tall, slim build, with short blonde hair. She was not wearing make-up. It was her outfit that caught Sophie's attention. She couldn't help noticing the very smart trouser suit. It made Sophie feel dowdy in the casual 'at home' clothes that Richard had frequently complained about. On the other hand, she hadn't expected any visitors that day.

'Detective Inspector Trussell, Kent CID,' said the man, offering a warrant card as he stepped into the hall, 'and this is Detective Sergeant Joynton, It's Mrs Blaxstone, isn't it? Can you just run through what happened?'

Sophie recounted the sequence of events, led them into the kitchen and showed them the broken window, the chipped wall and the flattened bullet lying on the quarry tiled floor.

'There was nothing to warn you? Did you see anyone outside?'

'No, but now you mention it, I did see a flash in that small wood over there earlier.' She pointed to the trees a couple of hundred yards away. 'I'm quite used to seeing the birdwatchers, and I thought it was light reflecting off someone's binoculars. Although, now I think of it, they're not usually around on a weekday. It's more of a weekend activity.'

'I see,' said Trussell. 'We'll need to look over there.'

He located the chip in the back wall, and standing in front of it, lined it up with the bullet hole in the window.

'Certainly came from that direction, Jackie,' he said, turning to his colleague, who had been busy writing in her notebook. 'Could be a professional hit - if so, someone would need a pretty serious reason. We'll take a look over there as soon as uniformed get here. They can tape the area off. Then we can turn the Crime Scene Investigators loose on it. They may just find something that could help us.'

Turning to Sophie, he asked, 'Are there any other houses near those woods? We'll need to talk to anyone living there to find out whether they noticed anything - any strangers around today.'

'There are a couple of cottages over there. I know John Shalford. He lives in Ivy Cottage. He's on our action committee. We're trying to fight Burtonlee's proposed development on the farm land over there.'

'At what time approximately did this happen?'

'About 1.45, I guess. My 999 call should be able to confirm that.'

'Have you noticed anything unusual around here in the last few days?' Have you seen any strangers or had any uninvited callers?'

Sophie shook her head. She thought about the earlier call on her mobile and mentioned it.

'Do you have any idea who might have any sort of grudge against you or any reason for something like this?'

'I've upset quite a few people in my time.'

While he was speaking, Trussell had been studying her intently. He was struck immediately by her piercing blue eyes. *Fortyish*, he thought, *about five feet eight inches tall, casually dressed in old well-worn top and jeans, with her light brown hair dragged back. No make-up, yet still attractive.* He thought she looked vaguely familiar.

'I've seen you somewhere. Was it on television?'

'Yes,' said Sophie, 'I'm involved with a consumer programme these days.'

'Of course, *'Ask Sophie.'* You're Sophie Breckton. I didn't make the connection.'

'Blaxstone is my married name.'

'Have you contacted your husband yet?'

'No point. He left me about five weeks ago. It seems he's got another woman in tow. If he wants to speak to me, he has my mobile number, of course. There's always a slim chance he might have a change of heart at some time, but I'm not holding my breath. He's probably having a midlife crisis. There doesn't seem any reason to call him.'

'Is there anyone else you can talk to? What about a relation or friend? You can't stay here now. You'll need to move somewhere safer. This is now officially a crime scene. But we can talk about it shortly.'

'I'm quite alone now. I don't have any living relatives, and I haven't really made any close friends locally since we moved here a year ago. My work keeps me very busy. I do know some of the people in the local action group who're trying to resist Burtonlee's development of the land over there…' She pointed at the fields beyond the garden. 'It's ironic that I've been working on a whole raft of complaints from people who've bought Burtonlee homes elsewhere, and now the company want to build several thousand houses at the end of my garden.'

DS Joynton carried on noting this down as Sophie spoke.

'Well,' said Trussell, 'apart from putting Mr Burtonlee's nose out of joint, who else do you think you might have upset?'

'You only have to look at my Social Media pages,' she said. 'I've reported some of the threats and abuse in the past, but I'm afraid some of your colleagues were quite dismissive. They told me not to take them seriously. They referred to them as *just a bunch of nutters, trolls and keyboard warriors*. Well, maybe someone will start listening now and take them more seriously.'

'We'll have to look at all of them to find someone sufficiently motivated to actually do something about it. Do you have easy access to your old stories?'

'Yes, I work from my laptop now, so everything is on flash drives and backed up on a portable hard drive and the Cloud, these days.'

'I'm afraid you'll have to be prepared to spend a fair amount of time with us as we review those articles. You can't stay in the cottage. You'll have to relocate to somewhere more secure. I suggest you pack a couple of bags with everything you need and we'll move you out of here. Unfortunately, we can't offer you an official safe house - they don't exist in today's world.'

'What about the Castle Inn in the High Street, Jim?' said DS Joynton, 'That would be convenient to the station, and Mrs Blaxstone would certainly be safer there. As you know, I live just around the corner in that new block of flats, so I could see her safely into the hotel and make sure she's settled. I could even ride in her car, while you take yours back to the station. She might have to think about somewhere a little more permanent until this whole matter has been resolved, maybe renting a flat short term. She obviously can't come back here at the moment. She'd better call the Castle now and book a room.'

Sophie did as she was told and called the Castle Inn from her bedroom. Then she packed, reappearing twenty minutes later, having changed into something more presentable. She dropped a suitcase in the hall, and went back for another.

'I'll help you take them to the car,' said DS Joynton. 'Are you sure you feel up to driving now, Mrs Blaxstone?'

'Yes, of course. I'm OK now.'

When Sophie emerged from the front door, she noticed other, uniformed police officers had turned up, and they had already drawn official crime scene tapes around the cottage. Her cases were carried to her distinctive red BMW with personalised plates, and she stowed them in the boot.

'Perhaps you can wait inside while we have a quick look around the woods over there,' said Trussell. 'These officers will stay until we get back.'

Sophie hadn't even noticed the armed response team had gone. The time just seemed to have rushed past. She looked at her watch - five o'clock already.

She needed something to do.

'Can I make us all a cup of tea?' she asked.

'Good idea. Say in about thirty minute's time?'

Trussell and Joynton got into his car, and, followed by one of the other police cars, set off for the woods looking for the place where the shot had been fired from.

Half an hour later, they were back, just as the Crime Scene Investigator arrived with his assistant.

They put on the usual hooded paper suits and plastic overshoes before entering the cottage, carrying boxes with their equipment.

One of them greeted Trussell. 'Hallo, Jim. What've you got for us?'

'A shooting, but nothing much for you to see here, really. We reckon the weapon was fired from a couple of hundred yards away.'

He took them into the kitchen and showed them the broken window, the chipped wall, and the flattened bullet on the floor. He explained briefly what had happened, pointing out the woods in the distance. 'We've already been over there and taped off the area. The evidence certainly points to the shot being fired from that direction. Mind you the ground's very dry over there, as you'd expect at this time of year, so not much chance of footprints or any other tracks. The situation's complicated because Mrs Blaxstone tells us a lot of birdwatchers use the area, mainly at weekends. Anyway, see if you can turn up anything. We've uniformed talking to the people nearby to see if anyone noticed anything unusual.

'Shouldn't take us too long in here, Jim,' said the senior officer. There's just the kitchen to photograph. No point in dusting for prints or looking for anything else if there were no intruders. We'll be finished in ten minutes.'

As soon as they had gone, Sophie took the cups and saucers out to the kitchen and put them in the bowl to soak. 'Somehow, I don't feel like washing up now,' she said. 'It's too dangerous around here.'

As they prepared to leave, Trussell asked, 'Do you have an alarm? If so I suggest you set it and secure the house. We'll be leaving a couple of PCSOs here for a while to talk to anyone passing by, just in case someone saw or heard anything. They won't need any access to the house.'

Trussell climbed into his dark blue Skoda Octavia, an eight year old automatic, instinctively looking at the empty passenger seat next to him, where Annette had always sat. He still thought of her – he couldn't help himself. Snapping out of an all too frequent reverie, he turned the ignition key and moved the gear selector to drive. He pulled away from the cottage in the direction of Woodchester, followed by Sophie's red BMW with DS Joynton in the passenger seat.

The PCSOs left to watch the cottage had walked round the back to the garden for a moment to see where the shot had come from. As the two cars moved off down the narrow lane, neither driver noticed a silver Mercedes 4 x 4 with darkened windows appear from around the corner to follow them at a discreet distance.

5

Trussell parked in his allocated space and locked his car. Inside the station he went upstairs to the CID office on the first floor. It was a long room, divided in two by a double bank of back to back filing cupboards with a laser printer sitting on top of one of the low cabinets.

He turned right into the area occupied by his team, with its four desks all fitted with computer screens and keyboards. A table in the corner contained a kettle, coffee percolator, teapot and assorted cups, saucers and well used mugs. Standing alongside was a half full box of teabags and a coffee jar. A battered metal biscuit tin stood at the back.

He glanced at his desk in case there were any urgent messages. There weren't.

The two young detective constables in his team, Mark Green and Tim Beach, had been tidying up after solving their last serious case. They were a contrasting pair. Mark Green, in his late twenties, had joined the CID over a year ago after six years in uniform. Unsurprisingly he was more traditional and thoughtful in his approach to the job and was usually seen wearing sports jackets and what he insisted on calling slacks. Trussell believed that he had the makings of a good detective. His colleague, Tim Beach, just twenty one, had only joined the unit four months earlier and was still learning. He tended to favour informality, usually evidenced by jeans and either a hoodie or a leather jacket.

The older man was removing pictures from the crime white board on the wall at the back of the office and wiping it clean. Both looked in Trussell's direction when he walked in.

'The last of the Scoular files have gone off to the CPS, as you asked, Guv,' said Green. 'There's nothing more for us to do, unless they have any further questions. By the way, I took a picture of the board as a record, in case you need anything from it. All clear and ready when something else turns up. Suppose we'll have to look at some of the historic stuff for now.'

'Well done, Greeno. Timing is everything! Get on your computer and download a photo for your nice clean board. We have got something serious to look into tomorrow.'

Green looked at him quizzically.

'Give me a name, Guv?'

'Sophie Breckton'

'You mean the woman on the telly?'

'One and the same. But use her married name, Blaxstone, on the board. Spelt with an X. Someone tried to kill her this afternoon at her cottage. A shot was fired at her while she was standing in front of the kitchen window. Looks like it could be a professional job at the moment. I want it kept quiet for now. The press don't know about it yet and I want it to stay that way as long as possible.'

'OK. I'll organise it, Guv.'

Satisfied they had completed their preparations to set this new investigation in motion in the morning, Trussell told the two detective constables to go home. 'You may as well pack up now. You'll have to get used to putting the hours in again from tomorrow morning. Jackie's taken Mrs Blaxstone to the Castle Inn, so we'll have a team meeting in the morning, when she gets in. Then we'll have a better idea where to start.'

When the others had left, Trussell looked around, nodded his satisfaction and walked out and down the steps to the car park. He had a plan. Since his wife, had died - about six years ago after a short, unexpected illness - he had tried to immerse himself in his work. Liz, his daughter, had gone off to University last year and his house seemed a very lonely place, so he rarely cooked for himself these days. He preferred to work late and spend as little time at home as possible now. He also had little appetite for office socialising these days, despite Jackie's efforts to change things, although she had managed lately to get him to the pub with his team.

This evening was different – he had some research to do, so he stopped off at his local Tandoori to pick up a takeaway. They had got to know him quite well recently. As he opened the door, he sniffed the usual heady aroma of mixed spices with the appreciation it deserved..

'King Prawn Biryani, Mr Trussell?' the manager asked. 'The usual Peshwari Nan bread as well?' Trussell inclined his head. 'Certainly, Sir. Ten minutes. Would you like a drink while you are waiting?'

'No thank you, Ranjeet. I'm in a hurry tonight. Work to do.'

He tapped his debit card on the reader and sat down to wait.

The meal appeared as promised ten minutes later in the usual paper carrier bag with the restaurant's name, *The Golden Elephant*, emblazoned upon it. Trussell took it from the waiter, smiled his thanks, and headed for his car, which was right outside. Thank goodness there was no one else he knew in there. He didn't have time for chatting tonight. He needed to concentrate on one subject and only one – work.

Ten minutes later, he pulled onto the drive of his semi-detached house on the outskirts of town. He and Annette had bought it fifteen years ago, and as new estates went, it wasn't a bad place to live – if only it wasn't still so full of memories for him.

He took the bag containing his meal from the floor carpet where he had put it to avoid marking the seat, got out of the car and carefully locked it. Turning the key in the front door, he looked down at the mat to check for post and then stepped inside. He carried the food through to the kitchen, left it on the worktop just inside and then took off his jacket, putting it on a hanger in the under stairs cupboard. He went straight to the fridge for a beer, put the food on a plate and the plate on a tray. He then settled down in his favourite armchair. Switching on the television, he found the catch up channel and surfed through the programmes until he found what he was looking for. It was the entire previous series of *Ask Sophie*.

I may as well start at the beginning, he thought. *Episode1. This should give me a better idea of what we're dealing with. Get some idea of how she operates.*

Within minutes he was thinking, *So this is the real Sophie Breckton. She looks a bit different to today's victim.* She was smart, attractive, articulate, smooth, and self-assured - totally at ease with her studio audience. She seemed quite unflappable in her interrogation of the dodgy traders and the others she'd was interviewing in the film clips. *Those piercing blue eyes must seem quite intimidating to anyone she's pursuing.* They showed real character and determination. She was obviously hugely popular. *Almost an institution these days.*

His phone rang. He picked it up and glanced at the screen. The caller was his daughter. He hit the stop button on the television remote.

'Hi, Liz. Nice surprise. How's Uni? Working hard, I hope. Not too much partying?'

It was nice to hear her voice. He knew she had a life at University, and couldn't expect her to call him too often but they had always been close and he missed her.

'Yes, I'm fine, love. I've been busy today with a new case. Can't say too much as it involves a rather well known personality…Yes, a lady. Good guess! I'm just doing some research while I eat my dinner…Yes, at home. I picked up a takeaway. You know me. I can't be bothered to cook for one.'

He listened intently, pleased Liz had rung. She always seemed to show an interest in what he was doing these days. She knew his sergeant, Jackie Joynton and had shared her concerns about her dad. Although she missed her mother, Liz had frequently suggested to him that he should get out more, meet people. Maybe even try one of the online dating websites. Find someone on his own terms. She was concerned he was slipping into some sort of self-imposed social isolation.

He had pleaded lack of time but she knew differently. He was hanging on to memories and a sense of loyalty to her mother. His excuse was always the same. No one would be interested in a policeman. He had seen too many marriages destroyed by the life style and the hours. Liz wasn't fooled by that, though. She would persist until he did something about it because there must be someone out there for him. It was just a case of finding the right person.

'You're right about today,' he told her. 'It's going to occupy the team for a while…No, not a murder. But close to…Lots of lines of enquiry to follow up…Yes, it'll get into the press eventually, but I want to keep a low profile on this until we make some progress….Intrigued? You want to know more? You can phone again for progress reports? I'm always pleased to hear from you, of course, but you can't expect me to tell you everything that's going on.'

Trussell put the phone down and thought for a moment. Liz didn't usually show quite such a persistent interest in his work. Perhaps she was concerned for him. Wanted to know what he was doing. Hear his voice. Keep in contact. Show him she was thinking about him.

Anyway, back to the programme, he thought, picking up the remote again.

6

Sophie twisted the ignition key of the BMW and as the engine fired up it was accompanied by the unmistakeable sound of Mozart's Clarinet Concerto in A Major from the speakers.

'Ooops, sorry,' she said, turning off the music system. 'I'd forgotten it was in the CD player. It's still one of my favourites.'

DS Joynton smiled, but said nothing.

Sophie pulled away from the cottage, following Trussell's Skoda, which soon drew ahead of them and disappeared into the distance around a bend. DS Joynton wondered whether her sedate driving was inhibited by the presence of a police officer in the passenger seat. She was overly cautious for the owner of a sports saloon.

'I'm not in Traffic Division, Mrs Blaxstone. You don't need to hold back. I need to see you safely into the Castle Inn as soon as possible.'

Relieved, Sophie obligingly dropped a gear and put her foot down.

They were soon on the outskirts of Woodchester. They entered the town centre and drove along the High Street until they reached the hotel. It was an eighteenth century coaching inn: a white rendered building with a wooden sign swinging gently in the slight breeze, depicting a grey stone castle and proudly proclaiming its name and date. A Kent peg-tiled roof and the historic chimney style underlined the age of the place. It was a long building with a main door beneath the sign and a couple of other doors spaced along the facade. In the middle was an archway, originally the entrance to the stables in its coaching days, but now providing access to the car park, hidden away at the back of the building.

Sophie turned the BMW into the narrow opening, concentrating on avoiding the old walls. Coloured scrapes showed that other drivers had been less fortunate. She failed to spot the silver Mercedes 4 x 4 with darkened windows which paused briefly outside the archway, before continuing along the High Street.

Sophie found a vacant space, retrieved her two cases from the boot, and, with the Detective Sergeant's help, headed through the hotel side door to the desk in the hotel lobby.

'Good evening, Detective Sergeant,' said the receptionist.

'Hello, Trish, this is Mrs Blaxstone. She's booked a room.'

'Oh yes. I've the paperwork here. How many nights will you be staying, Mrs Blaxstone?'

Sophie glanced at Joynton, who gave a slight shrug of the shoulders.

'I'm not sure at the moment. Until I find somewhere more permanent. I hope it won't take too long.'

'Can you just fill out the registration form, please? Are you using the car park? Can you include your vehicle details, please? I'll need to swipe your card.'

Sophie offered her credit card and this was returned to her a minute later with a copy of the paperwork and a room key.

'Room number 12 on the first floor. The stairs are on your right. Enjoy your stay.'

'I'll help you with the bags,' said Joynton, picking up one of the cases.

They found the room at the end of the corridor and Sophie opened the door.

Joynton went in first, looked around, and headed for the window, checking it was secure and not overlooked. A standard hotel room, not spacious but adequate. It was clean and tidy but the decor was bland with magnolia walls. There was a double bed, side units with lamps, a small table with a courtesy kettle, cups and assorted sachets of coffee, tea and the ubiquitous flat-screen television on the wall. Sophie was pleased to see a desk and chair. She opened the door to check the bathroom, which was windowless.

'You'll need to unpack, Mrs Blaxstone, so I'll wait downstairs in the lounge. It's just off the reception area. I think you might be glad of some company for a while after the day you've had. I live just down the road, so no problems for me getting home.'

'Please call me Sophie, Detective Sergeant. Everyone does. I don't think I really want to use my husband's name at the moment.'

'My name's Jackie,' said Joynton. 'That'll be easier. I think we'll be spending a lot of time together before we get to the bottom of things. By the way, I'll give you my card now. My mobile number is on there so you'll be able to call me if necessary. I expect DI Trussell will do the same tomorrow.'

7

Jackie went back downstairs and walked through the lobby into the lounge. It was very familiar to her with its old dark wood panelled walls, its subdued lighting providing a discreet ambience. Surprisingly, at this time of the evening, the room was deserted. She found a table in the far corner, away from the bar, where conversations would be a bit more private.

The bored, elderly waiter walked slowly over to the table, glad of the opportunity to talk to someone.

'Good evening, madam. May I bring you something?'

'In a moment, please. I'm waiting for a friend who should be here shortly.'

The waiter nodded and went back to the bar to resume his usual time filler, polishing clean glasses.

Fifteen minutes later, Sophie arrived and peered into the dimly lit room, looking for Jackie. The colour had drained out of her face and she looked somewhat shaken. She was holding her mobile phone and her hand was trembling.

'What's happened?' asked Jackie.

Sophie walked to the table and held out her phone. Jackie looked at the message on the screen. It said simply, 'You got lucky this time bitch. Next time will be different. If you meddle you pay.'

'We can run a check on the number to try to see who sent it,' said Jackie, 'but it's unlikely we'll be able to trace it. If a phone has been lost or stolen, particularly a pay as you go phone, then it's no problem for someone else to unlock it. Most High Streets are full of phone shops and street stalls offering the service. Chances are it's probably a burner, anyway.'

'It's the same number as the call I received before the shot was fired at me,' said Sophie as she sat down in the chair opposite the detective.

Jackie waved to attract the waiter's attention. 'Bring the lady a brandy, please, and I'll have a glass of white wine - Sauvignon Blanc, if you have it.'

'Certainly, Madam. Will New Zealand be alright?'

'Perfect, thank you.'

Sophie was still worried. 'Does it mean whoever sent that text has followed me here?'

'Not necessarily. The message could have been sent from anywhere. I'm sure you're safe here for the moment. I'd suggest you try to stay in your room as much as possible.'

The waiter appeared and placed their drinks on the table.

Jackie thought the best way to calm Sophie down was to encourage her to talk. 'Do you want to tell me something about yourself, Sophie? Talking about the past might just help in piecing this whole thing together. We'll be going through your old investigations tomorrow and we shall need to look at your social media pages as well. Why don't you start at the beginning? You said you're quite alone in the world. Can you tell me more?'

Sophie took a large sip of brandy from her glass and the welcome warmth spread its calming influence.

'OK, I'll give you my life story. My father was a senior executive with a major oil company. My parents spent most of their time abroad, usually in the Middle East, where I was born. As an only child, I rarely spent any time with them and was always left with a nurse or au pair, wherever we lived.'

'What about your education?'

Sophie's eyes filled with tears as she recalled those unhappy times, when her parents sent her to a series of expat schools from the age of five, changing frequently as they moved around with her father's job. Looking back, she wondered how she ever learned anything. She certainly hadn't been able to make any friends or socialise, which should have been so important to a small child growing up. It had had a greater effect on her than she could have ever imagined.

'I'm sorry,' she said, wiping away the tears and feeling somewhat embarrassed. She took another sip of brandy and regained her composure. This was not the confident television personality. She had revealed a vulnerable side.

Jackie tried to ignore Sophie's obvious discomfort and moved the conversation on. 'What happened next?'

'When I was eight, they sent me to a boarding school in the South of England, and I stayed there until I was eighteen. Looking back, I didn't make friends easily, and I rarely saw my parents. They'd come back to England occasionally and spend some time with me, but there always seemed to be some sort of barrier between us. They made sure I had everything I needed, except affection. It was as if they were just doing their duty. I've often wondered whether I was a bit of an unwelcome surprise.'

'So what did you do in the school holidays, then?'

'There were a few other kids in the same boat. We all felt a bit unwanted. The school staff did their best, of course, but it wasn't a very happy time.

'It must have been a very difficult time for you.'

'It made me determined to make something of myself, through my own efforts, if no one else was interested in me. I really concentrated on my studies, and eventually got a place at university to read English Literature - inevitably because books had become a major part of my life at school outside of lessons. The only other benefit of school was a love of classical music, thanks to a very friendly music teacher. She spent time with me and helped me widen my knowledge'

'What about contacts outside the school?'

'My godparents lived in the North of England, and they were sometimes in touch. I think my godfather was a very old family friend. She took another sip of brandy. It seemed to help. 'Anyway, my time at University made me very self-sufficient and I left with an Honours Degree. Then my godfather broke the news to me that my parents had died in a road accident somewhere in the Middle East. As their executor, he made all the necessary repatriation and funeral arrangements, dealt with all the paperwork and their wills. As you can imagine, in the circumstances, I found it quite hard to grieve, because I realised I hardly knew them.'

'So there was no family you could turn to at this critical time in your life?'

'No, neither of my parents had any living relatives. Looking back now, it all seems a bit odd.'

'It still must have been a huge shock for you.'

'Yes, it was. I found myself totally alone in the world. I'd made a few casual friendships at university, but those didn't last. When my parents' estates were settled, there was enough money to tide me over and put some in the bank, but it was obvious I would need to find a job. My godfather introduced me to one of his friends, Dan Janssen, who happened to be assistant editor of a national newspaper, *The Daily Enquirer.*'

'Do you have any contact with your godparents now?'

'No, that chapter in my life is closed.'

As she began to talk about her career as a journalist Sophie's whole demeanour changed. It was as if she'd been able to put the earlier unhappy time in her life back into its box. She became more animated as she narrated the beginnings of her very successful career.

'It turned out to be the best thing that ever happened to me.' Jackie drained her glass, waved to the waiter, and ordered another white wine. 'What would you like to drink, Sophie? Another brandy?'

'I'll join you in a glass of white wine, please. The brandy certainly did the trick.'

'Right, so you went to work for *The Daily Enquirer*?'

She talked about the early days as a junior reporter. How the Deputy Editor had encouraged and guided her so she was eventually promoted and started making important contacts. It had taught her the benefits of networking. She had an inquisitive mind and found she had developed an ability to dig up interesting stories.

'Where were you living at that time?'

'I rented a small, cheap flat just across the river in Walworth, South London. It was hardly paradise, but then I didn't spend too much time there. I was always out and about, building up contacts and interviewing people. As my stories began to appear more regularly on the front pages of the paper, I began to see the downside, as I told your Detective Inspector earlier. There were negative comments on my social media pages and I also received some threats. Nobody took them seriously at the time. In fact the police were quite dismissive.'

'So there were threats, even in those days?'

'Yes, but they predated the big stories I've been involved with in the last two or three years and the level of threats has certainly been ramped up. Anyway, I managed to buy my first property, a terraced house in a rundown inner London suburb. It proved a good investment, because there was the usual Yuppie invasion a little later and property prices went through the roof!' She recalled the rapid changes around her in the area as the old traditional neighbourhood shops had been transformed into trendy wine bars and coffee shops.

She continued. 'Anyway it seemed the media were taking notice of my work for the paper, and I was introduced to a television station to start a new series, investigating consumer complaints. It was a whole new experience appearing in front of the cameras for the first time although I began to miss the high profile side of my career so the producer allowed me to chase major scandals and exposés. A year ago, I decided to leave my job at the *Enquirer* to go freelance as the television work was rolling in. Dan Janssen insisted I took an annual retainer in exchange for the paper receiving exclusives and for sending them the occasional article.'

Jackie moved the conversation on to bring her story up to date. 'What about your personal life? How did you meet your husband? '

'About seven years ago I was invited to a major dinner in Docklands. I think the organisers needed someone with a high profile on each table to spark the conversations with the corporate guests. My husband, Richard, was on the same table. He was a partner in a City insurance broking firm he'd started a couple of years earlier with two friends.'

'That was where your relationship began, then?'

'Yes. 'Looking back, I guess I had an air of vulnerability about me, which probably explains marrying in my mid-thirties. Although I was totally driven by my career, I realised I really needed to share my life with someone. We seemed to get along alright that evening, and he suggested we meet again. He was a little older than me, and I didn't know at the time, he'd already been married. When I first visited his apartment in Docklands, there were photographs of her. She was called Jenny.'

'What happened to her?'

'It was rather sad. Richard seemed reluctant to talk about her at first, but eventually we did discuss it. She'd been killed in a road accident - a hit and run. The driver was never traced and I believe the case is still open. It must be nine years ago that it happened.'

Jackie made a mental note to look it up.

Sophie thought about those early conversations about Jenny. Richard had told her that all Jenny had wanted was to become a stay at home mum and raise a family, but this hadn't been part of his plans in those early days. She'd got the impression the subject had caused friction between them.

'Anyway, we seemed to hit it off and began dating. A year later, we were married – just a quiet registry office wedding with a couple of friends as witnesses, followed by a honeymoon in the Seychelles. Richard paid for it, although ordinarily he never seemed to have a lot of spare money. He told me everything was tied up in his firm, investing for the future. I didn't think anything of it. I was pulling in a decent income from my various jobs. When we returned, I moved into his rented apartment in Docklands and sold my house at a really good profit. The money eventually paid for the cottage and most of the cost of our flat in the Barbican. I took out a small mortgage for the balance.

'So, you moved out of London to the country. When was that?'

'About a year ago; around my fortieth birthday. We bought the flat in the Barbican at the same time so that we always had somewhere to stay overnight when we were in town. Things seemed perfectly OK between us - at least from my point of view. Then, quite suddenly Richard came home from work and calmly announced he was leaving me for another woman. I still have no idea who she is. Anyway, I couldn't persuade him to change his mind. He just packed his bags and left.'

Talking about Richard's departure had caused her to think in depth about their marriage. She had always been involved with the social side of his business, frequently attending dinners with both existing and prospective clients and had come finally to realise that he had used her as some sort of trophy wife. She was a nationally known television personality who could be wheeled out to impress people when he felt it would help him to clinch a deal. She was too modest to acknowledge the fact that she was very attractive as well.

She had also seen the ruthless side of him in his professional dealings, recalling his favourite expression, *There're no prizes for finishing second*. He was totally focussed on expanding his business. Perhaps this had been the attraction for her. They seemed to share the same driven approach to their careers.

'Were there no friends you could turn to?'

'No, I hadn't really made any where we live. I guess my work has made me a fairly solitary individual.'

Sophie thought about those early days again. The school had segregated the sexes as far as possible, so she later realised how naïve she was when she left. She had found it difficult to immerse herself in any meaningful relationship, always holding back, using her studies as an excuse. But now, she knew her lonely childhood and adolescence had had an even greater effect on her than she had realised at the time. There had been a deep rooted sense of being unwanted, worthless...

'Once I started work, I did have men in my life at times but nothing permanent. Nothing seemed to last. There was no one I could call on or rely on. Perhaps it was my fault. I was very career driven. I always felt the need to do more. Get more recognition. Be the best at what I did. I was competing in a man's world, after all.

'I find it hard to believe because I'm sure most men would find you very attractive,' said Jackie.'

'I think you've heard enough about me now, because I'm sure we'll have to revisit a lot of this stuff tomorrow,' said Sophie. 'What about you, Jackie? What persuaded you to join the police? You don't fit the stereotype for me?'

'I come from a police family so the future was pretty well mapped out for me. I joined as a fast track graduate straight out of Uni with a degree in Computer Sciences and eventually hope to join the Fraud Squad to work on Cyber Crime. I did the mandatory couple of years on the beat and then joined the CID. I passed the Sergeant's exam three years ago and somehow managed to avoid going back into uniform - that was a bit unusual - and I started working with Jim Trussell. I've learned a lot from him. He's a very experienced and intuitive guy.'

'I felt he looked a bit serious and intense, almost preoccupied, when you arrived today.'

'That's because he takes his job very seriously. You've got to get to know Jim. He's really nice behind the facade, very supportive of his colleagues. He lost his wife about six years ago, and I don't think he has fully come to terms with it, particularly as his daughter has gone off to Uni. Reading English Literature. I think she wants to write, or get into journalism. I don't think he's looking at the future with any sort of optimism. It's all left a huge void in his life.'

'How old is he then?'

'Early forties.'

'You said you live nearby?'

'Yes. I share a flat with my partner, Mike. He's in Traffic. We met on an advanced driving course. He teases me about my plain clothes work in the CID. Calls me the Fashionista! I've told him there's more to CID than scruffy hoodies and jeans, pulling drug dealers and shoplifters off the street. I don't need to look like the people I arrest.'

Sophie managed a nervous laugh. 'Did you include me in that?' she asked, conscious of the fact she was still very casually dressed. 'I promise to dress more appropriately for my interview tomorrow!'

Jackie smiled. 'I'm not the one who just dodged a bullet,' she said. She glanced at her watch. 'You seem a little more relaxed, Sophie. I'll leave you now and see you in the morning. One of us will call you and arrange to collect you in an unmarked car.'

She waved to the waiter and gave him her credit card to settle their bar bill.

'Thank you,' said Sophie. 'This has helped me push today to the back of my mind. Shall I bring my laptop and the other records tomorrow?'

'I'll phone you when I've spoken to Jim.'

The receptionist appeared at the entrance to the lounge holding an envelope in one hand. She looked around, caught sight of them and walked towards their table.

'Ah, Mrs Blaxstone. I was away from the desk for a moment, and I found this when I returned. I didn't see who left it.' She handed over a scruffy brown A5 envelope, addressed to Mrs Sophie Blaxstone.

'That's odd. Who could possibly know I'm here, apart from DI Trussell and you, Jackie?'

She opened the envelope and took out the folded paper inside. She smoothed it out, and a look of disbelief turning to horror crossed her face.

Jackie took it from her trembling hand by a corner and read it. It contained a random collection of letters, cut out from newspapers or magazines and pasted onto the paper. The words said quite simply *We know where to find you.*

'Who could have done this?' Sophie was rattled. 'That means I'm still in danger'

'You should be safe here in the hotel. There was no direct threat in the letter. It seems to be part of a plan to wear you down. We don't want to draw attention to you or alarm other hotel guests by putting a uniformed officer outside your door. I'll take this letter and envelope with me,' she added, producing a plastic bag from her handbag. 'We'll hand it over to Forensics to see what they make of it. They'll probably want to take your fingerprints to eliminate them from anything else they find on the paper.'

Sophie didn't look convinced.

'I'll see you to your room, Sophie, and then I'll be off,' said Jackie. 'I'll call you in the morning when I've spoken to Jim.'

8

Sophie looked at the clock on the unit next to her bed, as she had done all too frequently throughout a sleepless night. She had gone over and over the events of the previous day, yet she still couldn't comprehend what had happened to her. She had thought through her major cases and was still none the wiser. *Who could be behind this?* Perhaps the police would be able to make sense of it all.

She kept thinking about BurtonleeHomes – was it purely coincidental that her problems had only started when she began looking into the developer's business? She realised she was facing a difficult and intensive day. There would be many questions to be answered, not least because the police would want to look at her past articles searching for motives…She dragged herself out of bed, almost afraid to look in the mirror, and selected more suitable clothes for the day. She showered and dressed. A rumbling stomach reminded her that she hadn't eaten since the previous lunchtime, so a hotel breakfast seemed a good idea. Picking up her room key and ensuring her phone was in her bag, she quietly opened the door just enough to peer outside. The corridor was deserted. A CCTV camera blinked watchfully. She decided to risk it and left the room in search of refreshment.

She walked down the stairs into the lobby. The receptionist, behind her desk, was watching a man in bright blue overalls with a Woodchester Security logo on the back. He was standing on a step ladder working on the security camera which covered the lobby.

'Good morning, Mrs Blaxstone,' said the receptionist. 'I hope you slept well.'

'Yes, thank you,' lied Sophie, hoping that her makeup had sufficiently disguised the dark circles under her eyes. She obviously didn't want to draw attention to herself. 'Where can I get breakfast?'

'The dining room is over there.' The outstretched finger was pointing at a doorway in the far corner.

Peering cautiously around her, and hoping that was not too obvious, she headed for the dining room. There were only a couple of other people eating at a table and they paid her no attention. A waitress indicated one of the unoccupied tables and asked for her room number. Rather than say it aloud, she showed her the key. She was being ultra-cautious now. This was a new Sophie – she had never been this concerned before, even when pursuing serious wrong doers in the past.

She began to ask herself questions, trying to be logical. Was she becoming paranoid, or was this just a normal reaction to the previous day's events? All the time she was looking around her. *Must stop it*, she thought. *I don't want to draw attention to myself.* Luckily no one had recognised her so far. *Long may it last.*

She tried to concentrate on other things. There was her television programme. A new series was scheduled for a month's time, and there was a lot of preparation work still to be done. She would have to get in touch with her producer to talk it over. She would be unable to contribute to any discussions cooped up in a hotel room, hiding away.

She looked at the breakfast menu, trying to concentrate, but it was well-nigh impossible. She kept thinking about the sequence of events of the previous day. When the waitress appeared, she settled for scrambled eggs on toast and coffee. She just needed to get back to the safety of her room as soon as possible to await a phone call from Jackie Joynton about the timing of the day's plans. Sophie had been impressed by her quiet professionalism during their conversation last night. She had done her very best to put Sophie at ease, whilst encouraging her to talk about herself. Sophie definitely felt comfortable in her company. *What about the Detective Inspector?* Jackie's brief mention of his personal circumstances had gone a long way towards explaining his serious persona when they had first met at the cottage. Jackie seemed to hold him in high regard, so she would have to see where the enquiries went today.

She signed the bill, smiled at the waitress and headed back to her room to await Jackie's call.

9

Jim Trussell sat at his desk in the CID office, thinking about the previous day's events and the Blaxstone case, as it was now known.

The freshly cleaned white board, bare except for Sophie's photograph and a place, date and time, was a pointer to what lay ahead for the team that morning.

He had already put his two Detective Constables to work and both were glued to their computer screens. Mark 'Greeno' Green was busy researching Sophie Breckton and her social media pages, and Tim 'Sandcastle' Beach was looking through old newspaper reports of cases in which she'd been involved.

Walking in past Trussell, DS Jackie Joynton said, 'Morning, Jim,' nodding to the two younger men.

'You're late, Sergeant,' he laughed. 'Only to be expected when you only live ten minutes' walk away. Must have been a long night,'

'I spent a couple of hours with Sophie Blaxstone at the Castle Inn. I sensed she might want some company. It was pretty interesting and informative. Just as well I was there, because she received a rather nasty text message just after she checked in. I tried to put her mind at rest. Told her it was unlikely that whoever sent it had any idea where she was, and it could have reached her anywhere. I made a note of the number and I've passed it on, but hundred to one the phone was probably a burner. I tried to reassure her but she was badly shaken by it.'

'What did it say?'

Jackie consulted her notebook and read it aloud.

'Hmmm. Nasty. I can imagine it must have been quite upsetting for her, coming on top of her experience earlier.'

'It got worse, Jim. Just as I was about to leave, having calmed her down, the receptionist arrived with a letter addressed to Mrs Blaxstone that someone had left on the hotel desk when it was unattended. I've brought it with me, bagged up for Forensics to look at. It says simply *We know where to find you.* The usual cut out letters from a newspaper or magazine, pasted onto a sheet of paper. I handled it by one corner for safety.'

'How was she when you left her?'

'I tried to reassure her. I told her that I didn't think that it posed a direct threat and nothing would be achieved by putting any sort of guard there. The Castle has only a few rooms and there's CCTV everywhere, so any strangers trying to get in would soon be noticed. No one could have known in advance she'd be staying there. Perhaps we were followed from Foggenden. She seems quite tough mentally, once she's able to rationalise. She accepted what I said, so I saw her to her room and then left.'

'What about the CCTV?'

'I stopped at the front desk on the way out to ask the receptionist if I could look at the footage, hoping we could see who left the envelope. Unfortunately, the camera covering the lobby had been on the blink since late afternoon, and the security company were coming this morning to replace it. Sod's law.'

'Call her now to make sure she's OK and tell her we'll be in touch again shortly.'

'What's the next step, Jim? I told her she'd be spending a fair amount of time with us, looking through her old cases. I said one of us would drop by the Castle and collect her.'

'Give it an hour then give her a call to arrange a pick up. Ask her to bring her records with her.'

'Greeno,' he called, 'phone the duty sergeant and book one of the interview rooms for the rest of the day. There's no privacy in here with that lot over there.' He meant the second CID team at the other end of the office.

10

Sophie had just returned to her room after breakfast, when her phone rang.

'Morning, Sophie. It's Jackie Joynton. How are you today? I can come round to collect you. Shall we say about thirty minutes? I've spoken to Jim and brought him up to speed about last night. Can you bring your laptop and the memory sticks with you? I'll meet you by the hotel reception desk.'

Half an hour later, Sophie stood in the lobby of the Castle Inn, clutching a large tote bag containing her laptop and everything else she thought might be relevant.

Jackie arrived a couple of minutes later, smiling warmly. 'My car is out back,' she said, leading the way to the back entrance.

They drove straight to the police station at the other end of the High Street, found a space for the car and went through into the lobby. Jackie touched her ID card on the security pad and led the way through the double doors to the interview room where Trussell was waiting for them. It was a drab area with buff-coloured walls that hadn't been decorated for a while. It contained a table that had seen better days, firmly fixed to the floor, with four chairs, two either side. It was not meant to impress anyone unlucky enough to be brought in there for an interview.

Trussell rose to greet her, apologising for the somewhat Spartan surroundings. 'I know this isn't terribly comfortable, but at least it's private.'

He pulled out a chair for her.

Sophie put her laptop on the table and sat down.

'So this is where you sweat your suspects, then, DI Trussell,' she said.

'There'll be nothing like that today, Mrs Blaxstone! I hope you're a little more relaxed after yesterday's ordeal? Jackie told me about the text and the letter. I shouldn't worry about them for the moment. I believe the Castle is secure enough for you.'

Sophie forced a smile, trying to hide her concerns, but it wasn't fooling anyone. 'I'll need to carry on with my work. I'm getting ready for a new television series, starting in about a month. What do you suggest? A lot of people are involved. I can't hide forever.'

'Your safety is paramount. Let's get started and see where today takes us,' said Trussell. 'Have you got everything with you? Let's begin by making a list of your major articles and take it from there. Jackie will make a few notes.'

'Not a problem,' said Sophie, opening her laptop. 'Right, I'll find the stories that really caused a bit of a stir at the time. I'll just go through them quickly and then I can give you the details afterwards.'

She fished in her bag for some flash drives, selected one and inserted it in the USB drive. Her fingers flowed effortlessly and rapidly over the keys until she found what she was looking for. She scrolled down until she found the first entry. She turned the laptop round so that Trussell and Joynton could see it. The screen contained a front page from *The Daily Enquirer.*

The headline screamed 'Former Cabinet Minister jailed for 10 years on Secrets Charges'. Sophie's name was on the by-line as Chief Correspondent. 'This one involved Henry Alexander Kilhampton, M.P. and Government Minister,' she said. 'He came to my attention through one of my informants. I discovered he'd been passing sensitive information to a foreign power. He was being blackmailed about his private lifestyle which did not exactly accord with his public image, although he was handsomely paid for his treachery. Don't believe he was best pleased about my involvement in his fall from grace. He had a huge ego, like most politicians. He's serving a long prison sentence at the moment, having been convicted under the Official Secrets Act. I still can't believe it but his wife came to see me and pleaded with me to drop the story if he promised to resign. I won't repeat what I said to her, other than he was a traitor and deserved all he got.'

Trussell remembered the case. The public outcry which had followed Kilhampton's exposure and trial had caused a seismic wave in Parliament at the time. The subsequent fall out had caused a political crisis and almost brought down the government of the day.

She turned the laptop around, typed in another reference, and when she found it, showed them the next entry. It was another front page from *The Daily Enquirer.* 'Roger the Dodger,' was the headline, with 'City Boss flees after alleged wrongdoing' the sub-heading to the main article again credited to Sophie.

'That's about Roger Brownlowe-Jameson. You may remember him. About eighteen months ago. He headed up a huge financial and industrial group which he wanted to expand rather dramatically. Problem was he was manipulating the Stock Exchange and using a mixture of bribes and threats to get what he wanted. I broke the story at *The Enquirer* when a whistle-blower contacted me. He subsequently did a runner before anyone could grab him and no one knows what happened to him. I believe the police case is still open. Meanwhile, our boy's probably now relaxing in the sun on his yacht, beyond the law, where there are no extradition treaties and his fortune buys him protection. His businesses are being run by nominees, and the revenue is still rolling in while Roger sits on the beach pulling the strings.'

'That's right,' said Jackie. I remember it. The case is still open. No one knows what happened to the whistle-blower. Do people still hold up flyovers these days, Jim?'

Sophie refreshed the computer screen and brought up a third front page, about a year old, with her name once more prominently displayed below the headline. 'Major House Builder Scandal. Will nobody listen?' The article described how Burtonlee's building standards had slipped with huge numbers of complaints from buyers about shoddy workmanship and dodgy materials, corners apparently being cut everywhere.

'This is my current investigation which involves Burtonlee Homes. It's become very personal, for the reasons I mentioned yesterday. They've been very slow to resolve customers' complaints, where they've actually bothered. Even letters to the press haven't actually achieved very much.'

'I've seen it in the papers and on the national news,' said Trussell. 'Nothing seems to be getting better.'

'I've tried several times to get an interview with Terry Burtonlee, but he's dodging me. Now, to add insult to injury, he wants to build several thousand houses on my doorstep, destroying everything for miles around. It will turn our tiny hamlet into a small town - houses, roads, shops, and even a couple of schools.'

'What do the local council think about it?'

'Of course the development will generate a huge amount of money under Section 106 for them. That's the clause of the Town and Country Planning Regulations which ensures developers contribute funding to the local council. It's supposed to make the development more attractive to the local community in exchange for the granting of planning permission. It would help one or two of the councillors to catch up with some of their vanity projects that've been shelved due to lack of funds. It would certainly have its attractions for some of them, no question.'

'What about the local residents?'

'Nobody wants the development. I'm involved with the local action group, and Burtonlee Homes know it. I've received some information which could be quite damaging to him, both personally and legally. When Terry Burtonlee finds out about this, I know he won't be best pleased, to say the least. What I do know is he was involved in a high profile and very expensive divorce recently and he needs this development to stay personally solvent. If he doesn't build it, he faces financial ruin.'

'Will this form part of your next television series?'

'Yes, and in the press. I'm still writing occasionally for the *Enquirer* and other stories about Burtonlee have already appeared there under my name, as you can see.'

'What else are you working on?'

'Two other items at the moment. The first is an inquiry about illegal subletting of council flats at one of the big estates, linked with Benefit frauds. They call it Cuckooing these days. There are suggestions this might be organised crime which could be traced back to West Africa. I've been talking to the local council about it. I'd been approached by some of the legal tenants who were too scared to go directly to the council in case those behind the racket discovered their identities.

'The second is that I am trying to track down a one man builder, a local white van man, who's been ripping off pensioners. He gives out inflated estimates to vulnerable people, takes a deposit, and that's usually the last they see of him or their money. I've tried doorstepping him at all hours of the day and night with my cameraman but he seems to have gone to ground. Frankly, I don't see him as a threat in this context. Truth is, he's in hiding and probably more scared of me than I need be of him.'

'We'll arrange for one of the team to talk to the local council and then see if we can track him down.'

Jackie Joynton finished her notes and put the notebook down.

'It doesn't sound to me as if any of these people will be signing up to join your fan club any time soon, Mrs Blaxstone,' said Trussell. 'And it does give us somewhere to start.'

'Now let's look at the details. Jackie, we'll start with Mr Kilhampton. Can you look at the records of the case and find out where he's serving his sentence? We may need to visit him. Then there's our friend Roger. We obviously can't speak to him but we ought to talk to the Fraud Squad or the Serious Crime Agency to see what anybody knows about him. Find out who's running his businesses now and see if there are any regular communications between them. Lastly, there's Mr Burtonlee. It's too early to draw any conclusions, but he seems rather closest timewise to what happened yesterday, especially as Mrs Blaxstone's involvement with the local group is known to him. Oh, and ask Sandcastle to bring some refreshments in. Tea or coffee, Mrs Blaxstone?'

'Tea would be fine, thank you. Please call me Sophie. Everyone does. After my husband left, I wasn't sure I wanted to use his name anymore. Using my first name solves the problem for me.'

Jackie Joynton left the room and returned about ten minutes' later, holding the door open for DC Beach, who was carrying a tray with the tea. When he had gone, she handed a note to Trussell. It was a message in Mark Green's distinctively neat handwriting.

He scanned it quickly. It told him that the Crime Scene Investigators had trawled the woods the previous day, and had come up with some evidence, including a spent cartridge case. They had passed it to Forensics who'd be in touch with a written report tomorrow. Uniformed officers had spoken to people in the cottages near the woods - one neighbour, a Mr Shalford of Ivy Cottage, heard the shot, but took no notice. He thought it was one of the bird scarers that go off in the field all the time.

Jackie said, 'It seems that Mr Shalford also noticed a vehicle he hadn't seen round there before. He said the bird watchers tend to be the same group of people, probably a local club. But he didn't recognise this car, a silver 4 x 4 with darkened windows. He thought it was a Mercedes, but he couldn't be sure. Looked a bit out of place, he thought. Obviously he didn't take any notice of the licence plate. We've got his details, if we need to speak to him again.'

Trussell suggested one of the team follow that one up while it was still fresh in his mind. 'Let's send Greeno round to talk to him.

Jackie said, 'Sandcastle's already traced Kilhampton. He's two years into a ten year stretch in Barrington High Security prison. Category A prisoner.'

'Barrington? That's handy. I've known Fred Simpson, the head of security there, for years. We worked together for a while before he left the force. We'll need to get permission to see Kilhampton. We don't want to go the long route via the Home Office. It all depends whether he's prepared to talk to us. As he's not officially a suspect at the moment, he can refuse.'

'It could've been down to him, Jim,' said Jackie. 'Banged up in a high security prison with the wrong sort of people. He's already had two years to think about it and possibly become bitter and twisted - maybe even a bit obsessive and with revenge on his mind. He probably has the financial means, and he's living with people, day to day, who might have the right sort of contacts outside. There are people in there who are no strangers to contract killings. Maybe we need to check with the prison staff to see who's been to visit him and find out whether he's had access to a phone at any time.'

'Good idea.'

'What about Kilhampton's paymasters? They'd surely, have a reasonable motive for taking revenge on the person responsible for cutting off their source of important defence secrets?'

'No, that doesn't work for me,' said Trussell. 'It's a bit too obvious. We know who they are and our government's already done the diplomatic thing, chucking out a number of their senior people, including their Military Attaché. That resulted in the usual tit for tat response when their government expelled some of our Embassy staff. That's how it works in their circles. The diplomatic game has its own rules. The foreign power has nothing to gain at this point by killing the person who exposed Kilhampton back then. These days, they just tend to go after dissidents who've sought asylum over here. They've already caused enough of a stink without adding to the smell. But, we'll have to look at it as a possible line of enquiry. Maybe the Special Branch will have an opinion on it. I'll give Fred a call at Barrington to see what he says.'

'What about Roger?' asked Jackie. 'I could start the ball rolling. I know a couple of people at the Fraud Squad from my training days. I've kept in touch with them. Would you like me to have a word to see if they can give us an update on their enquiries? They're bound to know something about him. Brownlowe-Jameson would certainly have good reason to be upset with Sophie. After all, she has scuppered his business plans and effectively deprived him of his liberty as far as most of the world is concerned.'

'That's fine, Jackie, go ahead. One thing, though. I don't want to hear you've been using this as a means of networking and angling for a transfer. I need you here at the moment.'

Jackie held up her hands. 'No chance at the moment. I want to see this one through.'

Trussell turned to Sophie, who was sipping her tea. 'We'll leave you here for a short while so we can make a start. You won't be disturbed here if you want to work. Is there anything else we can get you?'

'That's fine. I've got my laptop. I'll catch up with a few things. I can't imagine a safer and quieter environment for me in the present circumstances.'

The two detectives left the interview room to head back to the CID office.

'She certainly seems quite calm now, Jim.'

Trussell just nodded, deep in thought. There just seemed to be so many options in the case. They must start eliminating some of them to speed up the investigation.

11

When Trussell and Joynton returned to their office, they noticed immediately that Mark Green had been busy on the internet. In addition to Sophie's picture, the white incident board now contained photos of Henry Kilhampton, Roger Brownlow-Jameson and Terry Burtonlee. The anonymous white van man was mentioned and there was a silhouette to represent the gunman.

'Right, Jackie, let's get started on the first two possibilities,' said Trussell. 'I'll speak to Fred Simpson at Barrington about Henry Kilhampton, and you get on to your contacts at the Fraud Squad about Brownlow-Jameson. You might ask them who's dealing with the case of the missing whistle-blower. It'll probably be someone in the Met. See if they have a contact name and number.'

'I'm on it, Jim.'

Trussell picked up the phone and touched the O button. The switchboard answered immediately.

'It's DI Trussell here. Can you find the number for Barrington High Security prison, please? I want to speak to Fred Simpson, Head of Security.'

'Planning a short break, Inspector?' said a woman's voice.

'Just get me the number, please, Maureen. I can do without your brand of humour at this time of the morning.'

'Putting you through…'

He heard a familiar voice at the other end of the phone.

'Security. Simpson speaking.'

'Morning, Fred. It's Jim Trussell.'

'Jim. It's been a long time. How are you? I was really sorry to hear about Annette. It must be at least three years now.'

'It's actually six, Fred.'

'I'm sorry. I didn't realise it was that long. How're you doing? You have a daughter, don't you?'

'Yes, Liz is nearly twenty now. It was very difficult for her at the time. It was all very sudden. But she's pulled through it, and gone off to university.'

'We really must try to get together sometime. But, what can I do for you? I presume this isn't a social call?'

37

'Correct. I want to talk to you about one of your guests. Henry Kilhampton. I understand he's serving ten years.'

'How can I help?'

'I'm investigating a rather serious matter which could possibly be linked back to Kilhampton's case. He's not officially a suspect, but I may need to talk to him, if only to eliminate him from our enquiries. I understand he doesn't have to speak to me at the moment, if it doesn't suit him. So I thought I'd have a quick chat with you first, to try to get some current information about him.'

'OK, what do you want to know?'

'What he's up to. How he's behaved since he went inside. What contact he has with other prisoners, any outside phone calls and whether he has visitors. If so who, and how frequently.'

'That's quite a list. I'll have to look at his file and get back to you. I do know his wife was a regular visitor when he first arrived, but she's been visiting less and less now. His most regular contact is the prison chaplain. He seems to have experienced some sort of Damascene conversion during the last few months.'

'Do you think it's genuine, or just enough to fool the chaplain?'

'Don't know about that. The Reverend Joe Hollister's a pretty experienced man. He's seen it all here. I doubt Kilhampton could fool him. Anyway, I'm not sure what it would achieve if it wasn't for real. It certainly won't earn him any extra privileges, or result in any early release on licence. If you're planning to visit, then it would be worth having a word with Joe. He'd be able to give you an objective assessment. Do you want me to see if Kilhampton would be prepared to talk to you?'

'Please. I didn't want to have to go the Home Office route. It would probably take weeks to get any sort of answer, and this enquiry can't really wait. Just between us, I think it's unlikely Kilhampton's involved, but I've to check and, hopefully, eliminate him as a potential suspect. He just might have spoken to someone in Barrington. I know you have some hard cases with connections on the outside. I'm talking about a possible hit man.'

'OK, I'll have a word with the management to clear it before I speak to Kilhampton. How much do you want me to tell them, and Kilhampton, if they agree you can come here?'

'Just say we're investigating a serious matter which has a very slight, possible link back to his case, and we want to be sure there's no connection, so we can move on to our other lines of enquiry. I would appreciate the courtesy of a brief meeting to eliminate him and progress the matter. You may stress to your management, Kilhampton's not a suspect at this point, but we need to be sure.'

'OK, Jim. I'll deal with it this morning. I've a meeting booked with the Deputy Governor in about half an hour, so that was good timing. Give me a number where I can reach you.'

'You had better call me on my mobile. I'm not sure where I'll be later this morning. We have a number of possible lines of enquiry, and I only have a team of three to help me. I'll talk to you later.'

Trussell hung up and looked across at Jackie, who was on her phone, scribbling notes on a pad while she was talking. While he waited for her to finish, he walked over to the two DC's, Green and Beach, still studying their monitor screens with rapt attention. 'Anything new?' he asked.

Mark Green looked up from his screen. 'The Brownlowe-Jameson case seems to have gone quiet, Guv, as you'd expect. It's been eighteen months now, so I guess it's no longer a front page story. His name does crop up occasionally on the City pages in the press when there are any major developments or announcements from any of his companies, but otherwise he seems to be keeping a low profile. It could be worse, spending all your time in the sunshine, awash with money and popular with the local politicians who don't like our government for some reason or other. Sounds like a tough life.'

'What about the other cases? Mr Burtonlee, for example?'

'Well, Guv, there really is a lot going on there. His company had been getting a lot of stick in the press - you know, letters from people who bought his houses and can't get the defects fixed. Snagging doesn't seem to be the company's strength. Coverage on TV - mainly news programmes. And, that was before Sophie Breckton got hold of it. She's certainly raised the temperature, and now she's become involved in her local action group. There are interviews with members of the group, a sort of unofficial committee. There's one guy whose name figures fairly prominently, Jack Finlay. He lives fairly close to the proposed development site and seems to have taken on the leading role in this little battle. If Burtonlee or his organisation is really behind the shooting, then you might expect Mr Finlay's name might crop up on their hit list sooner or later. He's retired, has lived in his house for about thirty years, according to the press, and has fought this sort of battle before with other developers who've wanted to build there. He's always managed to win up until now to preserve the land as it is. From what I've read, though, I don't think there has ever been anything on this scale before.'

'It might be worth talking to him for some background information.'

'Do you want one of us to deal with it, Guv?' asked Mark Green, looking in the direction of the other DC.

'Good idea, Greeno. You handle it. Anything you can find out, but don't mention the shooting at this stage. If he asks you any awkward questions, just hint we're looking at matters that might be connected with the development. Try to get the names of the rest of the Committee and some ideas about the local councillors. Sort out those who might be in favour of the development and those who are on the side of the residents. He's bound to know what's going on at the council. Try asking him what he thinks the councillors in favour might do with the windfall that will come to the local authority. We need to build up a picture of exactly what's going on in the background. It sounds like this Mr Finlay has fought this particular battle often enough in the past to have an opinion. Combine it with a visit to the neighbour, John Shalford, who saw the Mercedes leave the scene around the time of the shooting. Ask him if he can remember the vehicle and whether he got a look at the driver.'

DC Green got up, retrieved his sports jacket from the back of his chair, checked he had his car keys and headed for the door.

Trussell turned to Jackie, who had just put the phone down.

'What's the word on our man, Roger?'

'I spoke to one of my friends at the Fraud Squad, and they have referred me to the National Crime Agency. The whole thing was serious enough for it to be taken out of their hands. I made a brief call there to register our interest in Roger, and someone will call me back, hopefully with some info about the missing whistle-blower.'

'So, what does that leave us with? Mr Burtonlee's development plans and the other investigation into illegal subletting on one of the council estates. Plus the white van man who's gone to ground. We'll put Sandcastle on that one. It'll be good experience for him. I don't honestly believe one rogue trader ripping off pensioners over small building work would have either the resources, connections or the will to get involved in a shooting like this. We just have to eliminate him from the list. Tell Sandcastle to talk to the local Trading Standards Officer at the council and start looking for the builder. We need to know where he was at about 1.45 yesterday afternoon. Sophie has given us his name and address. Talk to the DVLA and get his vehicle registration details. When the word gets out the police are now looking for him, it's bound to get someone talking. With a bit of luck it'll flush him out from wherever he's been hiding. The Trading Standards people can take it from there.'

'So, which one shall we deal with first, Jim?'

'Let's look at the rent racket. I think it's a bit unlikely those behind it would hire a hitman to silence the investigation. They will just cut their losses and move on, leaving the little people on the ground to take the rap for them. They'd know it'll take the council quite a while to unravel all the details of the tenancies and arrange the evictions. Then they would have to clean up the mess and re-let the flats. I reckon those at the top will just disappear for now. The last thing they would want is to have the police involved in what's just a civil matter at the moment. Still, we need to check it out, anyway, if only to eliminate it from the list.'

'Is Sophie following that one up for her programme, or is she concentrating on Burtonlee at the moment?'

'She was talking about a trip to the estate to see if she could interview anyone there with any info about what is going on, but it's my guess they would want to speak to her anonymously, you know, the usual out of focus back view with an actor's voice over-dubbed so they can't be recognised. It takes a while to set that sort of interview up without raising suspicion and identifying the witness, apparently. I'm going to try to advise her against it. I knew the place years ago and I doubt that it's improved in the meantime. The place concerned is a bit of a sink estate with all of the usual drug problems and levels of crime. I honestly believe Sophie thought she was impervious to any threats until this shooting. I know she'd have her cameraman with her, but he wouldn't offer much protection with that weight on his shoulder. Bit of a dilemma for him, Drop the camera to help her and face a big bill for repairs, or hang on to it as a bystander witness and film anything that might happen. It's a difficult choice to make.'

'It doesn't seem to have stopped her in the past, Jim.'

'No one's taken a pot shot at her before. If she's determined to go ahead, then one of us should be there,' said Jim. 'I might be better prepared if there is a problem.'

'Shall we go back to the interview room and discuss this one in greater detail? Find out what she knows, how far the enquiry has progressed, and ask who she's spoken to so far.'

'The big question is, who else knows about it outside of her television programme? Sophie said she had always discussed their respective businesses and any associated problems with her husband. That seemed to be the norm in their marriage. Could he have mentioned any of her stories, even on a casual, chatty basis to any of his friends or colleagues? You know, something like *You'll never guess who my wife is chasing now? God help them when it hits the front page!* Just innocent remarks over a drink somewhere?

'Anyway we'll have to speak to him at some stage to see if he has any idea who might have been responsible. I don't believe Sophie's spoken to him yet about the shooting, given their recent estrangement.'

12

Trussell and Joynton returned to the interview room where they had left Sophie busy on her laptop, trying to catch up with her television schedule. She looked up and said, 'I do appreciate the use of your Wi-Fi, Detective Inspector. There's a really strong signal.'

'Tell me about your husband,' said Trussell. 'We're going to have to talk to him at some point. It's just a formality but as you've apparently discussed your work with him in detail, we might as well ask him if he's been aware of any threats. Anyway a bit of background detail about him might be helpful.'

'As far as I know, he's always been involved in the City insurance market. He came from a single parent home on a council estate, and never forgot it. He was an only child, and his mother passed away after he started work. I guess there were huge similarities between both of us in that respect. He started his working life, straight from school by joining a firm of Lloyd's Brokers. I think he was quite proud of the fact that he started at the bottom - you know, no advantages - didn't go to the right school - no family connections to help him up the career ladder. It was very much who you knew in those days - a very personal business.'

'He was ambitious even in those early days, then?'

'So it seems. He managed to persuade someone in the company to let him go into Lloyd's as a junior broker. He always described himself as the gofer in those days. His company gave him all the fetching and carrying jobs to do, sort of glorified post boy to begin with.'

'He was prepared to put the effort in and learn?'

'He got to know some of the more senior people in the market that way. I think they liked his cheeky, but respectful style. People were prepared to help him and he was a very quick learner. At that time he met his two future partners, Roy Jagger and Gerard Dalrymple. They were all working for separate companies, growing up together in the market. Although they were competitors, they still developed a close friendship. Roy was a bit like Richard, still the cheeky one, but Gerry had been to the right school. It was an unlikely triumvirate.'

'When and how did they decide to set up their own business?'

'Richard told me it all started as a bit of a laugh. They all felt they weren't getting the recognition they deserved. By then they had all built up impressive lists of clients for their employers, people they had got to know over the years, who had begun to identify with them. None of them could remember the exact date or time, or how it happened. Apparently, one day, after some sort of run in with senior management, one of them turned round to the others and said, 'Sod it, I'm done with this lot. I'm thinking of going it alone.' Knowing them all as I do, my money would have been on Roy. He's always been the impetuous and spontaneous one of the three. To his surprise, the other two admitted they'd been thinking along similar lines for a while.'

'So, how did they manage it?'

'Gerry was the one with the connections, and he introduced them to people prepared to put up some starting capital. Fortunately, none of their employers had tied them down to non-competing contracts, so they were all able to walk out of the door with their respective clients prepared to support this new venture. Since then, they've done very well. Gerry's still the man behind the administration of the company, and he keeps everything running properly, leaving Richard and Roy free to bring in the business. It seemed to me it was working very well.'

'Can we talk about life in Foggenden now and the problems with Burtonlee. Did your husband get involved with you in the local action group?'

'He did meet the other members of the action group when they came to our house, but he never got involved actively with our unofficial committee. He said he couldn't allow his name and his City connection to get into the public domain locally, because it might just result in embarrassing publicity for his firm. He was absolutely emphatic all my dealings with the local group should be in my maiden name, exactly like my television and press investigations. He was aware I had given Burtonlee Homes a fairly public airing on my programme. He met Jack Finlay, John Shalford and the others on a number of occasions and told them he was highly supportive of what they were trying to achieve. He just couldn't be seen to lend his name to it publicly.'

'Did he have any problems with any of them?'

'No. He has always been very friendly towards them. Pouring drinks or keeping the conversation going if I was making the tea or coffee. He was certainly very much up to speed with what was going on, both from a local planning perspective and the national problems with Burtonlee Homes.'

'Sophie, are you aware of any problems your husband may have had? Is there any possibility this attempt might have been connected with his business? Perhaps he might have upset someone in the past who might be using you as a means of getting back at him?'

'I think it's so unlikely that I believe you can discount it completely. I know there are huge sums of money whizzing around in the insurance business, but I've never heard of anything mysterious or overt happening to anyone. Business seems to be conducted in a fairly philosophical manner - you know, win some, lose some. Richard's often said it's been the case that they've been pursuing new clients and have left the back door open, so to speak, for someone to pinch one of their clients while they weren't looking. It's the way of the market. It seems there's always a slight turnover of their client base. Most are very loyal but there are always some who will listen to someone offering them the chance to save a bit of money, however short term. The intention is to always end up ahead on a financial basis and grow their business.'

'My next question, Sophie is, have either of you spoken to anyone at Burtonlee Homes at any time?'

'Richard would never have been involved in any contact with them. He's always kept a low profile publicly while being very supportive privately. It was down to me. I've tried several times to get a meeting with Burtonlee himself, but I can never get past his personal assistant, Jonathan Barlborough. He seems to be the fixer. '

'Have any of the other members of the committee had any dealings with Barlborough? Jack Finlay or John Shalford, for example?'

'They would certainly have met him at a Burtonlee presentation in one of the local halls. Burtonlee Homes have put on a number of these travelling road shows to try to convince the local people that the company's doing them a favour by dropping a new small town on their doorstep. Barlborough's always giving me the run-around. If I do manage to speak to him, he only wants to talk about the wonderful advantages of their project to the community. He's always stressing the sports facilities they will provide for the community, the country park, the schools, and the shops. In short, all of the wonderful amenities Burtonlee will so generously give to the community. The fact the land is criss-crossed at the moment with footpaths and public rights of way, conveniently goes over his head. I've seen him at a couple of their public presentations. I find him too smooth by half.'

'I assume you're still trying to get an interview with Burtonlee himself?'

'Yes, of course. He will realise eventually he can't keep dodging me, or other members of the Press for that matter, indefinitely. He'll have to talk to us sooner or later to put his side of the story and try to restore some of their reputation, which has certainly been suffering of late. It's just a case of getting to him. Barlborough can't defend him forever.'

13

Jim Trussell's phone rang. He picked it up.

'Yes sir, I'll be right up.'

He turned to Jackie and made a face.

'That was our Detective Chief Superintendent Watkins. He wanted to know whether I could spare him a couple of minutes and his wish is my command. It could be nothing - just a friendly chat because I've managed to avoid him recently - or something's up. Of course he may just want to know what's going on here.'

Trussell took the lift up to the hallowed eighth floor and made for the Boss's office. He tapped on the partly open door.

'Come in, Trussell,' said a loud voice. It didn't bode well.

'Sir?'

Old comradely familiarity seemed out of place. They had worked together when Trussell had started out as a Detective Constable in his first posting to an East Kent police station at Brandford. Watkins had been the Detective Sergeant. It had always been Charlie and Jim in those days; only it didn't seem to apply anymore. Nor had they been particularly happy memories. It was a tough place to police. The local estate contained more shoplifters, burglars and other petty criminals than most places. Then there were the more serious, hardened criminals. The police had had a difficult time there, trying to get people off the streets. Sometimes corners were cut to get the right result. Trussell found difficulty in the 'end justifies the means' philosophy adopted by some of his senior officers. The right criminals may have been removed from the streets but sometimes on less than the correct grounds. When Watkins had picked up the son of an important local politician during one of their raids, a deal was done behind the scenes, and his future was assured. He was promoted to Detective Inspector and then made even more rapid progress through the upper ranks. Now he moved in different circles. Trussell, as a newly arrived Detective Constable, was unimpressed by all of this and had asked for a transfer to another area. Now, ironically, he had found himself back, reporting to Watkins again, when he moved to Woodchester.

Watkins had settled into his administrative role in more ways than one. He had put on quite a few extra pounds despite regular appearances on the golf course and his thinning hair had a few grey streaks. Now he peered at Trussell over the reading glasses perched on the end of his nose.

I wonder if he's hitting the ball any straighter these days? thought Trussell, mischievously.

'Sit down. Now, what's going on downstairs at the moment? What's happening with that TV journalist woman? What's her name? Any progress yet?'

'Sophie Breckton, sir. There's nothing concrete to report at the moment. The Forensic report's due today, so maybe that will help. What we've found already is that she's upset a lot of fairly significant people over the last few years, so there are plenty of potentially motivated people out there. Threats have been made in the past, mainly through social media. We're working our way through them at the moment to see if we can narrow the list down a bit. It looks like a professional job at this point. We've been trying to keep the case under wraps for now. Don't think there's anything to gain at the moment by publicising it'.

'She's a bit high profile – in the public eye, and questions are being asked up here. I must have something to get the Assistant Chief Constable off my back. Keep me updated. I can't sanction any help or overtime for you. There are serious budgetary constraints at the moment,'

Trussell chuckled inwardly. He had noticed that the executive floor had been redecorated and some rather expensive looking modern furniture had appeared around the offices, so he had a fair idea where the money was going. With more political influence these days, it was obviously important to present the right image to any visitors.

'Well, Sir; we now have four people in the team, although two of them are recent arrivals. DC Mark Green joined us about a year ago but DC Tim Beach has only been with us about four months and he's somewhat lacking in experience at present. DS Joynton and I will cope. I know John McIndow's team is really busy just now, so I can't look to him for any help. We'll manage somehow.'

'Just let me know what's going on, Trussell.' And with that, he was dismissed.

He returned to the CID suite, puzzled.

'What did the Chief Super want, Jim?'

'News travels fast round here. Watkins wanted an update on Tuesday. I wonder how he found out about Foggenden? I thought we were trying to keep this one under wraps for as long as possible.'

'Well, he was a good detective once, Jim! Perhaps he really hasn't lost his touch despite all the politicking upstairs.'

'He also told me there wouldn't be any extra help or overtime. No money to spare'

'We'll manage.'

'I know that.'

'By the way, Jim, the Forensic report arrived while you were up there. I had a quick glance at it. Considering there wasn't very much around in terms of evidence, they've come up with some interesting facts and ideas. The cartridge case they found in the woods was American.'

She referred to the report. 'Here it is. It was a Black Hills Fusion 165 Grain. The remains of the bullet picked up in Sophie's kitchen matches the case in terms of weight. They've lifted some DNA from it, which will be useful if we find a suspect. The man who wrote the report seems a bit of an enthusiast - reads trade magazines and keeps up to date with the shooting lobby. He says this calibre is widely used in the States by deer hunters. He's taken an educated guess that the actual weapon would have been something like a Ruger .308, popular over there and readily available for about sixteen hundred dollars from gun shops. He said this would be a very suitable weapon for this type of job; relatively short barrel, adjustable stock and only weighing about nine pounds. They come with a telescopic sight, and have an effective range of about eight hundred to a thousand yards. And, he tells us, they've been used by US Special Forces. Sounds like the perfect contract sniper's weapon; compact, portable and lightweight. It might be worth finding out whether there's a registered importer over here and if so, how many have been sold. It doesn't sound like equipment for the run of the mill shooter readily available for hire here through the usual criminal sources.'

'What else was in the report?'

'As you said yesterday, Jim, the ground was very dry and it would have been difficult to find any meaningful signs or tracks. However, they did find that one of the low branches had been scraped, probably where the gun was rested for the shot. Location of the cartridge case would have corroborated that. It all lines up with Sophie's kitchen window.

They estimated the distance as about two hundred yards, so an easy shot for a professional with the right equipment but definitely rules out an amateur with a grudge.'

'I sent Greeno over to Foggenden yesterday to talk to the witness again about the Mercedes while it's still fresh in his mind. I asked him to find out exactly where he saw it. It may still be possible to find tyre tracks if we knew exactly where to look. Someone should also check with the bird watchers on Saturday, to see if they know anyone who might drive that sort of vehicle. We should ask whether any of them have seen a similar car there before. The driver might just have come down there earlier for a look around to work out his best position for the shot.'

'What about the committee members?'

'I also asked him to talk to Jack Finlay to get more information about his committee and the local councillors. Let's see what he has to say when he turns up.'

Almost bang on cue, DC Green walked into the office.

'Morning, Guv. I spent time with Mr Finlay yesterday to talk about his committee and the Burtonlee project. It was quite interesting.'

He dragged a notebook out of the depths of his pocket, opened it and read through the contents.

'He's not aware of any threats against members of his committee. He confirms his own objections are fairly well documented and freely admits he's had some slanging matches with one or two of the Town Councillors. He certainly doesn't pull any punches. He suspects them of all sorts of skulduggery. I had to rein him in a bit when he got into his stride. Told him I was only interested in facts and if he had any evidence of dubious practices, then he should show me the proof. I told him we would be prepared to look at it, but in the meantime, he should be a little careful about what he said to people, especially in public. I think I convinced him I was on his side and he got the message.'

'It sounds as if that went OK, Greeno. Did you get a list of his Committee members, and details of the Town Councillors and where they stand individually on the Burtonlee plans?'

Yes, they're all here,' he replied, tapping his notebook. 'I'll get everything typed up and printed off for you, Guv.'

'OK.'

'There's just one other thing, Guv. He did ask what was going on at Sophie Blaxstone's cottage. He mentioned he'd driven past on his way to town and had noticed the police tapes around it. One of the PCSO's flagged him down, asked him to identify himself, and then wanted to know whether he'd seen any strangers in the area. I told him I couldn't comment on an ongoing police investigation. He did ask about Sophie so I assured him she was OK and had moved somewhere else for the moment.'

'It sounds as if you said all the right things. What about the other witness, Mr Shalford?'

'I visited him as you asked, Guv. He's a widower and lives alone. I had a chat. Interesting chap. Ex-military, Used to be in the artillery, which has left him a bit deaf. He's OK with his hearing aids, though I had to knock several times to get a response. He really couldn't add anything to what he told the local uniformed when they spoke to him. He remembered seeing the Mercedes because it seemed new to the area, but couldn't say much about it beyond confirming it was silver and had darkened windows. He stated he hadn't seen it there before amongst the birdwatching group, but had no reason to note the registration plate. I did have another look around, but the ground was very dry. No evidence of tyre tracks on the ground or any mud on the lane. It'll all be in my notes.'

'Well done, Greeno. Put everything into a short report and I can add it to the file.'

14

Jim Trussell walked into the office. 'Morning, team. Looks like another scorcher out there today.'

'Morning Jim,' said Jackie. 'I've got some more news for you. The plot thickens. We've just had a call from uniformed. A body was found in the fields near Foggenden last night. That's the place where Sophie Blaxstone lives, the area Burtonlee wants to develop.'

'Obviously they've called us for a reason. Has the body been identified yet?'

'Yes. It was a John Finlay, a local house owner. He's one of the people on Sophie's committee – we've got him down as Jack Finlay. In fact, from what Sophie told us, Finlay was leading the resistance to the planning application. She said he was well known to the Burtonlee team from their travelling road shows.'

'The circumstances?'

'A dog walker found him, collapsed near one of the footpaths, about a mile from his house. He appeared to have been out for a walk when he just keeled over. The man called the paramedics, who arrived pretty smartly, given the distance, but they were unable to save him. He was pronounced dead at the scene. They thought he had suffered a heart attack, although they did specifically mention the look on his face. He looked frightened.'

'When did the local police turn up?'

'They were very quick. They arrived within fifteen minutes of the call. It was the paramedics who alerted them. They were able to identify him from his wallet. His wife arrived while all this was going on. She'd been concerned that he hadn't returned sooner, and had taken the family dog with her to look for him.'

'That was pretty distressing for her.'

'Do you think this is just an unfortunate coincidence, Jim, given his involvement with the Burtonlee development action group? Should we look into it?'

'The way this case is developing, Jackie, I don't believe we can rule anything out. I certainly think we should talk to his wife and to the man who found him, as well. Did uniformed give you any details? Have we got his name and contact phone number? I think we'd better follow this up as soon as possible. Find out where they took the body. There'll be a post mortem as a case of unexplained death. Find out who'll be carrying it out.'

While Jackie phoned the local police station for details of the witness, Trussell searched through the file for Finlay's address and phone number, which Sophie had given to him when they were reviewing her own notes on the development. He picked up the phone and rang the number.

'Mrs Finlay? My name is Detective Inspector Trussell of Kent Police. I'm sorry to trouble you at this very difficult time, but I wonder whether I could call on you for a brief word?...If you're sure? Then I'll come round this afternoon. Say 2.30 if that's convenient. Do you have someone there with you?...Good. Thank you.'

He hung up and turned his attention to Joynton.

'I've got the witness's details, Jim. His name is Victor Jarvis. He's retired, so should be available anytime. He lives at Bragdon Heath. It's a couple of miles from the place where Mr Finlay was found. From what I can gather from the local boys, the fields there are a popular place with dog walkers, joggers and even mountain bikers. We can ask him whether he saw anyone else. Never know. We might get lucky.'

'Give him a call. See if he's available this afternoon. Ask him if we can meet him at the scene. You never know; there might be something that will jog his memory.'

'OK, Jim, I'll do it now,' she said, picking up the phone.

She got through on the first attempt. 'Hello. Mr Jarvis? I'm Detective Sergeant Joynton of Kent Police. I'd like to speak to you about yesterday's events at Foggenden. I understand you spoke to the police at the scene, but we would still like to talk to you as this could form part of an ongoing investigation. Would it be convenient to meet you sometime later today? Preferably at Foggenden...Yes, of course you can bring your dog. I understand it's a regular exercise spot for you. I'll be accompanied by Detective Inspector Trussell. We're interested in what you might have seen yesterday. It could be relevant. Can we meet in the small car park on Foggenden Lane? What time would be convenient?...Three thirty would be fine. Thank you.'

She turned to Trussell. 'That's fixed, Jim. 'I'll get onto uniformed now to find out where they took Mr Finlay.'

Ten minutes later, after several phone calls, she had the answers.

'The paramedics took Mr Finlay to The Woodchester yesterday, where he was confirmed dead on arrival. The post mortem will be tomorrow. I've spoken to the consultant in A & E. He told me he was sufficiently concerned about the facial expression to note it down. He said he had seen this situation a couple of times before, over the years. There have been cases where the deceased had literally been scared to death. He started to explain it to me. Something to do with an adrenaline rush sending the heart into arrhythmia and calcium was involved there somewhere as well. I don't fully understand the biochemistry. He said if the victim had already got some sort of heart condition, then this could accelerate the problem. The details were a bit too complicated for me, I'm afraid. No doubt the pathologist will pick this up. It might be worth asking Mrs Finlay if her husband had any history of heart disease.'

'Right, Time for a quick update to see where we are. Do we have any further news on Mr Brownlowe-Jameson? Have we heard any more from the Agency? What about the whistle-blower who disappeared? Has there been anything more from the Met?'

'No, nothing has come back from anyone, yet Jim. I'll chase them.'

'OK. Maybe it's time we turned our attention to Mr Burtonlee. By the way, I think Sophie still plans to go to that estate to talk to the locals about the subletting racket.'

'I thought you'd tried to talk her out of it, Jim?'

'Not so far. It's part of her first programme in the new series and she's determined to get the story.'

'Has she indicated exactly when she's planning to go there?'

'Next week sometime, I believe, unless we can dissuade her. We can't organise any formal protection for her. Besides, if she turns up with a couple of PCs in tow, no one on the estate will want to talk to her.'

'Perhaps one of us should go in plain clothes. Don't really think it's one for Greeno or Sandcastle.'

'You're right, Jackie. It'll have to be me. I'll try to look like one of her crew. Have to get some advice on what I should wear. It's bound to be very casual behind the camera.'

'Never quite saw you as a TV star, Jim. A new career beckons!'

'I don't think so. Anyway, we'll just grab something in the High Street for lunch and then we'll head for Foggenden. Timing should be about right.;

'It sounds good to me - if you're buying, Jim.'

After a quick sandwich and a cup of coffee at a local cafe, they returned to the station to collect Trussell's car. They were soon heading out of town along the main road that led west. The lane signposted to Foggenden appeared and Trussell turned left into it.

'Watch out for tractors, Jim,' said Jackie. It's their playpen here - we know they always want most of the road.'

Trussell checked his satnav and looked around him. 'Finlay's house should be here somewhere. The system always just shows the centre of the postcode. Ah, here it is.' He indicated a small detached cottage with a gravelled area in front. Two cars were already parked there. He pulled into the remaining space. He looked at the house. It was quite small and had probably once been a farm labourer's cottage, although it had been extended and now had modern double glazed windows, carefully chosen to reflect the building's historic style. It looked well maintained.

Trussell and Joynton walked up the neatly paved path, flanked on either side by colourful, well-tended flower beds. He found the doorbell and pressed it.

A woman in her late sixties answered the door. She was very pale with greying hair and had on a floral dress. She was wearing glasses over swollen eyes but still contrived to appear outwardly composed despite the aura of sadness about her. A dog was barking forlornly somewhere in the house.

'Mrs Finlay?'

She nodded. 'I'm Rose Finlay.'

'Detective Inspector Trussell,' he said, offering his warrant card. 'And this is my colleague, Detective Sergeant Joynton. We spoke earlier. Thank you for agreeing to see us at this very difficult time.'

'Please come in.' She stepped aside pointing to the open living room door behind her.

Another woman half rose from a chair inside and subsided again.

'This is my sister, Elizabeth. She's been staying with me since yesterday evening. Our, I mean my son, lives in Australia. He's on his way back as soon as he can arrange a flight. Please sit down.' She indicated the large, comfortable sofa under the window. 'Now, how can I help you? I've already spoken to the policemen who turned up yesterday.'

'I'm sorry to have to ask you to go over the events yet again. I realise how hard it must be for you,' said Trussell. 'Can you tell me why your husband went out?'

'Jack received a phone call early yesterday evening. It must have been about five thirty. I heard him ask the caller several times for a name and how he'd come by the information he was offering. He stated several times that the committee certainly couldn't pay for anything, as they were a self-funded group of householders, only wanting to safeguard the area for themselves and the future. I heard him tell the caller he would meet him by the Dewpond - it's a fairly prominent feature over there. Then he put the phone down.'

'Did he say anything to you?'

'Only that the caller had told him he had some damning evidence that Burtonlee had been passing brown envelopes around to bribe certain councillors in connection with planning permission for their development.'

'Did he give you any more details about the conversation, or even the caller? Didn't give any name, I suppose?'

'No. Jack did say the man wasn't local. He seemed to have some sort of accent. American, he thought. But he couldn't be certain. As Jack said, *What would an American want with a development in Kent?* He said the man wasn't looking for money. Just wanted to make sure Burtonlee got what was coming to him. That it was personal.'

'How long was he out before you became concerned?' asked Jackie.

'I'd told him his meal would be ready in an hour. He said that was plenty of time. Fifteen minutes' walk each way, and a few minutes for the conversation. When an hour and a half had passed, and there was no sign of him, I began to worry. I put the dog on the lead and we went to out to look for Jack. When I arrived at the Dewpond, the paramedics were already there with the man who'd found him. They told me they were too late, and Jack had already passed away. Two policemen arrived shortly afterwards. They wanted me to identify him, which I did. I'll never forget the look on his face. He looked really frightened. I've never seen anything like it before.'

'Tell me, Mrs Finlay, did your husband have any history of heart problems?'

'Not that I've ever been aware. He was very fit. He walked a lot and took care of all the heavy work in the garden. He was always active.'

'Has he felt under any pressure with his resistance to the development? Has he had any contact with Burtonlee Homes? What about local councillors?'

'He may have met some of the Burtonlee people at their various exhibitions. But he hasn't had any direct dealings with them as far as I know. As far as the councillors are concerned, I do know he's fallen out with some of them publicly over the development, when it's been discussed at open council meetings. They're fully aware he's been leading the opposition to the plans. He's been fairly vocal in his opinions of some of them. A couple of times he was told by some of his colleagues on the committee to tone down his comments as they felt he was sailing very close to the wind and some of it might have been actionable.'

'Did that involve anyone in particular?'

'Councillor Jeremiah Blackley. Jack thought his support for the development was a bit too fulsome. He thought there was something going on behind the scenes.'

'Were there any representatives of Burtonlee present when he made these allegations?'

'Yes. They always seemed to have someone at those meetings. You don't think this has anything to do with his death, surely? That he was lured to the meeting at the Dewpond on the promise of evidence, just to get him alone in a secluded place?'

'That's one line of enquiry we're considering at the moment.'

Mrs Finlay's hand flew to her mouth and she looked at her sister in horror.

Trussell stood up. He handed Mrs Finlay a card.

'Thank you for your help at such a difficult time, Mrs Finlay. Should you recall anything else, please call me on this number.'

He nodded to her sister, who had remained silent throughout but had been listening intently to the conversation.

Jackie had been writing all this down in her notebook while they spoke. Now she stood up and followed Trussell towards the front door which Mrs Finlay closed firmly after them.

When they were back in the car, Jackie asked, 'Do you think this might turn into a murder enquiry, Jim?' If so, we'll have to consider getting her a family support officer. I know she has a sister and her son is returning to be with her, but she may need some protection from the press once this tragedy moves up a notch.'

'It's certainly beginning to look that way. The consultant's comments would seem to reinforce it. However, we'll have to wait for the results of the post mortem. We'll head for the car park now.' Glancing at his watch, he added, 'We've got a little bit of time in hand, I think. Perhaps we can take a look around before Mr Jarvis arrives.'

It was a ten minute drive to the small car park, carved out of the land to encourage more people to make use of the amenity. When they arrived, a few minutes before the agreed time, they noticed an elderly man already letting a dog out of his car and attaching a lead. The man, in his seventies, of average height and quite upright, with grey hair and glasses, was wearing a well-worn green waxed jacket, comfortable brown corduroy trousers and had put on a pair of walking boots.

They approached him and Trussell asked, 'Mr Jarvis?'

'You must be the two detectives.'

Trussell produced his warrant card and introduced himself and Jackie. 'Thank you for agreeing to meet us this afternoon at such short notice. We really appreciate it and thought it would much easier to discuss things here rather than at the station. We're hoping this might just help you remember something which maybe didn't occur to you yesterday when the tragedy occurred.'

'It was no problem, Detective Inspector. I bring Hunter over here most days.' He looked down and patted the brown and white Springer Spaniel sitting patiently by his side.

'Do you always use this car park? Were there any other vehicles here when you arrived?'

'There are usually two or three cars. I come at roughly the same time most days. One gets to know the regulars. Nodding terms, you know. Pass the time of day with them. Strangely enough, I did notice a car I hadn't seen before. It looked out of place. *A bit smart for dog walking*, I thought. Maybe it was one of those weekend posers.'

'Did you notice what sort of car?'

'Yes. It was a silver Mercedes - expensive looking with tinted windows and sun roof. *Top of the range job*, I thought. Just couldn't help noticing it. When I finally got back, after the whole tragic affair, the car had gone.'

Jackie and Trussell exchanged knowing looks.

'I don't suppose you took note of the registration number?' asked Jackie.

'I'm afraid not. It didn't occur to me at the time.'

'Perhaps we can walk over to where this all happened yesterday evening, Mr Jarvis, if you feel up to it. It must have been a very unpleasant experience.'

'It was. I don't think I'll ever forget the look on that poor man's face. I felt so sorry for his wife when she arrived with her dog. She was out looking for him, because she was worried he hadn't come home. It was a terrible shock for her.'

'So you called the paramedics?'

'Yes. They arrived very quickly. The police arrived about fifteen minutes later.'

'You mentioned you tend to see some regulars around here when you're out. Was there anyone about as you walked over here?'

'I saw a couple of the usual people in the distance with their dogs. They waved to me. Doubt they'd been to this part. Otherwise they'd have raised the alarm before me.'

By now they had reached the Dewpond where Jack Finlay's body had been found. It had not been treated as a crime scene by the local police but as an unfortunate death which appeared to them to be due to natural causes.

'Tell me how you found the body, Mr Jarvis,' said Trussell. 'This is a bit of a hollow, below the normal line of sight.'

'It was Hunter. I'd let him off the lead. These Springers are bred as gun dogs. Very obedient, but need the exercise. He got ahead of me and disappeared into this dip. I heard him barking, so I came over after he didn't respond to my voice. It's quite unusual for him. That was when I saw the poor man, lying there. He wasn't moving, so I called the emergency service on my mobile phone. The rest you know.'

'Apart from the people you saw in the distance, the other dog walkers, did you see anyone else about?'

Jarvis stopped to think for a moment as he looked around him, and then pointed in the direction of the car park.

'There was someone. I didn't think to mention it yesterday to the police officers, with everything else that was going on. I remember now. I saw someone over there.' He was pointing to a path leading back to the car park.

'Can you describe that person?' asked Jackie. 'Was it male or female? How were they dressed?'

'That's the odd thing, now I come to think about it,' said Jarvis. 'It was a man. I thought at first he was out jogging. He could have been running. As if he wanted to leave the place as quickly as possible. I really didn't pay much attention. There was far too much going on at the time.'

'Nothing strange about that, surely?' asked Jackie.

'No. But he wasn't dressed for it. I'm used to seeing people out exercising. This time of the year, they're usually wearing vests and running shorts, or maybe jogging bottoms. But this chap wasn't. He was quite smartly dressed in a brown leather jacket, smart jeans and trainers. Not running kit at all.'

'Can you describe him?'

'Not really. He did have dark hair and a darker complexion. Sort of olive-skinned. What we might call Mediterranean appearance.'

Jackie busied herself, noting all this down.

Trussell asked Jarvis to show them exactly where he'd found Jack Finlay.

He glanced around but there was nothing much to see. 'Nothing more to be seen here now, Jackie,' he said. 'Thank you, Mr Jarvis. You've been very helpful. I'll give you my card. Please give me a call if anything else occurs to you. It could be important. We'll leave you to your daily exercise now.' He stroked the dog's ears. 'Well done, Hunter.'

The dog licked his hand, liking the attention and his gaze followed the two detectives as they took the path back to the car park.

'I think we can now rule in foul play, Jackie' said Trussell, as they climbed into the Skoda for the trip back to Woodchester. 'We need to pay more attention to that mysterious Mercedes. It seems to be increasingly involved in this case. Things are getting more complicated by the day.'

'Should we tell Sophie?'

'Yes,' said Trussell. 'She needs to know. We'll go to the Castle now. I also need to talk to her about the trip to the estate next week. I'll try again to dissuade her. But if she won't listen, then, I'll suggest I go along to keep an eye on things. Let's see what she says.'

15

Twenty minutes later, they drove carefully through the arch at the Castle Inn and found an empty space in the car park.

Jackie had phoned ahead and Sophie met them in the lounge. She had found their usual corner table unoccupied, despite the fact it was Friday and the hotel was quite busy, with guests enjoying a pre-dinner drink and she waved as they walked in through the archway from the lobby.

'Evening,' she said. 'How's your day been?' She seemed relatively cheerful after a busy day, discussing her television programme with her producer. Then she picked up on their subdued mood. 'What is it? Has something happened?'

'Bad news, I'm afraid, Sophie,' said Trussell. 'We've just come from Foggenden. Your friend, Jack Finlay, was found dead near the Dewpond last night. The paramedics who attended thought he had died of natural causes. A heart attack, maybe. However, we now believe otherwise. We're awaiting the results of the post mortem to be sure.'

Sophie's reaction was one of total shock. Her hand went to her mouth, she gasped and the colour drained from her face.

'That's awful,' she said. 'Poor Rose must be devastated. Is anyone with her? Their only son lives in Australia. Is there anything I can do? Should I go to see her?'

'We've been to see her this afternoon,' said Trussell. 'Her son is on his way back. In the meantime, her sister's staying with her. Sophie, I don't want you to leave this hotel on your own. There's a lot going on that we don't fully understand at the moment. I think we need to discuss Mr Burtonlee. We haven't got any real reason to talk to him officially yet. There's no evidence that he or his company is actually involved in this at the moment, whatever we may think but there are too many coincidences already.'

'I still have to go ahead with my preparations for the new series. I'm going to the estate I mentioned to you. We've had some positive feedback from some of the tenants. They're prepared to talk to me. I need their testimonies to move the investigation along. They're prepared to give me names and details of which flats and houses have been illegally sublet.'

Jackie interrupted her. 'Jim and I've been talking about this. We don't think it's a very good idea. But, if you're still determined to go, then we think one of us should be there while you're doing your interviews. We know you'll have your cameraman with you, but he's unlikely to be able to help you if anything happens. Just film the events. No good to you. I'm sure you can see that. Anyway, it seems I'm going to miss out on my television debut this time. Jim's pulled rank on me. He thinks it would be better to have a man there.'

'My idea is to stay very much in the background,' said Jim. 'Just try to look like any member of the public who's curious about the idea of a television camera on the estate. I'll be someone who just wants to watch. Question is, what do you think I should wear to melt into the background?'

'I suggest you wear the scruffiest clothes you can find. Old jeans, dirty tee-shirt, baseball cap. Oh, and don't shave for a few days. That should help. The baseball cap should help to disguise your hair. It looks far too smart for the Brandford Estate.'

'Thank you for that. I'll take it as a compliment,' he said, smiling. 'Which day have you arranged to go?'

'I need to talk to Dennis, my cameraman. But I was thinking about next Tuesday, the twenty-fifth.'

'What time?'

'I'd aim to get there sometime mid-morning so I'm planning to leave the hotel at nine-thirty. I'd want to start at about ten-thirty and wrap it up before the kids get out of school - at least those who can be bothered to attend. I think there's a high level of truancy there. *Educated in the University of Life*,' she said. 'A lot of them have found that running drugs for others pays for all of their designer gear. Most of them aren't bright enough to realise everything is counterfeit, anyway. I expect some of them are running drugs for one of the County lines. It's not a very nice place. I feel so sorry for the decent people who have to live there. If you're seriously thinking about coming with me, DI Trussell, then you'll have to turn a blind eye to a lot of what you see going on and concentrate on what we're doing. Leave the day to day problems for the local police to handle. I'm sure they already have a pretty good idea what happens there the rest of the time.'

'You'd better call me Jim to avoid your cameraman becoming suspicious. Just pass me off as a minder suggested by the producer. DI Trussell when we're on official business.'

'OK, Jim it is,' she said, looking at him and smiling.

Was there something more to that smile? Jackie wondered.

Sophie waved to catch the barman's attention. 'We'll have a drink to celebrate Jim's entry into the world of television. Let's hope it passes off smoothly. This programme is very important to the innocent people who live on the estate whose lives are being blighted by the illegal tenants who've moved in, bringing more drug dealing and other crime into the area.'

Official business over, thoughts turned to the weekend.

'What have you got planned, Sophie?' asked Jackie. 'I suppose you'll be working on your programme. If not, I could drop by tomorrow, if you'd like me to.'

'That's really kind. You're correct though. The programme's keeping me fully occupied, although I owe the *Enquirer* a follow up article on the Burtonlee problems and my email inbox is filling up with yet more complaints. I do need to catch up with them. More emails to Jonathan Barlborough. All I get from him is even more platitudes. *We're doing everything we can to fix these problems. Please ask your complainants to contact me directly.* I've done that countless times already, but he just shrugs them off. *'I promise we're doing our best to catch up, but we're in other peoples' hands. Delay with deliveries of the materials we need. Tradesmen overloaded. Labour shortage.'*

'It sounds as if he's just soaking it all up. Like a sponge.'

'That's right. It's frustrating enough for me. Heaven knows what it's like for those poor people who've bought their houses. Do you think Burtonlee is involved in my problems? And now there's poor Jack to consider. What is there about his death that's made you suspicious?'

'The answer, Sophie, is we can't rule anyone out yet. I don't want to discuss Mr Finlay's death until we have the results of the post mortem. There's always one held in the case of any unexplained death. We're still looking at your friend, Roger, as well, although information is a bit slow reaching us at this level, because of the complexity of his particular brand of sin. The file on the whistle-blower is certainly still open.'

'Lovely turn of phrase, Jim,' said Sophie. 'You should become a journalist. If Burtonlee or one of his people has caused harm to that poor man, then he would certainly be capable of doing something to me.'

'One journalist in the family is enough, I think. I'll leave it to my daughter, Liz, if that's what she really wants to do.'

'It's not such a bad career, you know, Jim. It's very rare for journalists to get themselves killed! I just seem to be unlucky at the moment.'

'Jim,' said Jackie, 'If Sophie is OK, then I'll be off. It's one of those rare evenings. Mike and I both have a free Friday night, and I think he has plans for us. You've got my number if you need me, Sophie.'

Trussell nodded. 'That's fine, Jackie. I'll see you on Monday. If anything important comes up, I'll call you. I'll stay here for a while longer.'

With that, Jackie stood up, smiled at Sophie and walked out of the lounge.

As she turned her head at the archway and looked back, she saw they were already engaged in an animated conversation.

Maybe I'll hear all about it on Monday. Or maybe I won't, she thought, *seeing Jim laughing with Sophie. They look very comfortable in each other's company. Jim'd better be careful. We're already on a fairly informal basis with Sophie due to the nature of the case so I wouldn't want him to cause any problems for himself by getting involved. On the other hand Jim's a widower and Sophie's alone now. She's a very attractive woman. Why not? It's difficult for me to say anything.*

16

Sophie's mobile warbled. It was Richard. Warning bells rang.

'Why've you phoned me, Richard?' she asked, taking the initiative. 'You haven't contacted me since you left. You know what a terrible shock it was to me. I thought I'd never get over it. Now, just as I'm getting my life back together, you call me. Why? What do you want? Are you just twisting the knife? What are you trying to do to me? Haven't you hurt me enough?'

That familiar voice. 'I've been confused. I think I've made a mistake. I've missed you. I know I said some unkind things when I left last month. I could blame the pressures of our two different careers and the fact we've spent too much time apart. I've always been concerned about your work and the potential dangers you might have been exposed to. But, how've you been getting on?'

It was that same familiar persuasive voice with the intonation and the careful choice of words. Richard, the consummate broker, was using all of his professional charm to make a convincing case. He knew which buttons to push.

'Just fine, Richard, apart from the fact that someone tried to kill me a few days ago.'

There was a gasp, followed by a stunned silence.

'What do you mean? What happened? How could you be sure it was deliberate?'

'Someone taking a shot at me and ruining our kitchen window seemed pretty deliberate to me, Richard.'

There was a sharp intake of breath. He sounded totally shocked.

'When did this happen? Were you hurt? Why didn't you phone me? I assume you called the police? What did they say?'

'Oh yes, they arrived very quickly. They sent an armed response unit. They're looking at my old investigations and press articles to see if they can find out who was responsible.'

'Well, Sophie, you always did have a knack of upsetting important people. I remember all those online threats. Do the police have any clues, yet?'

'I don't know. If they do, they're keeping pretty quiet about it. At least they're taking it seriously this time.'

'Look, Sophie, I really do think I've made a huge mistake. Would you be prepared to meet me to talk things over? Perhaps you could come up to town for lunch soon so we can discuss it?'

'I'll think about it. You've hurt me badly and I'd need to be sure you're being totally honest and serious about reconciliation. If not, forget it. I'll move on. I still have my career to think about. If I do decide to meet you, where should it be? At our flat in the Barbican? Or would that inconvenience your girlfriend? What was her name?'

'Victoria. No, we'll meet somewhere else. I'm having the flat redecorated at the moment.'

'It's a shame you didn't discuss it with me first. After all, I do own half of it. In fact, as I remember, I put up most of the money to buy it.'

'You know the decor was rather tired when we bought it. The job was on our *to do list*. It just seemed the right moment to organise it.'

'Sounds like you were trying to paint me out of your life, Richard. I'll think about your suggestion and send you a text. I need to be absolutely convinced you're serious about getting back together.'

'It's important we get together - there's a lot to talk over. We could meet at our favourite wine bar in Leadenhall Market. The company rents a private room there and I can find out when it's free. It'll give us a chance to talk to see if we can work things out. I'll send you a text with some dates. Would that suit?

'I'll think about it, Richard, but don't get your hopes up.'

12.30 p.m.

Sophie's phone warbled the usual message notification.

It was from Richard, telling her he'd be able to book the private room at the wine bar for the following Tuesday, the twenty-fifth, or the Wednesday at one o'clock. Would either be OK? Could she confirm it was convenient for her? It was signed off with a couple of kisses.

She thought about it seriously for a few minutes. Did he really mean it? She made her decision and then sent a text, telling him Tuesday wasn't any good, as she had to go to Brandford that morning for her television programme, but confirmed she'd meet him on the twenty-sixth at one o'clock.

17

Jackie's phone rang. It was Jim Trussell, calling from home.

'Morning, Jackie. I've decided to take a day's leave to catch up on a few things and prepare for the trip to Brantford tomorrow. Keep the team on track following up on Brownlowe-Jameson and ask Sandcastle to pursue our white van man. He should have enough time today to get that enquiry started. Sophie gave us the man's name and address. Tell him to contact the local Trading Standards to see whether they already have any complaints registered against the man. If not, tell him to give them the details. He should get on to the DVLA to get the registration of the man's van. Greeno is busy at the moment looking at Mr Barlborough of Burtonlee Homes.'

'It's fine, Jim. We can manage. That is, unless we get yet another unexplained event. Certainly seems to be a feature of this case. Good luck tomorrow at Brandford. Let us know when you've finished there.'

'Thanks. By the way, I'll contact Sophie in a moment to make sure she's OK. If anything's changed, I'll call you straight back.'

He was looking in the mirror, yet again. He felt somewhat self-conscious about his appearance with three days' growth of stubble. Not a good idea to go into the office looking like that. Jackie could keep things under control. She was very efficient and had a good rapport with the two younger Detective Constables. He was still concerned she was ambitious and he knew she had her heart set on joining the Fraud Squad. He wouldn't stand in her way but he needed her to help him solve this case. He still hoped, privately, she might stay on and make her career in the CID.

She certainly had the ability to progress.

18

Monday 24th June. 9.15 a.m.
In the City.

Richard Blaxstone put on his raincoat, picked up his executive case and left the flat in the Barbican. He couldn't wait to get away from the pervasive smell of paint left behind now the redecoration was finished. The meeting he'd arranged with Sophie for Wednesday was very much in his mind. How should he play it? Trying to win Sophie back would be a major challenge. He needed her more than she might realise.

After reaching street level, he walked around the tube station and crossed Moorgate. He continued southwards along the street and turned left into London Wall. Another ten minutes took him to the traffic lights at Bishopsgate. He crossed the road and reached St Mary Axe. He turned right and walked past the Gherkin, paying the iconic building no attention as he was still deep in thought. He needed to get Sophie on his side again and was still wondering how he could do it. At the top of the road, he turned left onto Leadenhall Street and a couple of minutes later, had reached his office building. He took the lift to the third floor, and then walked through the frosted double glass doors carrying his company name into the reception area. The scent of the daily fresh flowers was very strong.

'Good morning, Mr Blaxstone,' said the cheerful young receptionist.

Richard nodded, his mind elsewhere.

'Good morning, Richard,' said Jo, his personal assistant, from her desk outside his office. 'Roy and Gerry were looking for you. They're in the boardroom.' She didn't seem her usual bubbly self and looked a bit embarrassed.

Strange, he thought. *Must talk to her and ask her if she's OK.*

Richard dropped his case by his desk, hung his raincoat on the coat stand, and retraced his steps back through the reception area to the boardroom on the other side.

The door was open. His two partners were sitting on the other side of the long polished dark wood table. Roy Jagger was below average height, mid-forties, fair hair and with a boyish look that had never left him. The other partner, Gerard Dalrymple, of a similar age, was tall and cadaverous, with a long, lugubrious face that had earned him the nickname of *Horse*. He was still occasionally seen in the market, looking after some of his long standing clients, but he had now assumed the administrative responsibilities in the partnership. He had a sheaf of papers on the table in front of him. There was a very definite atmosphere. Roy was even wearing his jacket, something he seldom did around the office.

'Morning boys,' said Richard. 'You look a bit serious for this time of the morning. What's up?'

'Morning, Ritchie,' said Gerard. 'Please close the door and sit down'. He indicated the chair opposite them.

'What's going on? Have we lost a major client? Has someone dumped us in it? I hope one of the juniors hasn't landed us with a Professional Indemnity claim?'

'No, nothing like that,' said Gerard, shuffling the pile of papers in front of him.

'Ritchie, it seems you've a problem. We're just in the process of closing the end of year accounts, and John Swingle has brought something to our attention.'

'Which is?'

'We have a problem with some substantial expenses You've signed. They involve fairly large sums of money spent in casinos over the last few months.'

'That'll be money spent on Hank Zarkowski of Bravura Shipping when he was over. He's not a dining or club man. He prefers a night at the tables. He's our biggest client, after all. He pays us millions every year.'

'Even so, it's a hell of a lot of money. Don't forget it's coming out of our pockets as well.'

'I never query any money you spend on your clients. I thought we all trusted one another.'

'We know, but we think it goes a bit further than that, Ritchie,' said Roy Jagger.

'What do you mean?'

'We looked through your diary,' said Roy, 'Jo refused to hand it over at first. She resisted us. But we told her the facts of life. Reminded her who pays her salary. Loyalty can only go so far.'

'I see…'

'Some of these expenses were certainly run up during Hank's visit. But how do you explain these other dates? We didn't have any clients in town, so why do we have these hefty bills from the casino? Ritchie, do you have a…problem? Have you been going there on your own and charging the bills to the company? We need to know what's going on. We've told John to bring any more of these bills to us before they're paid. We know we've always made joint decisions about the company. The three of us started it and built it up to what it is today, a privately owned market leader. But we can't have it destroyed if one of us has a gambling habit which is out of control. We also can't afford to have our company reputation dragged down in this way. Just imagine the damage if this got out into the market, let alone the press. Is there anything you ought to share with us?'

Richard just stared back at them, unsure.

'Does Sophie know about this?' asked Roy Jagger.

'She's thrown me out,' he lied. 'I'm living in the flat in the Barbican now.'

'Well, We're not going to settle any further bills from this place, so we would strongly suggest, no, insist, that you keep away from the place from this point on. When you visit Hank in his backyard, do you go to any local casinos?' After all, he lives in New Jersey. Isn't Jersey City the home of gambling on the East Coast?'

'No, he tends to be very family oriented at home. Usually he invites me out to his home for dinner with his wife. It's a palatial place with a housekeeper. She's an excellent cook.'

'Exactly. So there will be no more visits to casinos when he comes over here. I'll speak to him, if necessary,' said Gerry. 'We won't discuss this any further now, and everything stays within this room between the three of us. It's hard enough for us with all the competition out there without creating problems for ourselves'

Richard rose from his chair, looked hard at the other two, and said, 'If that's all for now, I've got things to do.' And with that, he walked out of the boardroom and back to his office.

Roy and Gerry exchanged glances.

'Don't want to revisit that one,' Said Gerry. Hope Ritchie has taken it on board. We can't have a falling out over this. There's too much at stake. If he needs help, like Gamblers Anonymous, then we must see he gets it as soon as possible.'

'Is everything OK, Richard?' asked Jo, as he walked past her desk.

He managed a wan smile. 'Yes, fine. What do we have today? Any calls for me?'

'I'm sorry about the diary. They left me no option but to hand it over.'

'That's OK. I understand. Now, what was in this morning's emails and post?'

'I've passed copies of the emails to the team for action. Just a couple of phone calls you need to be aware of. Costas has bought another company, managing two ships. It needs urgent attention. It seems he's decided to diversify. They are high end cruise ships. The company is called Diamond Shipping, but he's changing it to Diamond Cruises. The two ships are being renamed *Diamond Alexa* and *Diamond Eleni* after his wife and daughter, but I guess you would know that.'

'He never gives us any warning. I'll have to talk to him about it. This deal must have been in the negotiation stage for quite a while. He didn't just pop into a supermarket and buy two ships on a whim!'

'There was one other call, Richard. A man called and said he would phone later. He said his name was Antoine. You would know him.'

A concerned look flitted across Richard's face before he regained his composure. 'Yes, I know who he is. He works for the casino where I take Hank. I'll talk to him when he calls again.'

He walked into his office and closed the door. He needed time to think about the conversation with his two partners and the anticipated call from Antoine. He made a decision and picked up his phone.

Jo answered immediately.

'Yes, Richard?'

'Jo. I need to take care of a few things in here. Can you hold all my calls, unless Antoine phones.? If so, put him through.'

'Certainly, Richard. Do you need anything? What about some coffee?'

'No thanks. I'm fine.'

19

The phone rang on Trussell's desk. Mark Green picked it up.

'CID. DC Green speaking. How can I help you?'

A look of surprise crossed his face as he reached for a pad and pen.

'I see...When did this happen?...Last night? Who found the body?...I'll pass that on to the DI when he comes back. Where can he reach you? A name and contact would help...OK. I've got it. Thanks for calling. Bye.'

'Who was that, Greeno?' asked Jackie.

'It was someone from Sussex police. Apparently they found a body at the bottom of Beachy Head this morning.'

'It seems to be a regular event there, unfortunately. The third most popular place in the world for suicides, apparently, if you believe the media. It was nice of them to share the information, though. But, what's it to do with us?'

'It was one of the Woodchester councillors. They found his car in a layby on Beachy Head Road. His name was on the list I gave the DI.' Mark Green searched through the pile of papers on the side of his desk. 'Here it is. Councillor Jeremiah Blackley. He was one of those trying to push the Burtonlee development planning application. There were unsubstantiated rumours about his motives and a possible link to Burtonlee and some of the allegations that've been flying around. If he was really implicated, he certainly won't be picking up any more brown envelopes, for sure.'

'Jim will want to call them back. We'll need to know whether anyone else was seen nearby. It'll be too much of a stretch if the silver Mercedes appeared again, but the question will need to be asked. The car is beginning to remind me of that Spielberg film.'

'Which film was that, Sarge?'

'What was it called? Oh yes, *Duel*, with Dennis Weaver. It was Steven Spielberg's first film. It was the one where a rogue truck pursued a commuter on the roads in the States. I must have seen it three times.'

'Never saw it, Sarge.'

'That Mercedes just keeps turning up. I wouldn't be in the least surprised if it was there. You'd better leave Jim a note, reminding him of what you've just mentioned. Probably means we'll have to interview all of the other councillors to see whether Blackley had been acting strangely, or had received any calls or messages. Now this comes on top of the death of that local resident, Jack Finlay.'

'It looks like there's a bit of a pattern emerging, Sarge.'

'I expect one of us will have to make a trip to the seaside on this one, before the trail goes cold there. If it was suicide, then someone must have really put the pressure on him. Or, do you think he was more affected by Finlay's death than anyone realised? Perhaps he thought the whole thing was getting out of hand. There's apparently been more violence and mayhem surrounding this planning application than anyone round there's ever seen. We'll need to get into Councillor Blackley's car to look for evidence. Can you contact whoever you spoke to at Sussex Police and ask them to move the car somewhere safe so we can look at it?'

'I'll do it, Sarge. Do you want me to go down there now?'

'Actually, sounds like a good idea, Greeno. Give them a call now to arrange it then get down there as quickly as you can. Talk to the locals while everything is still fresh in their minds. Have a look where the car was found. Talk to the police who found it. You could ask them whether they saw any other vehicles parked there. A Silver Mercedes, for example. We'll also need to know where they've taken Councillor Blackley's body. His personal effects might offer some clues. Some idea of why he was there. Arrange for the car to be brought back to Woodchester so that Forensics can look at it.'

'OK.' Mark Green picked up the phone to speak to the contact at Eastbourne. When he'd finished, he looked around his desk to make sure there was nothing else needing immediate attention.

'Right, Sarge,' he said, 'everything organised. I'll leave now.' He picked up his jacket from the back of his chair. 'Here are the details of our contact in Sussex Police. Oh, and just one other thing. The locals found a large amount of cash in an envelope under the driver's seat.'

20

It was already quite warm with the promise of another hot June day to come.

Sophie and Jim stood on the pavement outside The Castle's main door, waiting for Dennis, the cameraman, to turn up in the anonymous van they used on these occasions. Sophie was smartly dressed in a blue blouse with dark tailored trousers. Her hair was neatly pulled back and held with a jewelled clip. Her sunglasses were perched on top of her head. Jim, by contrast, was unrecognisable. He had followed Sophie's advice and was wearing an old tee-shirt, jeans and comfortable trainers. As suggested, he hadn't shaved since Friday and was sporting a very dark stubbly growth on his face. This and an old baseball cap he had found at home, together with a pair of sunglasses, had completely changed his appearance. He hadn't been involved in any sort of surveillance work since his early days as a Detective Constable. It was like turning back the clock.

Sophie looked at him approvingly. 'Your team wouldn't recognise you today.'

'Have you told your friend, Dennis, about me?' Jim asked.

'Of course I have. As agreed, he believes you're a minder just along to keep an eye on us. Dennis has no illusions about our destination. He was quite pleased you were coming with us. He knows nothing at all about what's happened. He probably would've called in sick if he did, knowing him.'

'Good. Let's hope today goes without a hitch.'

'By the way, Jim, you certainly look the part. Amazing what the lack of a shave does for a man.'

A dark blue van pulled up next to them and the passenger window rolled down.

'Ready, Sophie?' said the young man behind the wheel.

Sophie opened the door and climbed up onto the bench seat, leaving room for Jim to follow her. She made the introductions.

'It's nice to meet you Jim. Just hope we don't need your services today.'

'Don't worry. It'll be fine. I'll just hang around out of camera shot and keep an eye on what's going on. Just forget I'm there and help

Sophie get her story.' He used a slightly deeper, assumed voice. It made Sophie turn towards him smiling.

'How long will it take to get there, Dennis?'

'About forty five minutes, Sophie. What time have you arranged to meet the people you'll be interviewing?'

'I told them we'd be there about ten-thirty. Timing will be perfect.'

Jim studied Dennis discreetly. He was in his early thirties, and of average height with a fresh complexion, very short light brown hair and fashionable designer stubble. He was casually dressed in a sports shirt and jeans, and certainly seemed self-confident.

As they pulled away from the Castle, none of them noticed a silver Mercedes 4 x 4 with darkened windows pull out of the side street opposite the hotel and follow them at a discreet distance.

Nothing much was said during the drive, with Dennis concentrating on the road and Sophie skimming through her notes on her iPad.

Jim was determined to keep quiet and maintain his aura of anonymity. *Was this the way tough guys played it on the screen?* Jim thought, in a whimsical moment.

The time passed quickly and they soon arrived at the edge of the estate in East Kent.

'The estate starts just over there. Maybe I'll park here. Don't want anyone kicking lumps out of the van or slashing the tyres,' said Dennis, the first words he had uttered since they left Woodchester.

Maybe he was feeling the tension. The estate certainly had an effect on anyone unlucky enough to visit it. It had been built in the sixties and exuded a general air of decay and despair. Tall, multi-storey blocks of flats, interspersed with rows of terraced houses occupied by those fortunate enough to escape the towers. There was graffiti everywhere. What open grass spaces existed, were full of litter and the odd upturned supermarket trolley. Feral dogs roamed at will. Jim noticed a few youngsters in a bunch in the distance, with their off road bikes. A silver car appeared several hundred yards away and a black youth in a shell suit left the group and jogged over to meet it. Jim's experienced eye told him another drug deal was probably going down.

Not my problem today, he thought. *Have to leave that to the locals.*

As the youth reached the car, the driver, tidily dressed, spoke to him, and it looked like money was changing hands. It confirmed Jim's view of the likely cause of its presence.

Sophie was busy on her mobile phone, calling one of her interviewees. 'Can you get the other two together and meet me across the road? What's this street called, Dennis? Brandford Street. We're in a dark blue van. We can do the interviews right there, if you like. There's no one about.' She turned to Dennis. 'You've got ten minutes to set up the camera. They'll be right over.'

They all climbed out of the van. Dennis opened the back door and unloaded his shoulder held camera. He put on a set of headphones.

'Can we do a quick sound check, Sophie?'

She took up a position by the side of the van, with the estate framed behind her, microphone in hand.

'Testing, testing…This is Sophie Breckton reporting from the Brandford Estate in East Kent. I'm here to speak to some of the legitimate tenants who are concerned about the illegal sub-letting of flats and houses here. This is seriously impacting their lives in a negative way, with an increase in drug dealing and other crimes. How's that, Dennis?'

'Perfect. We'll just wait for your customers to turn up.'

'Dennis, I want you to film me asking the questions from behind my guests, so no one can recognise them from their rear views. Just show their heads and shoulders. You know the drill.'

He nodded in agreement.

Jim was looking around, studying the area. Years of training and experience had given him a different perspective. He noticed the black youth he had seen earlier talking to a man was now sauntering in their direction. He was still a couple of hundred yards away. The man had turned away and was walking back towards the silver car parked in the distance. *Surely it couldn't be a Mercedes?*

The three tenants arrived. Two middle aged women and an elderly man. One introduced the others. They all looked apprehensive.

'As agreed, we won't show your faces or name you,' said Sophie, trying to put them at their ease. 'Even your voices will be changed by our sound engineers before the interviews go out on the programme. We know the risks and understand how hard this must be for all of you. We really appreciate you agreeing to meet us and tell your stories.'

Jim was still keeping an eye on the youth, who was walking across the grassy area towards them. There was something strange about him and his gait. Warning bells began to ring for Jim and so he gave the youth his full attention.

In the meantime, Sophie had started her interview. Dennis had his camera trained on her from behind the three local residents.

The youth was getting closer. Jim had a bad feeling something was going to happen. He positioned himself closer to Sophie, but out of camera shot.

'You ain't wanted 'ere,' shouted the youth. 'You oughta stay out of our business. I'm gonna make sure you don't come back.'

Jim noticed his eyes. They were staring, almost vacant. His experience told him the youth was probably high on drugs. With that, the youth pulled out a knife. A kitchen knife, maybe eight inches long.

And he lunged at Sophie.

'I'm gonna cut yer, I'm gonna kill yer,' he screamed.

Jim stepped forward between them and grabbed the youth, trying to disarm him. The youth slashed at him with the knife and Jim received a cut across his right forearm before he finally subdued him, wrestling him to the ground. It felt as though someone had seared his arm with a red hot iron.

Sophie stood there, microphone in hand, mouth open, rooted to the spot. She was totally shocked.

Dennis placed his camera carefully on the ground and rushed to assist.

'Phone,' shouted Jim. 'Get some help here.'

Roused from her reverie, Sophie reached for her phone, tapped in 999 and gave the police the brief details.

'There'll be here as soon as possible,' she said, as Jim and Dennis held the youth on the ground.

By now, Jim was bleeding quite badly from the wound on his arm.

Sophie, recovering her composure, looked in the van for a first aid kit.

The three local residents, their moments in the sun interviews disrupted by the sudden attack, seemed to shrug it off. They were almost disinterested onlookers.

'Suppose that's the end of our interview,' moaned one of the women. 'Bang goes our chance of getting anything done now.'

'Better call an ambulance as well. That cut looks nasty,' said the elderly man. 'Now you have some idea of exactly what happens here, almost daily. Knife crime is one of the real problems.'

The youth, clearly drug fuelled, was still struggling as Jim and Dennis continued to restrain him.

Then they heard the sound of a police siren.

A patrol car pulled up and one uniformed officer got out. He took one look at the situation and reached for his handcuffs. Once cuffed, the youth stopped struggling but still continued to rant.

The policeman looked at Jim's arm.

'We'll need to get you to hospital to get it looked at. It'll probably need stitching, as well as a tetanus injection. You never know what these people do with their knives round here. I'll call an ambulance.'

Jim thought he should identify himself. He took the PC aside and showed him his warrant card.

'Today's little fracas is probably part of an ongoing enquiry We're running in Woodchester. I shall need to talk to him,' he said, pointing at the youth, who was sitting in the back of the police car, handcuffed and quieter now. 'I'm not convinced it was a spontaneous effort on his part. I think someone put him up to it. He's obviously under the influence of drugs. I need to question him. A charge may be the least of his problems. I believe his target was that lady,' pointing at Sophie. 'I should appreciate it if you don't identify me to her cameraman or the others.'

'Very good, Guv,' said the PC. 'Will you want him transferred to Woodchester?'

'Take him to your local nick, and I'll be in touch as soon as possible. The charge may well be attempted murder. It will certainly be GBH for starters. I'll sort it with the CPS. I'll want to question him to find out who put him up to it before we actually charge him. I thought I saw him talking to someone over there, by those cars, but that individual's gone. It looked as though money was changing hands. *Just another drug deal*, I thought at the time - *not my problem today*. Now I'm not so sure.'

'OK, Guv. I'm expecting some backup shortly. They'll probably send the van.'

'Tell your custody sergeant our client must have a drug test as soon as he arrives. Oh, and no bail.'

Sophie had finally found the first aid kit in the van and was trying to staunch the flow of blood from his arm.

'You saved my life, Jim,' she said, looking at him with a new respect. Not quite the serious and intense individual she had described when she spoke to Jackie at the Castle that first evening. A bit more of an action man than she'd thought.

A crowd of spectators had begun to assemble, drawn by the arrival of the police car, and now the police van. Some of the younger ones were overtly hostile.

'Why've you got Emile in de car?' screamed one of them. 'You let 'im go now. He ain't done nuffin'. You don't want no more problems. People get real angry when you come 'ere.'

The first police officer was now radioing in for more support. 'Bit of a crowd gathering now over our arrest. We'll need some help in case it kicks off here.' He turned to Trussell. 'Not unusual on this estate. Knife crime's a real problem here.'

He resumed the call on his radio. 'No problems with any idea of guilt. He's used a knife on someone in front of everyone else. His problem now is the victim is a DI working undercover. He helped to arrest him despite a nasty cut on his arm. It's a straight forward case of GBH. It shouldn't be a problem for the CPS.'

'We'll need the knife for evidence,' said Jim. 'Make sure it's bagged up and sent to the nick.' Then he turned to Sophie. 'I think you'd better wrap this one up for the day. I don't feel you'll be able to continue now. Your witnesses won't just be able to pass themselves as casual onlookers now that a crowd's gathering. The important thing is to get you and Dennis out of here before anyone works out who you are. You'll have to speak to those people on the phone later and maybe arrange to meet them somewhere else on another day. I suppose Dennis caught the whole thing on video. I know it may be important evidence, but I should appreciate it if the tape doesn't get into the public domain at the moment. Don't want to see it on the local television news tonight. We're trying to keep your case under wraps as far as possible and I certainly don't want to be identified.'

'I can see that. I'll talk to him and make sure the tape doesn't go anywhere when we get back. He'll listen to me. Hopefully there'll be enough evidence without the tape. After all, Dennis and I saw the whole thing. I still can't thank you enough for what you did.'

Jim looked embarrassed. 'Good job I was here, then,' he said. 'I'm concerned now about the sequence of events here. If that yob was paid to attack you, how did they know you'd be here today? Who was in the loop?'

'Well, obviously, my producer and director knew. Dennis knew. The people I'd arranged to meet and interview today knew. I can't believe they would have set me up. Certainly the television company wouldn't. Where does that leave us?'

'Well,' said Jim, 'I thought I saw that yob talking to someone over on the other side of the estate. See where I'm pointing?' indicating a couple of cars parked on the other side of the grassed area. 'I thought I saw him with a man who didn't look like he belonged here. And there was a large silver car nearby. It could have been a Mercedes. I thought at the time it was another drug deal in progress. Way of life here.'

'It can't be that same car, surely. How would the driver know where I was going?'

'It leads me to the conclusion the Castle's being watched. We had begun to suspect this from the off, when that scruffy envelope was delivered to you on the first night.'

'Is it still safe for me to stay there?'

'I'm still convinced you're safe enough inside. I don't believe anyone would try anything there - it's too public and too many security cameras. No, I just think it's being watched. Someone's keeping track of your movements to provide an opportunity somewhere else. Can't think where the individual, if it's just one, is getting his intelligence at the moment. But I will work it out. You didn't discuss today's outing with anyone else? What about your newspaper editor friend? Did you mention it to your husband, for that matter?'

'I did mention it to Richard in passing on Sunday when he phoned me. He offered me two dates to meet him in London to discuss our futures. Lunch, either today or tomorrow. I told him I couldn't manage today as I had to do some television interviews at Brandford. That's all I said. I didn't mention any times. He couldn't have known my plans.'

'I'll talk to the uniformed at Woodchester. Arrange for the foot patrols and PCSO's to keep an eye out for any silver Mercedes 4 x 4's with tinted windows around town. Note the registration numbers of any they see. Even better if they catch a glimpse of any driver, a description would help. I'm not pinning all our hopes on that, but it might just tip the odds in our favour. If the car is in and around Woodchester, where does it go over night? Where's the driver staying? Can't be too far away, or he wouldn't be able to keep up with your movements. I'll talk to Jackie. She's the modern thinker!'

'I think you're being a bit modest, Jim,' Sophie said.

The ambulance had turned up and the two paramedics appeared, carrying their bulky equipment bags. The PC directed them towards Jim.

The covering Sophie had put on the wound hadn't completely stopped the flow of blood.

'Let's have a look at that, Sir,' said the male paramedic. Donning his rubber gloves, he eased the temporary dressing away.

'What do you think, Katie?' he said to the other paramedic. 'Can we fix this without troubling A & E?'

She looked at it dubiously. 'Better off in hospital. He's bound to need a tetanus jab. I'll cover it and we'll take him down to the Royal. Best to let them deal with it.

'Do you want us to come, Jim?' asked Sophie. 'You'll need a ride back.'

'No, it's fine. I'll call Jackie. She can pick me up. I need to bring her up to speed anyway. You pack up and go straight back to the Castle now and I'll catch up with you later. Tell Dennis to say nothing to anyone about the whole thing. As far as your studio is concerned, the interviewees didn't show up, so you came back.'

The paramedics had applied a temporary tourniquet and dressing. They helped him into the ambulance and closed the doors. No siren or flashing lights. They made their way to the Royal hospital, conveniently only a ten minute drive. The paramedic, Katie, contacted A & E on her radio to let them know they were on their way. She stressed the injury needed urgent attention.

On arrival, Jim was taken straight through the double doors and handed over to a doctor, while the paramedics gave him a brief summary of what had happened. Jim sat in a chair while a nurse removed the temporary dressing and cleaned the wound up.

'That's going to need a few stitches. You'll probably have a bit of a scar after it heals, I'm afraid,' she said. 'Good job you don't have a tattoo on that arm like most of our customers these days. The scar would fairly ruin the artwork. Were you in a fight?'

'Official business,' said Jim, showing his warrant card. 'It was all in the line of duty, as they say, although not quite what I expected today. I was only supposed to be watching.'

'Where did it happen?'

'On the Brandford Estate, about half an hour ago.'

'A regular source of business for us here,' said the nurse. 'We're used to it, unfortunately. Lots of knife crime. Drug overdoses. Domestic violence of all types seems to be the local pastime. Not a nice place at all. Whatever were you doing there?'

'I'm afraid I can't tell you,' said Jim. 'How long before I can leave here? I need to arrange a pick up.'

'We should be done in about twenty minutes. I bet your tetanus isn't up to date. You'll need an injection as well.'

Jim reached for his phone and tapped in Jackie's number.

'Hi, Jim. How's your morning going?'

'It didn't run quite to plan, Jackie. I need you to collect me in about half an hour.'

'OK. Where are you?'

'I'm in A & E at the Royal. The interviews at Brandford didn't go quite as we expected. Sophie's OK. I've sent her back to the Castle. Her cameraman is dropping her off.'

'A & E? What's happened? Are you OK?'

'I got in the way of some yob's knife. They are just about to stitch my arm up now. Should be done by the time you get here. I'll fill you in with the details on the way back. I'll just say I think our favourite car turned up again.'

'OK, Jim. I'm on my way.'

The arm was stitched, a fresh dressing applied and the tetanus injection had just been given when a very worried looking Jackie walked into the room. She did a double take at Jim's appearance: old clothes, stubble, and now a substantial bandage on his right arm.

'Are you OK?' she asked, looking concerned. 'You look rather pale.'

'He's lost quite a bit of blood,' said the nurse, 'but he should be fine in a day or so. He'll need to arrange for the stitches to be removed in about ten days. His GP should be able to deal with it.'

Jim thanked the nurse for her attention and he and Jackie walked out into the sunshine. It was hot now. Reaching the car, Jackie opened the passenger door for him and tried to help him with his seat belt.

'I can manage, Sergeant,' he said, trying to make light of it, but Jackie saw him wince as he stretched the belt across with his right hand before clicking it in place.

Jackie drove out of the car park and headed for Woodchester. Jim filled her in with the details of what had happened that morning, including his possible sighting of the silver Mercedes.

'We'll need to be in touch with Brandford nick to make sure they're hanging on to our suspect. I'll need to interview him as soon as possible. I'll also want to make sure he's been tested for drugs already. There's no question in my mind he was bribed in some way to attack Sophie. We need to ask him some serious questions about it.'

'We can organise that when we get back, Jim,' said Jackie. 'In the meantime, we've had a call from Sussex Police. One of the Woodchester councillors, Jeremiah Blackley, was found dead at the bottom of Beachy Head. His was one of the names that had come up in Sophie's investigation of Burtonlee's affairs. Greeno took the message. I've sent him down to Eastbourne to talk to the locals and he's trying to arrange for Blackley's car to be brought to Woodchester for examination.'

Jim whistled in amazement.

'Stuff keeps piling up, doesn't it? There's something else at work here, I'm sure. Just need to figure it out.'

'Do you want to go straight to the station, or do you want to stop off at home and clean up first. Not sure about the current DI Trussell. Think I prefer the old one. I can wait for you. No problem. You do have a public persona to maintain. Not sure what the team would think about your new image.'

After a quick stop at his house for a shave and a change of clothes, and with his image restored, they went straight back to Woodchester police station. He had put on a short sleeved shirt as the bandage prevented him from wearing a jacket for the time being.

'You'll have to report your injury, of course, Jim.'

'More damn paperwork. Not sure what Charlie Watkins will make of it. He's a stickler for rules these days.'

'Even if it's moved the case on a bit?'

'Only a matter of time before he starts asking questions again. Anyway, we'll get the team together for an update when we get back. We need to look at Burtonlee's business and decide the next step. We can't just breeze in there and ask him if he's trying to arrange for Sophie Breckton to be killed. We'll have his lawyers on our backs before we even leave his office. We have to find another way of looking at the problem.'

'Sophie did mention his front man, Jonathan Barlborough. Should we do some digging there? See if anything is known about him. My guess is that if Burtonlee is behind this, then he won't want to get his own hands dirty. He'd rely on someone like Barlborough to organise it. Maybe Burtonlee himself knows nothing about it. From what Sophie told us, he's had his hands full with his personal life recently. Barlborough has probably got himself quite a cosy niche at the

83

company, wielding the power day to day while the boss is preoccupied. If the company's in financial trouble, then Barlborough's little empire will be going down the tubes. He wouldn't want to throw all of that away. Perhaps he might know someone who drives a silver Mercedes?'

'Good idea. We'll look at the fixer first.'

Jackie parked the car in Trussell's allocated space and they walked into the building. The duty sergeant on the counter looked at Jim's arm.

'Fighting again, DI Trussell?

'Don't even ask, Alan.'

Jim's phone chirped. It was a message. He pulled the phone out of his pocket and looked at the screen. It was from Sophie. *How are you? How's the arm? Have they managed to fix it? I won't ever forget what you did for me today. It deserves some sort of official recognition. Please let me know.* It was simply signed *S*. Jim felt rather embarrassed about the whole thing. He certainly could do without any further complications in the middle of this investigation.

'Problems, Jim?'

'It's a text from Sophie enquiring about my health. Last thing I want at the moment.'

'From what you've told me, I expect she feels some responsibility for what happened. After all, you did try to dissuade her from going to Brandford.'

'True. But in a way, it has produced some more evidence.'

Jackie opened the door to the CID office for him.

'What's happened, Guv?' asked Mark Green. 'Are you OK?'

'Yes, thank you. I'll live. Jackie has told me about our councillor. How did you get on at Eastbourne? Is Blackley's car being brought here?

'That's all in hand, Guv. They've given me his personal effects - contents of his pockets and so on. Odd thing is there was no trace of his car keys.'

'I suppose he could've thrown them away. After all, he wasn't going to need them anymore. Unusual, though.'

'I'll collate all the information and leave it on your desk, Guv.'

'Good effort. When you've typed up your notes, Greeno, I've another job for you. I know you prefer your computer screen to real policing.

'That's a bit harsh, Guv. What do you want me to do?'

'Time we turned our attention to Burtonlee. First of all, I want you to find out as much as you can about his fixer, Jonathan Barlborough. We need to look at his life. Find out where he lives and whether he has any family. Where does he bank? See whether he has any form - even a parking or speeding ticket. Where did he come from? How long has he been with Burtonlee? I want a complete picture of the man.'

Sandcastle asked whether anything else was needed.

'I need full information about Councillor Blackley. Contact details for his address. I assume there's a Mrs Blackley. I shall need to talk to her. Can you get in touch with her and find out whether she's prepared to see me later; say, six thirty this evening, if convenient? Say all the right things, Sandcastle. The poor woman has just lost her husband.'

21

Trussell and Joynton walked to the Skoda in the car park. He handed her the keys.

'You'd better drive, Jackie.'

'What was the address, Jim?'

He read it off the piece of paper handed to him by Tim Beach. 'It's Wisteria House. Church Lane, in Upper Forge. It's just two miles out of town. Close enough for Mr Blackley to qualify as a Town Councillor.'

'I know the village, Jim. Take us about twenty minutes at this time of day. There's bound to be lots of traffic. It's the middle of the rush hour. Everyone's going home.'

Jackie soon found the turning off the main road and they headed down the narrow winding lane towards Upper Forge. With the usual high hedges, it was hard to see what was around the next bend.

When they arrived at the green it was to find a chocolate box village with period houses around it. Jim pointed to the church tower, just visible behind one of the houses. 'Church Lane must be over there.'

Jackie drove slowly up the narrow lane. They both scanned the houses either side, many of them impressively large.

'There it is,' said Jackie, pointing to a gravelled drive between high hedges. 'Wisteria House.'

There was a discreet varnished wooden board by the gate. The name was burned into it in old English script and picked out in black paint. She turned into the drive. The property was a substantial, well-maintained, double-fronted house; old brick with a Kent peg-tiled roof. The chimneys gave a clue to its age, dating it to the eighteenth century. An ancient wisteria clung to the front of the building, spreading out on either side, its purple flowers hanging down in clusters. There was ample parking space in front. The tyres crunched softly on the gravel as they approached.

'This looks a bit expensive, Jim. Wonder what Councillor Blackley did for a living? It looks a bit above a councillor's budget, I would have thought.'

'I'm sure we'll learn more shortly. This will probably be another difficult discussion. Just like the one we had with Mrs Finlay. We'll need to proceed carefully. We can hardly ask her outright whether her husband was taking bribes from Burtonlee. Doubt whether she'd have known anyway.'

They got out of the car and walked to the front door, their shoes scuffing on the gravel.

'This is just like the beach at Dungeness,' said Jackie. 'Without the Sea Cabbages!'

There was a substantial metal studded wooden door with several lock holes in it, reminiscent of an old church. To the left there was a cast iron bell pull. Jackie gave it a sharp tug and a bell rang somewhere inside.

The door was opened by a woman. Mid-fifties, wearing a drab dark dress. Her medium length dark brown hair, with undyed greying strands, hung loose. She had a pale complexion. No make-up. She was wearing glasses, but they could see the strain in her eyes.

'Yes?'

'Mrs Blackley? '

'Yes, I'm Sally Blackley.'

'My name is Detective Inspector Trussell, Kent Police,' he said, offering his warrant card, 'and this is Detective Sergeant Joynton. May we…?'

'Of course,' she said, trying to recover her composure. 'Please do come in.'

She showed them into a comfortable living room, overlooking the front drive. It was elegantly furnished. The latest edition of *House and Gardens* magazine was prominently displayed on a highly polished coffee table.

'We're very sorry to trouble you at such a difficult time. I'm sure you understand there are a lot of unanswered questions about yesterday's tragic event.'

She seemed ill at ease. Maybe it was more than just shock at her husband's death. 'What can I do for you?' Said with an odd emphasis on the personal pronoun.

'I'm going to ask you some questions and my sergeant will make notes. Did you have any prior hint that your husband intended to take his own life yesterday? Did anything happen? What was his mood?

'Jerry came home later than usual yesterday. He did look a bit preoccupied.'

'Was this from a council meeting?'

'Oh no, it was from work. He owns a chain of estate agents around Kent. Blackley Jenkins. The main one's in Woodchester.'

'We're in a bit of a property boom at the moment. More houses being built,' said Trussell. 'Is the firm doing well? Or did he have any business worries?'

'There were none I'm aware of. The company has always seemed pretty good, even in difficult times for the market. He has a junior partner, Morris Jenkins, but essentially, Jerry ran the business day to day.'

'Did anything happen after he got home yesterday afternoon?'

She thought for a moment. 'There was a phone call for him earlier, before he got home. I took it.'

'Who was the caller?'

'He didn't leave his name. He just said he would call back later. I think the voice was disguised but it seemed as if the caller had a foreign accent. I thought he sounded American. I haven't been aware of Jerry having any American contacts or customers. It did seem a little strange, now I think about it.'

'What time was this?'

'About three o'clock. Jerry came in about seven. I mentioned it to him. He looked a bit thoughtful. Preoccupied, I'd say.'

'Did the caller phone back?'

'The phone rang about seven thirty. Jerry picked it up, and then said he would take the call in his office, as it related to a business deal. I didn't think anything of it. It wasn't unusual, and he does keep all of his paperwork in there.'

'Did he say anything after he'd finished?'

'No, only that he had to go out unexpectedly, and couldn't stop for dinner.'

'How did he look?'

'We've been married for thirty years, so I think I should know him pretty well by now. I think he looked worried. Frightened even, I thought.'

'He didn't mention where he was going?'

'No. He just said it was about an important deal that was in the pipeline which was too good to miss. He walked out and it was the last time I saw him.' She removed her glasses, dabbing at her eyes with a paper handkerchief.

'You have no idea what this was about? Did it have anything to do with council matters?' Trussell was determined to try to see whether there was any link to Burtonlee without actually mentioning his name.

'I do know Jerry has been involved with supporting a rather controversial development in Foggenden. He thought it would be good for the community and bring in a great deal of very much needed revenue for the council. From what he tells me, it's a constant balancing act, trying to deal with the financial problems. The revenue base just isn't there. He saw this as a means of redressing matters. He takes his responsibilities as a Councillor very seriously.'

'You're aware there has been considerable opposition to this, particularly from the people who live in Foggenden, near the proposed development?'

'Yes. I understand Jerry was involved in one or two confrontations in council meetings with some of these people. Shouting matches, I understand. I wasn't there.'

'You may also have heard the gentleman who was involved in this was found dead last week?'

'Yes. Jerry mentioned it. He was quite upset. He's never been one to harbour personal grudges, even though some fairly harsh things were said at the meetings.'

'I'm sorry I have to ask this question. Are you aware of any business dealings your husband may have had with Burtonlee Homes? Was he hoping to be offered the chance to sell any of the houses through his agency?'

'I wouldn't know. I don't get involved in his business. I'm not sure he would've wanted it mentioned, if it were the case. It would look bad for any councillor to be involved before any planning permission was granted by the appropriate committee. He would have been obliged to declare his interest before any vote, and then abstain.'

'I don't think I've any further questions at this time. Thank you for your help, Mrs Blackley. I'll give you my card. I can be contacted at either of the numbers on it. Please give me a call, if anything else occurs to you that may shed any further light on this unfortunate matter. We would be particularly interested to hear if the anonymous caller with the American accent should phone back. Do you have anyone who can be with you?'

'Yes. Our daughter's been here to support me, and my sister lives nearby.'

Trussell looked at Jackie. 'Any further thoughts? If not, we can return to Woodchester.'

She shook her head.

'Then thank you for seeing us, Mrs Blackley. We do understand how difficult it must be for you. Should anything else occur to you, please give me a call.'

'Thank you, Detective Inspector,' she said, showing them to the door, and closing it quickly behind them.

As soon as they got back into the car, Jackie looked at Trussell. 'There's a lot going on there, Jim. There's that phantom American again. Where does all this fit in?'

'The question is, did Blackley leave home to collect something, or was he threatened with exposure and decided to end it all rather than the truth coming out?'

'It seems unlikely Blackley would involve himself in this, Jim. If it came to a vote in the council, then he would have to declare an interest as the leading estate agent in the area, and probably abstain. It would be natural for Burtonlee to gravitate to him to help to sell the new Foggenden estate, or whatever they're going to call the new place. He surely couldn't be seen to vote in favour of the project and then the world at large would see the houses advertised in the windows of his shops. That would be so obvious it would be laughable. It would surely be followed by corruption charges at the earliest opportunity.'

'That's a brilliant explanation, Sergeant. Your Fraud Squad aspirations shone through that one,' said Trussell.

'Unfair, Jim,' she laughed. 'But what do we do about the allegations of brown envelopes being passed around?'

'It seems to me it doesn't quite fit with what we now know. Sophie seemed to home in on that one. Is someone dropping red herrings around? If that's the case, then who else would want to discredit Burtonlee? Is it just possible there's another developer lurking in the background, letting Burtonlee take the heat?'

'It's an interesting question. It might be worth contacting the owners of the land to see whether there've been any other offers or even any other interests at work. A question we might even put to Sophie. Who would want to lead her in another direction?'

'Anyway, we've had enough of this speculation. Moving on, in the morning, we'll see what Greeno has found out about Mr Barlborough. Maybe it'll offer some clues in trying to draw the strands together. The whole case seems to become more tangled with every day that passes. If we look back to the first day, we believed we were confronted with a relatively simple case of attempted murder back Now look at us.'

22

Sophie searched through the limited wardrobe she had managed to cram into the two cases she had brought with her. Eventually she decided on a yellow, floral-patterned summer dress and found the matching yellow shoes in one of her cases. A rather expensive pendant and matching earrings given to her by Richard completed the outfit. She took even more care than usual over her hair and make-up. She knew she had to look her best after Richard's blunt criticism on the day he'd left her.

Thirty minutes later, she picked up a smart jacket and her laptop, thinking that an hour and a quarter on the train would give her some valuable working time. She grabbed her bag, checking she had her car keys, and walked down the stairs to the lobby.

She stopped at the desk to hand her key in to the receptionist.

'Good Morning, Mrs Blaxstone. What a lovely dress. Are you going somewhere special today?'

'Morning, Trish. Thank you. Yes, I'm off to London for a meeting. Think I'll drive to Headcorn and leave the car there. It's just a bit closer to London on the line.'

'Have a nice day. See you later.'

Sophie walked out of the side door and headed for the car park. She climbed into her BMW and looked in the glove box for one of her favourite CDs - Vivaldi's Four Seasons by Nigel Kennedy. She started the engine, reversed out of the space, and accompanied by the opening notes of *Spring*, she turned right out of the archway into the High Street heading for Headcorn railway station. She reasoned it would probably be easier to park there. She expected the trip would take about twenty-five minutes along the A274, long enough for all of *Spring* and *Summer*, and maybe some of *Autumn*. She loved that piece of music.

Back at the hotel, the phone rang at the desk and Trish picked it up.

'Good Morning. This is the Castle Inn. How may I help you?...Mrs. Blaxstone? I'm afraid you've just missed her...Do I know where she has gone? Yes. She's on her way to London by train. She said something about picking the train up at Headcorn. Can I give her a message?...No?...You're welcome. Goodbye.'

The road to Headcorn was fairly quiet, and, absorbed by the music, Sophie paid little attention to the traffic following her. She passed the aerodrome and then eventually drove onto the bridge over the railway line. Another couple of minutes and she reached the station entrance on the left, opposite the Texaco garage. As usual, there was a double decker bus at the stop on the left in the station approach, and she had to wait while the driver performed his usual complicated U turn to leave the station. That gave her room to get into the station car park. She parked, locked her car, and walked over to the station to get her ticket and pay for the parking. Lost in thoughts about what lay ahead that day, she failed to notice a silver Mercedes 4 x 4 with darkened windows drive into the car park.

Having organised her ticket, she walked along the platform and over the footbridge to the London line and found a seat. It was a warm morning in late June, so why not enjoy the sunshine after the confines of her room at the Castle. There were quite a few people waiting for the train and she paid them little attention, just glancing at the indicator board to check on the train's arrival time. On a whim, she sent a text to Jackie, telling her where she was going and why, in case she or Trussell tried to contact her. Sophie was sure they would understand.

When the train arrived a few minutes later, Sophie was lucky enough to find an unoccupied seat with a table. She settled herself and opened up her laptop, knowing she'd have time to catch up with today's emails and do a bit more research for the forthcoming series. She still needed to work out a way to get an interview with Terry Burtonlee but first, she had to get past his gatekeeper, Jonathan Barlborough. An experience she was not looking forward to. Frankly, the man gave her the creeps. This was quite a judgement, as she'd been obliged to deal with a large number of awkward and unsavoury people over the years.

'Tickets, please,' said a loud voice next to her, breaking into her thoughts. It was the inspector. She offered her ticket and it was duly punched. With a smiling, 'Thank you', he moved on to the next passenger.

Her concentration destroyed for a moment, she twisted her rings again as she thought of Richard and their lunchtime meeting. She had deliberately kept them on her right hand, and this would, hopefully send a signal to Richard, that she was not to be trifled with. That is, if he even noticed...

Concentrate, Sophie, she thought. *There's work to be done. You have no control over Richard. The scene will just have to play out. You've made the effort. It's up to him.*

The journey seemed to rush by as she was immersed in her work. She heard the announcement that the train was approaching London Bridge, so she collected everything together, replaced the laptop in its case, and rose from her seat. Stepping down onto the platform and following the crowd towards the escalator down to the main concourse, she was jostled but paid no attention. It was just one of the hazards of commuting.

Putting her ticket through the exit barrier, she decided that, today, she'd take the tube to the Bank, rather than cross over London Bridge. She walked down the tunnel lined with shops to the Northern Line entrance, passed through the barrier and walked towards the escalator. This had to be one of the highest and steepest in the Underground system, she thought. She had made this journey countless times and mentally switched off.

It was very crowded. *Where have all these people come from?* She moved to the right, leaving the left side free for those people in too much of a hurry to stand still all the way down. People were continually rushing past, and she felt the occasional contact - a shoulder or an elbow followed by a muttered apology, sometimes. As an unending line of people rushed past her, she suddenly received another push – in the back this time.

She fell forwards, desperately trying to find something to hang on to, to get her balance. It was a very long way to fall.

It was her good fortune that the man standing in front of her, two steps down, was rather substantial. As she lurched into him, he not only managed to keep his balance, but broke her fall.

'Are you OK?' he asked, as he helped her stand upright.

'I think so. Thank you. That could have been nasty,' she managed in a shaky voice. 'Did you notice who pushed me?'

'No, first thing I knew was when you fell forward into my back.'

'I'm sure it was a deliberate push,' she said. 'Why? Who would want to do something like that?'

'Unfortunately, there are some strange people around these days. That's how they get their kicks.'

Sophie was unconvinced. Her recent experiences made her think otherwise. She must share this with Jackie Joynton and Jim Trussell as soon as possible.

They reached the bottom of the escalator and she turned right toward the northbound platform.

A train had just left, so there were only a few people waiting as she made her way towards the white line painted on the platform. She was aware of more people joining all the time, until the platform was quite crowded. The usual jostling as a rush of air preceded the rumble of the approaching train. The crowd surged forwards. The slowing train was only about fifteen yards away when Sophie received another violent shove which pushed her towards the edge of the platform. She felt someone grab her jacket to break her fall. Disaster was again narrowly averted. 'Careful,' said a voice behind her 'It could have been serious. Did you stumble or trip or something?'

Sophie turned round to see a young man still holding onto her jacket while the girl with him had turned white.

Not wanting to cause a fuss, Sophie just said 'Thank you so much. I must have tripped as everyone moved forwards. I'm fine now.' There seemed little point in saying anything else. She stepped into the train for the short journey to the Bank and tried to collect her thoughts. She definitely needed to talk to Jackie now. She resolved to call her as soon as she reached street level and got a signal on her phone.

She exited the Bank station by the Royal Exchange stairs. She had become even more wary now, looking around, treating everyone around her with absolute suspicion. She reached in her bag and found her phone, tapped in Jackie's number and waited for a response.

'Hi, Sophie. I got your message. I presume you've arrived in the City by now.'

'Yes and I'm lucky to be here.'

'What do you mean?'

'Things were fine until I reached London Bridge station. I decided to take the tube today instead of walking over the bridge. It was a bad decision. Someone tried to push me down the escalator. Luckily the man standing in front of me broke my fall.'

'Are you sure it was deliberate?'

'Oh yes. I had a repeat performance on the platform ten minutes later. Someone shoved me in the back just as the train was arriving. It was only a quick thinking young man standing next to me with his girlfriend who grabbed me and stopped me from falling in front of the train. No one saw who did it. I obviously had to pass it off as my own clumsiness, tripping up as I moved forward.'

'I'll have to speak to Transport for London. They have CCTV everywhere. It may be possible to spot whoever was responsible. Who knew you were going up to the City?'

'Well, Richard, of course. But he wouldn't have had any idea of the timing of my arrangements or where I would be travelling from. All he knew was I would meet him at the wine bar at one o'clock.'

'We had already considered the possibility that the Castle was being watched. Where did you travel from?'

'Headcorn. I drove there and left my car in the station car park.'

'Did anyone at the Castle know where you were going? You didn't leave any message with the reception desk?'

'Actually, I did mention to Trish, the receptionist that I was going to London when I handed in my key. We did have a short chat. The people there have got to know me now. I'm almost a resident.

'I'll talk to Jim and we'll contact TfL. Maybe I'll talk to Trish at the Castle. About what time did these incidents occur?'

'It would have been about half an hour ago.'

'OK. We'll look into it. Enjoy your lunch. Hope you get the answers you want. Call me when you're on your way back.'

'Right, I'll do that. Bye for now.'

With that, Sophie rang off and put her phone back in her bag. She started walking up Cornhill towards the traffic lights at the junction with Gracechurch Street. Richard's office was a couple of hundred yards the other side of the junction on the left hand side, but no doubt he would be at Lloyd's at that moment, involved in some negotiation or other. They were meeting at the restaurant in Leadenhall Market, so she crossed the road to take the Gracechurch Street entrance to the Market.

She walked past the open shop fronts. How the place had changed. It was mostly restaurants, wine bars and sandwich shops these days. At least *The Lamb* had survived. It always reminded her of an old John Wayne film. *What was it called? Brannigan. That was it. A visiting American policeman who got into a fight in The Lamb and almost singlehandedly destroyed the pub.*

She pushed open the door of the wine bar, so familiar. It was where Richard would take her for lunch in those early days when she was working in Fleet Street for *The Daily Enquirer*. There were so many memories. The Moretti poster on the wall behind the bar, The Chianti bottles on the shelves above. She looked around the restaurant. At forty-one, she was still a very attractive woman, capable of turning heads. A man waved from a table at the other end of the room. Was he one of Richard's underwriting friends? What was his name? Alan? Alexander? Anthony? She couldn't remember. It must be at least five years. She acknowledged him with a smile and a slight nod.

'Ah, Signora Blaxstone. How are you? It's been a while.' The owner appeared and greeted her like a long-lost friend, which was probably how he thought of her.

'Hello Luigi. It's nice to see you.'

Picking up a couple of menus, he led her upstairs and opened the door to the private room. It had been rearranged and a small table was centre stage, laid with two places. He took her jacket and guided the chair as she sat down. 'May I bring you something to drink? I'm sure Signor Blaxstone will not be long.'

'Thank you Luigi. I'll wait for him.'

Sophie sat in the small, intimate room, alone with her thoughts. What should she say to Richard? Should she wait for him to make the opening move? Of course, he was the ace negotiator. She must not allow him to seize the initiative.

The door opened and Richard bustled in, looking flushed. He had obviously been hurrying. His expensive tailored suit seemed a bit tighter than she recalled. His whole demeanour oozed embarrassment. He looked down at his feet and shuffled them. There was an awkward silence.

'Hello, Sophie. You look terrific. How've you been?'

'Well, Richard, apart from being cooped up in temporary accommodation which is rather inconvenient, and the fact that someone seems to be absolutely determined to do me harm, I guess I'm fine. What about you?'

'Never mind me. What's been happening?'

She told him about the attempts on her life and drily mentioned the hazards of travelling on the tube these days.

'Have you told the police? What are they doing to protect you? Didn't you have some problems in the past with threats? I remember we spoke about them a number of times. As I recall, the police weren't too concerned in those days. I hope they're taking them more seriously now. Do they have any clues?'

'If they do, they aren't sharing them. They've been working their way through my old cases to see if they hold any clues.' She gave him a searching look. 'Can I remind you that it was your idea to meet you to discuss our future? Perhaps we can start by talking about the flat. You told me you're in the process of redecorating it. Don't you think I should have had some input into your plans? After all, I paid for the damned place and it's half mine. Or has your girlfriend chosen everything for you?'

'No. I've finished with Victoria. It's all over. I should have realised it was never going to work. Is there a way for us again, Sophie? Will you let me back into your life?'

'It's certainly not going to happen just like that. I need to be sure.'

At that moment, the waiter came into the room. 'Ah, Signor Blaxstone, you are here. May I bring you drinks?'

Richard looked at Sophie.

'A glass of white wine, please. Pinot Grigio?'

'Make that two,' said Richard. 'We'd better look at the menu. Can you come back in a couple of minutes, please?'

Sophie sensed Richard was feeling even more uncomfortable than she'd expected. He seemed preoccupied and was unable to look her in the eye. She tried to generate some sort of conversation to get him to engage with her but it was difficult. He pretended to study the menu when she knew he could probably recite it to her without even looking at it. She had a fair idea of what he would order anyway. She needed to get his attention; to get him talking. Tell her what was really on his mind. 'So, how have you been?'

'The last six weeks have been difficult for me,' he began. 'I've had all the usual pressures at work and demanding clients and then the realisation that my relationship with Victoria wasn't going anywhere.'

'I told people I thought you were going through some sort of mid-life crisis.'

'What about you? What've you been doing?'

'I've been attempting to prepare for my upcoming television series. I'm still trying to get hold of Terry Burtonlee. In the meantime our committee has suffered a bit of a setback. Jack Finlay is dead.'

'What? Jack dead? What happened? Was he ill? Or was he in an accident?'

Sophie related the circumstances of Finlay's death. How he had been found by a dog walker who had called the emergency services but they'd been unable to save him. She mentioned that the police were now treating the matter as suspicious.

'That must have been a terrible shock for his wife. Do the police know how it happened?'

'They're following up some information given to them. That's all I know.'

'So, where does that leave your resistance to Burtonlee and his development?

'The rest of the committee are still very much involved and John Shalford has taken over the reins, temporarily.'

'The chap who lives in Ivy Cottage? The ex-military man?'

'Yes. Anyway, We're getting away from the reason for us being here. Please give me some compelling reason why I should believe you really want to come back. You hurt me badly. It was totally unexpected. We hadn't disagreed about anything. As far as I'm concerned, it came completely out of the blue. Now, just as I'm getting my life back together, you want us to return to where we were. I need to be sure you're sincere to even consider it.'

The waiter arrived with their wine and took their lunch orders. When he had closed the door behind him, Richard looked at Sophie, even more embarrassed than earlier. 'Sophie, I've a confession to make.'

'Is there something else, now?'

'Yes. I need to raise a very large amount of money. One of our original investors has decided he wants to pull his money out. We're surprised, as he's been getting a decent return on it. I've to put my share in, like Roy and Gerry, to buy him out. It would be really helpful if I could use the flat as collateral. Do you think you'll be able to help me by agreeing, so I can talk to the bank?'

Sophie was thunderstruck by the selfish blatancy of the suggestion. 'Richard, I don't believe you're in the least interested in us getting back together. You dragged me up here to see if I could offer you some financial help. If that's all there is to it, then I'm not staying to hear any more.' Furious, she stood up from the table and stormed out of the room, slamming the door behind her leaving Richard, dazed still sitting at the table.

'I'm not staying for lunch,' she told the waiter as she walked back down the stairs.

The owner appeared as she emerged into the restaurant proper. 'Is anything wrong, Signora Blaxstone?'

'I'm afraid so, Luigi. I regret I can't stay for lunch. May I have my jacket, please?'

Taking it from the astonished man, she walked out into the street, and headed for London Bridge and the train back to Headcorn. After her experiences earlier, she decided the walk would be safer and also give her a chance to clear her head. *The very nerve of the man*, she thought, *dragging me all the way up here just to try to get money from me.*

After the initial sense of anger passed, it turned to a feeling of sadness. She really had believed Richard had been serious when he had spoken about reconciliation. She would have to try to forget him now and move forward with her life.

She walked along Gracechurch Street and onto London Bridge itself, looking around her all the time, wondering whether she was being followed. This constant need for vigilance was beginning to play on her mind. Jim Trussell had told her she'd be safest at the Castle Inn but she couldn't go on hiding forever. She had a job to do. People expected it of her, although no one else knew what was really happening to her. Only Dennis, her cameraman, had witnessed the events at Brandford yesterday, and he had been told in no uncertain terms to forget what he'd seen.

I wonder how Jim Trussell is today, she thought. *That was a nasty cut on his arm. He saved my life yesterday without any thought for himself.*

There were too many such thoughts chasing each other around her head to take any notice of the train journey. She was far too preoccupied to even open her laptop and think about work. She left the train at Headcorn, got into her car and headed for the safe haven of the Castle Inn. She still kept a watchful eye on the road and checked her rear view mirror frequently. There was no sign of any car following her and she arrived in Woodchester without any further problem, parked her car behind the Castle Inn, collected her key at reception and went straight to her room. Only there did she feel safe once more.

23

Wednesday 26th June. 9.00 a.m.
Woodchester Police Station.

Trussell walked into the CID office. He still looked rather pale after the previous day's events.

'Morning, Jim,' said Jackie. 'I thought you might have given yourself the day off. How's the arm?'

'Painful, but I'll live. We have too much to do today. Can you call Brandford nick and set up an interview over there with our knifeman? I want to question him as soon as possible.'

Jackie picked up the phone, asked the switchboard to connect her, and within thirty seconds, was speaking to the duty sergeant at Brandford. 'We'd appreciate your help. You arrested a youth yesterday on the estate after he slashed DI Trussell's arm. We'd like to come over as quickly as possible to interview him. Yes, this is part of a very serious ongoing enquiry. We don't believe this was a random attack.'

She listened intently, and then said, 'I appreciate the background info. Would eleven o'clock be OK? That will give you a chance to organise a brief for him. By the way, what grounds did you give for his arrest? Causing GBH? The charge could well be upgraded to attempted murder, so make sure you hang on to him for us. Thank you.'

Jim looked at her expectantly.

'All fixed for eleven, Jim. Apparently your friend, one Emile Osugu-Francis, is well known there. He's one of their regular customers. They've pulled him in for the usual - shoplifting, possession, and a few other minor things. The duty sergeant says he's never known Emile to use a knife like this before. Oh, and by the way, they carried out the drugs test yesterday when he arrived at the station. It was definitely a fail on his part.'

'OK. I'll just see if there's anything else here that needs attention, then we'll be on our way. You'd better drive, Jackie,' he said, offering her the keys.

They were soon in Trussell's Skoda, heading for Brandford. He knew the station from his early years as a Detective Constable. Nothing much had changed there.

'We used to call this place the Alamo when I was here, Jackie. Even in those days. God knows what it's like now.'

Jackie looked at the building. Drab. It looked Victorian. No money had been spent on it for a long time. She found a parking space and they walked up the steps into the public area.

Trussell recognised the duty sergeant from years ago. 'Are you still here, Brian? Couldn't you find anywhere else to take you? I doubt things are any better here today.'

'Jim Trussell. Well I never! It's a name from the past, come back to haunt us. What were you doing on our manor yesterday, upsetting our upright local citizens? Not to mention taking the edge off Emile's knife as well!'

'Well, we're here to talk to your friend Emile. Hope it's all laid on. Has the duty lawyer arrived yet?'

'Interview room is over there. I'm sure you know the way. I'll phone the custody sergeant and ask someone to bring Emile up. The lawyer should be here any minute.'

'A bit nostalgic for you, Jim?' asked Jackie. 'Was it a tough place to police? I bet you have a few stories about this place.'

'Better left untold,' he said, pulling a face. 'We've enough on our plates without raking over old ground.'

Trussell led the way to the interview room. It made the one at Woodchester look positively luxurious. With just one fixed window, the walls were a faded cream colour and a green line was painted all the way round at hip height. Indeterminate marks on the paintwork hinted at problems with previous customers. The table bolted to the floor, contained a recorder. The lightweight tubular chairs, two each side, were not built for comfort.

He pointed to the chairs. 'We sit this side with our backs to the window. In the unlikely event of any sun reaching in here, it will be in the accused's face. One of the few advantages we're allowed these days.'

The door opened and yesterday's assailant came in, flanked by two uniformed PCs. He looked heavy eyed and dishevelled. He was still wearing the shell suit from the previous day, although it now contained traces of Trussell's blood on it. He glared balefully at him when he caught sight of the bandage on his right forearm.

Trussell motioned to the chair opposite him. 'It's nice to see you again, Mr Osugu-Francis. Or would you prefer I call you Emile? I understand you're fairly well known around here.'

'I ain't talkin' to you wivout a brief,' he said.

One of the two PCs said,' He's on his way, Guv. He should be here any minute.'

Jackie inspected the recorder and made sure there was a fresh disc in it.

'We can wait,' said Trussell. I think Emile is going to have to get used to a lot of waiting in places like this.'

'Whaddya mean?'

'It'll keep till your brief gets here.'

The door opened as he spoke and a small, dark Asian man entered the room. He was in his fifties with thinning black hair and dressed in a blue suit with a dark red tie. He placed his briefcase on the table and produced a pair of glasses from his top pocket. 'What have you been up to this time, Mr Osugu-Francis?' Without waiting for a reply, he turned to Trussell and introduced himself. 'My name is Chopra. I am the duty solicitor today.'

'I'm Detective Inspector Trussell, and this is my colleague, Detective Sergeant Joynton. We're both from Woodchester. You're obviously acquainted with our guest?'

'Yes. I've met him here on several occasions. What has he been up to this time? Has he been charged?'

Trussell indicated his right arm.

'Your client attacked me with a knife yesterday on the Brandford estate. I've ten stitches in my arm, thanks to him.'

'Oh dear. So has he been charged yet??'

'We've heard from the CPS. The details were passed to them yesterday when he was brought in. He'll be charged with causing Grievous Bodily Harm. It's likely other charges will follow.'

'Is this a holding charge then? Will he be offered bail?'

'Certainly not. It's quite likely a more serious charge may be preferred.'

'Being?'

'It could be attempted murder. You'll no doubt acquaint your client with the fact that the present charge can carry a maximum sentence of life imprisonment. Wounding a police officer is taken very seriously by the courts. I would also point out there were five independent witnesses to the event, so his future comfort, courtesy of Her Majesty, is assured. It was even captured on video.'

'So, if you have this evidence, why the lesser charge?'

'I want your client to give me some truthful answers. There is much more to this than the stabbing of a police officer. I want to give him the opportunity to tell us what we need to know. The extent to which he assists us will determine the way we decide to proceed in terms of charges.'

Emile sat there, somewhat bemused by all of this.

Chopra looked at him quizzically, and then turned to Trussell. 'May I've five minutes alone with my client, Detective Inspector?'

'Of course, Sir.'

Jackie and Trussell stood up. One of the PCs opened the door, and the four officers left the room.

'Outside, Trussell asked the older constable, 'Do you know anything about our client?'

'Yes, Guv. I've watched him grow up on the estate. He comes from a single parent family. No one was interested in him. He's always been a bit mouthy. Feral's the word. He's done a bit of drugs like most of the kids over there, dealt in them too. Bit of petty theft. He's never done anything like this before. I guess they all find their way into something serious as they get older.'

'I haven't seen his details. How old is he? I assume he's unemployed?'

'Just coming up nineteen, I believe, Guv. No job, like most of the kids his age over there. They make a living out of running drugs and petty crime.'

'So not much has changed on that estate over the years, then?'

''I'm afraid not.'

The door to the interview room opened and Mr Chopra asked them to come in. 'I have spoken to my client and he now realises the seriousness of his position. He's prepared to cooperate to the best of his ability.'

The two detectives sat down and Jackie switched the recorder on.

'This is a record of an interview at Brandford Police Station on Wednesday 26th June, commencing at 11.15 a.m. Would everyone identify themselves, please?'

'Detective Inspector Trussell, Kent Police.'

'Detective Sergeant Joynton of Kent Police.'

'Rajinder Chopra, duty solicitor, representing the accused.'

All three looked at Emile. Chopra prompted him.

'Emile Osugu-Francis,' he muttered.

Trussell launched straight into the questions.

'Mr Osugu-Francis, when you attacked me yesterday on the estate and slashed my arm with the kitchen knife you were carrying, I wasn't your target, was I?'

The prisoner looked confused.

'You intended to harm Sophie Breckton. Maybe even kill her? I just got in your way. Isn't that the case?'

Chopra looked at his client who in turn just looked down at his feet.

'I suggest you answer the officer,' he said.

Emile nodded.

'For the record, the prisoner nodded in agreement,' said Jackie.

Trussell persisted.

'Just before you walked over to us, I saw you talking to a man by a silver car. I saw money changing hands. I thought it was another drug deal, which was not my concern yesterday. But it wasn't drugs, was it, Emile? The man was paying you to harm Sophie Breckton.'

'Where's your evidence, Detective Inspector?' asked Chopra.

'The money was taken from him when he was arrested. It's been logged with the rest of his possessions in the custody suite. Your client is in serious trouble at the moment, Sir. This all forms part of a much larger enquiry. It's in your client's interests to tell as much as possible. My intervention probably saved him facing a murder charge.'

Emile now appeared distinctly uncomfortable. He looked around him wildly, his eyes showing fear.

'I want to know about that man, Emile. And I want you to tell me about his car. What did he say to you? How much did he pay you to attack Sophie Breckton? Had you seen him before on the estate? Come on, Emile. We need to know about him.'

He looked even unhappier and turned to Mr Chopra, eyes pleading.

'If you know anything Emile, tell the officers now, whispered Chopra. 'You may not get another chance.'

'I can't. I can't. He'll kill me. He's a real serious dude. I wouldn't want to mess with him anytime.' He looked around him, clearly panicking. He was perspiring heavily.

'Come on, Emile, tell us about the man. He won't be able to reach you where you're going.'

'He told me if I said anything, he would come back to kill me. He opened his jacket and there was a gun in a shoulder holster. He's a professional. Not the cheap handguns like we see round here. He told me he knew how to use it. Said it was what he did.'

'OK, Emile. This is progress. Describe him to us.'

'He was taller than me. About five ten, I'd guess. Dark straight hair and olive skin. He had an accent, Sounded American. He was dressed in expensive clothes. He had a brown leather jacket, jeans and classy trainers.'

'And how much did he pay you?'

'He gave me a bundle of notes. I didn't get a chance to count it.'

'What about his car?'

'Expensive wheels, man. A Merc with dark windows. Bit of a risk bringing a car like that round here, usually. But one look would tell you not to mess with the guy.'

'Did you only meet him once?'

'No he came round the day before. He asked me if I'd seen that Breckton woman on the television. He said she had caused him a problem and wanted to teach her a lesson. He said he had asked around the estate and people had told him I was the man. He gave me some quality Spice. It was mine to use or sell. Managed to get rid of most of it and then used some myself yesterday morning. While I was talking to him, he saw the blue van and told me the Breckton woman was there. He handed me the money and the kitchen knife and told me to go do it. You know the rest.'

'If you know anything else, Emile, then tell the officers,' whispered Chopra. 'You're already in serious trouble. Anything may help you.'

'I can't say anymore.'

'Did he phone or text you?' asked Trussell.

'How did you know that?'

'Where's your phone?'

'They took it when I cum here yesterday. They've got my money, too.'

Trussell motioned to Jackie to stop the recorder. He got up and left the room.

'Interview paused. DI Trussell has left the room.'

He returned ten minutes later, holding a mobile phone.

Jackie switched the recorder back on.

'Interview resumed at 11.42 a.m. DI Trussell has returned to the room, carrying a mobile phone.'

'Is this your phone, Emile?'

He identified it, and at Trussell's request, turned it on.

'For the record, the prisoner is now identifying a mobile phone as the one in his possession when he was arrested,' intoned Jackie for the benefit of the recording.

Trussell scrolled down the list of incoming calls.

'Show me the calls he made to you.'

Emile identified them and Jackie wrote down the numbers.

'We can compare these against the other one we already know about,' said Jackie.

'Right, Mr Chopra,' said Trussell. 'This phone will now be seized as evidence. I'm now going to charge him, additionally, with the attempted murder of Sophie Breckton. He will of course also be charged with causing grievous bodily harm to a police officer, viz, me. This will be as much for his safety as anything.'

'I thought you said that you might reduce the charges if he cooperated?'

'That may well happen. But, as I said, this is for his safety. 'I can't have an important witness wandering off and possibly getting himself killed.'

He nodded to Jackie, who spoke to the recorder.

'Interview terminated at 12.15 p.m.'

Trussell called the two PCs in and told them the prisoner could be returned to the custody suite. 'I'll join you down there so he can be charged and the paperwork organised. Are you coming with us, Mr Chopra?'

As they passed the station desk, Trussell spoke to the duty sergeant.

'I certainly appreciate your help today organising things, Brian. We're just going down to custody to sort out the charges and then I'll need to speak to the boss man.'

'OK. When you come back up here we'll fix that.'

Fifteen minutes later, charges and prisoner processed, Trussell returned to the front desk.

'I've spoken to the Super about Emile,' said the sergeant. He can spare you a couple of minutes right now. I'll take you to his office.'

'Thanks, Brian,' replied Trussell, following the sergeant along a still very familiar corridor.

The sergeant stopped, knocked on a door, bearing the name, Superintendent Ross, and opened it. 'Detective Inspector Trussell, Sir,' he said to the uniformed figure behind a large desk, a grey haired, heavy-set man, obviously no longer pounding the beat, who put down the paper he'd been studying, took off his glasses and motioned to the chair in front of his desk.

'Thank you, Brian. Take a seat, Trussell. Now what have you been up to on our manor? I understand you spent time here a while back?' The duty sergeant had obviously primed his boss with that information.

'That's correct, Sir. I'd like to apologise for causing problems for you. It was all a bit unexpected, really. This all forms part of an ongoing serious enquiry at Woodchester into a shooting and two unexplained deaths. Not to mention one of your regular customers opening up my arm yesterday. But I wasn't the target. I just got in the way.'

'So what more do you need from us then, Trussell?'

'Well, Sir. Your guest has now been charged. There are plenty of witnesses. I just want him up before the magistrates tomorrow, so he can be remanded in custody. It will be mainly for his protection. I've reason to believe a lot of our problems have been caused by a professional killer. Emile has actually met him and was able to give us a description. So we can't have him loose on the streets, for his own safety. We have enough on him to put him away for quite a long time. If we deal with it quickly, at least he'll be off your hands. We'll just need the arresting officer to pop along to the court tomorrow, to give evidence. Shouldn't think it will take too long. The prosecution must oppose bail. Then he'll be out of your hair, and he'll just become my problem at Woodchester.'

'Sounds reasonable to me. Glad we were able to be of assistance. By the way, how's the arm? Lots of stitches, I understand.'

'Thank you for asking, Sir. It's a bit sore but it'll be fine. We have too much going on with this case. I can't stop to worry about the arm. The developments are coming at a pace. I'd just like to thank you and your team for your assistance in this part of the enquiry,' he said, rising from the chair.

He walked out, closing the door behind him. Back down the corridor to the front desk to thank his former colleague and collect Jackie, who had been chatting to the sergeant.

'Right, Jackie, back to Woodchester. Who knows what else has happened while we've been away from the shop? There's bound to have been something.' He turned to the sergeant. 'Thanks again, Brian. Good to see you again after all this time.'

As they walked out of the station and down the steps to their car, Jackie said, 'I had a call from Sophie, Jim. She's gone to London this morning to see her husband. Apparently he wanted to talk about reconciliation. She's meeting him for lunch in the City.'

'Let's hope it works out for her, 'said Trussell.' She could do with some support at the moment. She's already been through a lot.'

'It gets worse. Someone tried to push her down the escalator at London Bridge tube station, but the chap in front of her stopped her falling. Then, when she reached the platform, someone gave her a shove as the train arrived. She was caught by a young couple standing next to her. We'll need to contact TfL to look at their CCTV images if they're available.'

'We'll have to speak to her when she gets back. There is a question that needs to be answered. Who knew she was going up to the City? That is, apart from her husband? Let's get back to Woodchester now. You can text Sophie to find out when she's due back at the Castle.'

24

Trussell and Joynton returned to the office after their visit to Brandford.

Trussell checked his desk for any messages and asked Jackie to text Sophie about meeting later on and to ask her to let them know when she was safely back at the Castle.

Greeno caught his attention. 'I've begun looking at Burtonlee Homes, as you asked, Guv,' he said. 'Thought I'd see what I could turn up on this character, Barlborough. He seems to be the gatekeeper as far as Sophie Blaxstone is concerned. It's a rather unusual name, to say the least; Jonathan Zachariah Barlborough.'

'I'd agree with that.'

'Well, Guv. Here's where the mystery starts. My father's been working on our family history for about twenty years. About a year ago, when I came here, he told me that, as I was the detective in the family now, it was about time I gave him a hand. Once I got involved, I was amazed at the amount of information available through the online family history websites. It certainly taught me a lot of new skills very quickly.'

'That's impressive, Greeno. But aren't we straying away from today's business?'

'Not really, Guv. I looked at Barlborough's name again in a slightly different way when some of the information came in. I decided to research it, using his apparent date of birth, on one of the family history sites I use. It was a relatively unusual name. Do you know, I only came up with one hit in the records?'

'Not surprised to hear that. Guess his parents must have had a sense of humour, or maybe it's a family name. What's your point?'

'Well, Guv, this particular individual didn't make it to his first birthday. This wouldn't be the first time a dead child's name has been taken by someone changing their identity because they had something to hide.'

'Are you saying that Barlborough may not be his real name?'

'Exactly.'

'Well done, Greeno. I'll give you ten out of ten for initiative. It might be helpful if we could establish his real identity. We can't just pull him in and fingerprint him or ask him who he really is. We need to go to

110

Burtonlee Homes and meet him. Perhaps something with his fingerprints or DNA might just accidentally come our way. What have you discovered about him?'

'There's another thing about Barlborough, Guv. I'm beginning to get the impression he wields a fair amount of influence at the company. You know, day to day. I wonder if it extends to the company's finances. I've already mentioned that a lot of money seems to be going through his account before it's sent somewhere else. Could this be the reason why the company's in trouble?'

'You might have something there. If Burtonlee's been involved in an expensive divorce, as Sophie mentioned, then the financial and personal costs of that might have meant he took his eye off the ball for quite a while. If he left it all to his capable assistant Jonathan, to look after things in his absence… If he's been running the company into the ground by skimming money off and diverting chunks of it through one of his own accounts, it would certainly explain why he's kept Sophie away from Burtonlee himself. It would also provide a motive to get rid of Sophie. A way of stopping her asking questions and trying to meet Burtonlee.'

'Well, Guv. We've looked at his bank accounts, found out where he lives, and we're trying to build a picture of his life outside the company. He's not short of money, but as soon as it comes in, he seems to move it somewhere else. Nice house, with a modest mortgage. He drives a classy motor – a company car of course.'

'Paying off someone?'

'It's possible, Guv.'

'Do you have any idea where the money came from?'

'The bulk of it seems to have come from Burtonlee Homes.'

'I doubt whether Terry Burtonlee has sanctioned it, or whether he actually knows that his trusted assistant has been emptying the company accounts. I wonder where he's sent it.'

'We'll have to start asking questions.'

'Does it mean that we'll have to involve the Fraud Squad in this part as well? We've already got them involved with Mr Brownlowe-Jameson. At this rate, Guv, we'll be taking them away from all of their other business.'

'If Barlborough's been stealing money from the company, then we shall certainly need to bring them in to look at things. It'll require forensic accountants to go through the books and Barlborough's bank accounts.'

'I suppose there's always a slim chance he was moving the money on Burtonlee's instructions. Especially if he knew the company was in financial trouble and wanted to safeguard his own future after his divorce.'

'What about Barlborough's family?'

'There isn't one, apparently. He lives alone.'

'Plenty of opportunity to do whatever he likes then without someone looking over his shoulder. Does he travel? What about holidays? No visits to the States, I suppose? We'll need to check with the Passport Office. See if he has a passport.'

'I've already done that, Guv. They have confirmed he does hold a current passport, so I've asked for a copy of the documentation he provided to obtain it. Unsurprisingly, it included a copy birth certificate. In the meantime, I've contacted the Public Record Office for a copy of the birth certificate for the entry I found online, together with a copy of the child's death certificate. I stressed the urgency and they've promised to email me copies tomorrow with originals to follow by post in a few days. If the two match with the birth certificate he used to get his passport, then we can at least haul him in for fraudulently obtaining the passport. As you know, that's worth two years inside on conviction. He probably used it to get his driving licence as well. Gives us an opportunity to get his fingerprints and we may be able to establish his true identity. Meanwhile, I'm still waiting for a lot of other questions to be answered. '

'You've done a good job on this. It's beginning to look a bit promising, Greeno. Don't suppose you've got around to Burtonlee himself, yet?'

'No, but removing Barlborough temporarily will certainly give us legitimate reason to call on the man himself.'

'That's right. Good effort, Greeno. Anyway, Jackie and I will be talking to Sophie shortly and we'll see what background information she can offer us on Burtonlee.'

He turned to Jackie. 'I think we'd better talk to Sophie now. Find out what happened to her today and see what further action we need to take about that. Then we can talk to her about Burtonlee and Barlborough. See if she can shed any further light on them.'

Jackie tapped in Sophie's number and waited a few seconds.

'Hello Sophie. It's Jackie. Are you back from the City yet?...Yes? OK. Jim and I would like to talk to you about Burtonlee. We need to find out what you know about him before we try to arrange a meeting with him. Can we meet you in the lounge at the Castle in, say, about fifteen minutes?...Good. Thank you. See you shortly.'

'That's fixed, Jim. She'll be there in fifteen minutes.'

'We can leave in a moment and walk down there. We'll let Sophie talk about her day first. From what you told me earlier, it's been an uncomfortable one for her.'

25

Jim Trussell and Jackie Joynton left the station and walked along the High Street towards the Castle Inn.

'This case grows more complicated by the minute, Jim,' said Jackie.

'I have an open mind at the moment,' he answered. 'But I grant you, it's certainly becoming more interesting.'

'I'll have to get some details from Sophie about her accidents on the Underground this morning so I can contact TfL about their CCTV.'

'Once you have the exact location details and timing from Sophie, then give them a ring. You may have to go up there to look at the recordings, if they have them.'

Sophie was waiting for them in the lounge at the Castle. She was still wearing the smart yellow summer dress and looked completely different from the woman they had grown used to dealing with during their interviews. Jackie couldn't help noticing Jim's reaction. It was almost a double take. Sophie seemed to have made the corner table her own now. She had already ordered tea for three and the pot, milk, cups and saucers were on the table.

Jackie noticed the way she looked at Jim first. Was that a hint of a blush, a slight reddening of her face? Maybe she had imagined it.

'How's your arm today, Jim? I'm surprised you haven't taken some time off.' were Sophie's first words as they walked through the door into the lounge.

'Still a bit sore, but I really can't afford to be away. This case is moving so quickly, I daren't miss a moment of it.'

Sophie belatedly smiled a greeting at Jackie, but her priority was obvious. Jackie's thoughts returned to that moment when she left them alone on Friday in the lounge. The last thing she wanted was for Jim to make a fool of himself over some television personality. It just didn't seem to fit his character although she grudgingly admitted to herself that Sophie was an attractive woman and, despite her self-assured air, certainly fitted the damsel in distress category at the moment.

'Well, Sophie, how did you get on today? Asked Jackie. 'Tell us about your trip to London.'

'Not so well. Apart from the two unfortunate events at London Bridge, my lunch with Richard was a bit of a disaster.' She recounted the

114

sequence of events from the moment she left the Castle until she arrived back again.

'Do you want to talk about your lunch?' asked Jim.

She started pouring tea for them all. It gave her a few seconds to collect her thoughts.

'When Richard arrived, and after we had indulged in the usual small talk, he claimed his affair with the other woman was over. I told him about the shooting. Not surprisingly, he wanted to know exactly what had happened to me and whether the police were making any progress in finding whoever was responsible. Then before we had even ordered our meals, he cut to the chase, to use one of his favourite expressions.'

'And?'

'He told me he needed money urgently. He said one of the original investors who had lent them money when they started the broking firm, had now changed his mind and needed to take it out. Richard said the three partners would have to come up with equal shares to buy him out. I must say I found it slightly odd. The company had been doing rather well, and I would have thought they had enough credit with the banks to raise the money that way, if necessary.'

'That must have put a dampener on your lunch.'

'Certainly did. He wanted me to agree to put our flat up as collateral with the bank. Naturally, I refused. It was obvious to me Richard wasn't really interested in reconciliation. He'd just lured me to London on a pretext so he could persuade me to help him find some money. Naturally, I told him it was totally impossible.'

'What was his reaction?'

'He was disappointed, to say the least. I think he expected me to agree to his request as a condition for allowing me back into his life. The sheer bloody cheek of the man was unbelievable! I told him if he wasn't really interested in trying to make a go of our marriage, then he had been totally wasting my time. So I just got up and left the restaurant. I walked to London Bridge this time, caught the train to Headcorn and arrived back without any further problems.'

Jackie had been watching Jim's face during the conversation. Did she detect a sigh of relief when Sophie told them the attempt at reconciliation had failed? Or was she reading too much into a look?

She thought this was a suitable moment to move the conversation on. 'Who knew you were going to the City today, apart from Richard? Did you mention it to anyone else?'

Sophie thought for a moment. 'Well, I might have mentioned it in passing to Trish in reception when I handed my room key to her on my way out.'

Jackie pushed her chair back. 'I'll have a quick word with her, Jim.'

She returned just two minutes later, looking serious.

'Apparently there was a phone call, just after Sophie left, asking to speak to her. Trish has admitted she told the caller she was going up to London. She mentioned Sophie would be driving to Headcorn and picking the train up there.'

'I don't suppose for one moment the caller left a name or number?'

'No, Jim. But she did say the caller had a foreign accent. Possibly American, but she couldn't be sure. She offered to take a message but the caller rang off.'

'If she can remember exactly when the call came in, we might be able to trace it from the phone records. We'll need to deal with that while the matter's still fresh in her mind.'

'What can you tell us about Burtonlee and Barlborough?' Jackie asked.

'Well,' replied Sophie, 'I can tell you very little about them personally. Barlborough's been the real obstacle. He seems determined to keep me away from his boss at all costs.'

'Have you ever met Burtonlee?'

'Not to have any sort of conversation. I did follow up his divorce. I went to the court and listened in for several days. It was all a bit unsavoury. I think it was the usual problem of a man with plenty of disposable money trying to prove he was actually younger than he looked. Got involved with one woman too many and his wife cleaned him out.'

'You saw his wife at court?'

'Yes, and two of their three grown up children were there to support her. I think our friend Terry's burnt his bridges as far as his family are concerned. I must say he seemed to take it really badly. He looked totally crushed by the whole thing. I honestly believe he aged visibly during the proceedings.'

'What about your whistle-blower? How did he contact you? Who is he?'

'He had worked for Burtonlee Homes for quite a while and I think was a bit miffed when Barlborough joined about four years ago. He felt he'd been passed over for promotion, and really didn't like the new man and the way he assumed control there. Like any journalist, I'm unwilling to identify my source!'

'Did he hint at the idea that brown envelopes were being passed to certain councillors at Woodchester?'

'No. It wasn't him. That suggestion came to me anonymously. There was a voice message on my phone from a withheld number. I still haven't a clue where it came from.'

'Did you mention it to Jack Finlay? We understand he was making similar allegations. According to his wife, he said rather too much at one of the Council meetings. His friends had to warn him he was sailing a little too close to the wind, and he should tone down what he was saying.'

'No, I certainly didn't mention it to him. I'm treading a rather difficult path, supporting the local community resisting the planning applications while trying to pursue my professional enquiries. It's absolutely essential I keep the two totally separate.'

'Well,' said Jim, 'I can tell you some information has come into our hands and we should have proof tomorrow. That should enable us to start making enquiries of Burtonlee Homes. We've been concerned up until now how we could approach them without any definitive reasons. We couldn't just breeze in there and ask Terry Burtonlee whether he or his assistant had been shooting at your cottage.

'I don't suppose I can persuade you to share this new information with me?' asked Sophie, more in hope than anything else.

'I certainly can't provide any exclusives on this one,' laughed Jim. 'I'm sure you'll discover the truth at the appropriate time.'

'What about the kid who attacked you with the knife, yesterday?' Sophie asked.

'We interviewed him this morning and he was quite talkative when his solicitor pointed out the gravity of his situation. He did confirm you were the target.'

'What will happen to him?'

'He's been charged with attempted murder and grievous bodily harm. He'll appear before the Magistrates tomorrow morning and will be remanded in custody to a high security prison, more for his own safety than anything. There will be no application for bail. I believe the man he identified is actually the one who's been making your life difficult, and I think may have been involved in Jack Finlay's death. He might possibly even be connected in some way with Jeremiah Clarke's death as well.'

'Am I still safe here?' asked Sophie, looking understandably concerned.

'I honestly believe so,' said Jim. 'We now have more details of the individual and his vehicle, and we have people looking for it. I don't believe anything will happen while you're at the Castle.'

26

Jackie Joynton put down the phone as Trussell walked in. 'Morning, Jim. You just missed an interesting call.'

'Oh, yes? Not more bad news, I hope?'

'Not today, for a change, although I'm not sure whether it will help us or not. That was the Met. I spoke to them a couple of times about the Brownlowe-Jameson case. You remember I asked them about the missing whistle-blower? They have some news at last.'

'Not another body?'

'No. Quite the opposite, for a change. They've found the man. He's alive and well, living in the West Country. He chose to disappear and has been in hiding, living a totally different life. Surprisingly, he hadn't even changed his name, though. Talk about hiding in plain sight'

'So, how did they find him?'

'Devon and Cornwell Police carried out a routine stop after a local traffic accident. Someone made the match on the missing person when they put his name into the PNC. The Met are on their way to interview him, to see if he has any further information about the original case. At least we won't have to worry about dismantling any flyovers!'

'I expect Sophie will be pleased to hear the news. He came to her first when the story broke. I got the impression she felt some sort of responsibility for the man.'

'Where does that leave us regarding our friend, Roger, as a likely suspect in this case?'

'Good question. My thinking at the time was if he could dispose of a witness, then he'd be quite capable of trying to kill Sophie. In the light of recent events, I think things are moving too quickly for Roger to influence or orchestrate from his overseas base. We can't completely eliminate him at this stage, though.'

'Do you think we should concentrate on Burtonlee at the moment, Jim?'

'I think we should, in the absence of any other immediate leads. We'll see what turns up after we've spoken to Barlborough.'

27

Jim Trussell looked around the office. It was prison visiting time.

'Right, Jackie,' he said. 'I'll borrow Greeno to drive me to Barrington. I'm sure he can catch up with what he's been doing when we get back.'

'That's fine. I was wondering how your arm would stand up to a longer drive.'

'Grab your coat, Greeno. I'm going to let you look inside a prison.'

They got into Trussell's car in the police station car park. Greeno got into the driver's seat, turned the key, pulled the gear lever into drive, and they headed out of the gate in the direction of the North Kent coast, their destination Barrington High Security Prison on the Isle of Sheppey. About a forty-five minute trip along the A249 if the traffic behaved.

The Head of Security at the prison, Fred Simpson, had spoken to the Assistant Governor as promised, to secure permission for Trussell to meet Henry Kilhampton, currently serving ten years at Her majesties' pleasure thanks in no small part to Sophie Breckton's investigation.

Now Trussell wanted, hopefully, to eliminate him from his current suspects list. Kilhampton was not officially one of course, and it remained to be seen whether he would even see Trussell despite having agreed to the meeting.

The traffic was light on the A249 and they soon arrived on the Sheppey Crossing, the bridge opened in 2006. Another fifteen minutes and they arrived at the prison where they found a space reserved for police visitors in the car park. Trussell took a file from the seat. Greeno locked the car and they headed for the main entrance where they produced their warrant cards and told the Officer in reception that Fred Simpson was expecting them. After the usual checks and passing through the airport-style metal detector, Simpson appeared and greeted Jim warmly.

Fred had visibly aged since Jim had last seen him. He had put on quite a few pounds and the dark, unruly mop of hair he remembered was now liberally streaked with grey. Jim wondered whether the obviously more sedentary life style really suited Fred, despite his original assertions that he wanted a quieter life, away from chasing criminals.

'It's been ages since we last met, Jim. Can't believe how time's flown. Whatever have you done to your arm?'

'I had a run in with a young hooligan on Tuesday. It was connected with our case. I had to take his knife away from him. That's the reason I've brought DC Green with me, as driver today.'

The introductions made, Simpson shook Greeno's hand and then turned back to Jim. 'You're getting a bit too old to be involved in street fights, Jim. Glad you're OK. Anyway, everything is ready for you. Kilhampton's happy to see you, and the interview room's reserved. Someone will bring him down when we're ready. However, if you recall, me saying I think you should speak to the prison chaplain first. If you would care to step into my office for a moment, I'll ask Joe to pop along.'

They went into Simpson's office which seemed quite austere. It contained little more than a desk with a couple of trays and a telephone on it, two tall locked filing cabinets standing against one wall, a high backed swivel chair behind the desk and three other three simple tubular chairs that were obviously not designed to allow anyone to get too comfortable. Trussell noticed that, despite being in the executive wing of the prison, the windows still had steel bars.

Simpson motioned Trussell and Green to sit, picked up the telephone, tapped a couple of buttons and waited a moment until the call was picked up at the other end.

'Ah, Joe, it's Fred. Jim Trussell has arrived. Can you spare us a moment, please?...No, there won't be any coffee!'

He turned to Trussell.

'Joe will be along in ten minutes. In the meantime, I've looked into our guest's file and spoken to the team on that wing. Kilhampton has never really mixed with the other prisoners there. He prefers to keep himself to himself. The Officer in Charge there thinks that in the beginning, he was rather in denial about what had happened to him, and saw himself as a cut above his fellow guests, whom he considered just criminals. He just didn't make the connection.'

'Has he had any contact with the outside world?'

'At first, his wife came to see him every month without fail, but after the first year, her visits became less frequent. She hasn't been here for at least four months, now,' said Simpson, consulting Kilhampton's file on the desk.

'What about other visitors?'

'His solicitor came here last month.'

'Wonder what that was about? Surely he's not considering an appeal and it must be too early to think about an application for parole? Or maybe Kilhampton still owes him part of his fee for his defence,' said Trussell facetiously.

'No idea. There was no one present at the interview. That's what the rules say. Any solicitor would be very quick to remind us if we tried to listen in.'

'Have you got his name and telephone number in the file? I could try asking him why he came to visit his client, but he'll probably plead client privilege.'

Simpson passed the details over and Trussell tucked the paper inside his file.

'So Kilhampton hasn't had meaningful contact with any of his fellow guests? Anyone who could arrange for someone on the outside to have an unfortunate accident? Does he have any access to a mobile phone?'

'That wing is swept pretty frequently and nothing has ever been found in his cell. On the contrary, he keeps it unbelievably tidy, compared with the others. He tends to read quite a lot, so there are a fair number of books.'

There was a tap on the half open door, and the prison chaplain came in. Above average height, greying hair and a pair of twinkling blue eyes that stood out from his ruddy complexion. He was wearing a check jacket over a blue grey clerical shirt which had the familiar half dog collar on it. Grey chinos and a pair of dark hush puppies completed his outfit.

Fred Simpson made the introductions. 'Jim, this is our Chaplain, The Reverend Hollister.'

'Please call me Joe,' he said. 'No formalities here.'

Trussell in turn introduced Greeno.

'Joe, Jim is here to see Henry Kilhampton. He's agreed to the meeting.'

'How can I help?'

'I can't say too much, other than that we're investigating a serious crime which has possible links to a number of previous cases, one of which was Kilhampton's. I obviously have to keep an open mind at this stage, and say I believe it's unlikely he's involved, but we just have to check, and hopefully eliminate him. What can you tell me about him?'

'I saw him when he first arrived here. He's another member of my flock, of course.'

'What was your impression of him then?'

'He genuinely seemed a bit shell shocked by what had happened to him, but I also sensed some sort of relief that the whole thing was over. It was quite a spectacular fall from grace. A Cabinet Minister who was apparently being tipped as a possible future Prime Minister. Suddenly, in here, he became just another face.'

'Did you talk to him a lot in those early days?'

'I visited him on a weekly basis. I try to see everyone, if they agree. At first, he was just distant and polite. Then we talked about his interests. He had been to Oxford and obtained a degree in Medieval History, and I believe he saw his interests might be a way to deal with his time here. I brought him books and, inevitably, our talks became more frequent and began to turn to the subject of early Christianity. That was when he started asking more questions and showing an interest.'

'What about visitors? His wife's visits became less frequent, I understand, and stopped a while ago.'

'Henry told me his wife had said she couldn't continue, and now wanted a divorce. I don't think he was really surprised.'

'Is that why his solicitor came here last month?'

'That's quite possible. You'll have to ask him. I believe you'll find him quite open and forthcoming.'

'What about other prisoners? Did he have any specific contacts with anyone?'

'No, he tended to shun them.'

'I have one last question, Joe. On a strictly confidential basis, do you think Kilhampton is capable of wanting to harm anyone? Do you think he might harbour any grudges?'

'I don't think that has ever been the case since I've known him, and certainly not now. He has turned increasingly to his faith and it has become very important to him. In my experience and opinion, it isn't something he can fake. He has nothing to gain by it. I honestly believe he's had an opportunity to think things over, reconsider his life and refocus it. He wouldn't be the first. There are some fairly well documented cases in prisons.'

'Thank you, Joe. I really appreciate your time and insight. Well, Fred, perhaps we can talk to him now.

They shook hands with the Chaplain, who waved a nonchalant farewell to Fred Simpson as he left the office ahead of them.

Down a corridor they came to a barred door. A uniformed officer unlocked it, let them through and relocked it after them. This was repeated as they walked further into the prison, accompanied by another officer. Finally Simpson stopped and opened a door into an interview room containing a table, two chairs and another chair by the door.

'Right,' he said to the accompanying officer, 'Can you bring Kilhampton down?'

Five minutes later, the door opened and Kilhampton came in. He was tidily dressed in his own clothes, a short-sleeved blue shirt and a pair of grey casual trousers. He was wearing a pair of loafers on his feet. Trussell had seen pictures of Kilhampton when he was still in office, and he was shocked by the transformation. The man had lost a lot of weight and his dark hair was turning grey. He held out his right hand to Trussell, who took it after a second's hesitation, The hand was dry, the handshake firm. Trussell winced slightly, but tried not to show it.

'Thank you for agreeing to see me, Mr Kilhampton. This is Detective Constable Green, who's assisting me with our enquiry.'

Kilhampton nodded to him.

Jim and Fred Simpson took the chairs opposite Kilhampton at the table and Greeno stood silently against the wall, listening to the conversation.

'It's my pleasure, Detective Inspector. I don't get that many visitors so I'm happy to see anyone from the outside world. But, I'm intrigued. How can I help you?'

'I'm looking at a particular event at the moment that might have had a tenuous link to your case, amongst others, so I wanted to eliminate that at the beginning.'

'Tell me more.'

'There were a number of people who were in some way involved in your case. How do you feel about them?'

'Do you know I was actually relieved when all this came out. I was in a position which was very uncomfortable. The foreign agents were putting a huge amount of pressure on me to give them more, paying me whilst threatening to reveal my private life to the world if I didn't deliver. That placed me between the proverbial rock and a hard place. The situation was becoming intolerable for me and it began taking its toll on my health.'

'Are you saying you were glad when it all came out?'

'Yes most definitely. Whatever the cost, the burden's been lifted. In answer to your question, they were all doing their jobs as they saw it so I can't blame them. I've rediscovered my faith now, and realise I was guilty of at least four of the seven deadly sins; pride, envy, lust and greed. So, you may be surprised to hear that I don't bear them any ill will, whoever they are. This has given me the chance to reconsider my future and perhaps in some way, rebalance my life and start giving back. In fact, I've had long discussions with the Chaplain as to how I can achieve this, perhaps by turning to the cloth in some way.'

'What about your wife? I understand she's stopped visiting you?'

'That was inevitable. Our marriage was in trouble long before this happened. This has given us the opportunity to put things right. We're getting divorced. I've let her use my problem as suitable grounds, although I've known about her affair for a long time. It just seems tidier. My solicitor came to discuss it last month.'

'Thank you for your candour, Mr Kilhampton. I don't believe I'll need to trouble you any further in this particular matter.'

'I hope you manage to solve your problems fairly quickly. I know from my time as Home Secretary that you have a mass of rules to follow.'

Fred Simpson opened the door and the officer waiting outside indicated to Kilhampton that the interview was over. As he left the room, he turned and said, 'Goodbye, Detective Inspector. Good luck with your enquiry.'

Simpson led them back through the labyrinth of locked doors until they finally reached the executive wing.

'Are you happy with what you heard today, Jim?'

'I think so. I never really believed he was involved. But, you know how it is. We have to eliminate all the possibilities until we're left with only one solution, however unlikely it might seem. Didn't Sherlock Holmes say something similar in one of his stories?'

'Blowed if I know, Jim. I see it's lunchtime. Do you fancy a quick pint and a sandwich before you head back to Woodchester? Our local pub five minutes from here does pretty good food.'

'Thanks, Fred. I'll pass on it this time. We have to get back but we must stay in touch. You have my number. Thanks again for your help today.'

'Good to see you. Say hello to Liz for me.'

They shook hands and an officer opened the door for them to leave the building.

Instinctively, Jim took a deep breath of the fresh air outside. He had only spent just over an hour inside, but he could imagine now exactly how a prisoner might feel after being released. There was definitely a sense of claustrophobia for someone unaccustomed to life inside. For him, it was the constant unlocking and locking of doors as he had made his way deeper inside the prison which seemed intolerable.

They headed for his car and Greeno took the wheel for the journey back to the station.

Trussell wondered whether Jackie would have anything to report about the Brownlow-Jameson case. What should be the next move? To an extent it would depend on Sophie and what she planned.

He tapped in Jackie's number on his mobile.

'Yes, Jim?'

'We're on our way back from Barrington. We've seen Kilhampton. He was very open and what he told me tied in with the information from Fred and the Chaplain, who know him pretty well. I'm satisfied he had nothing to do with the shooting and certainly didn't order it. Surprisingly, he seems to have found some sort of peace or closure in his current situation. Anyway, we'll discuss the next step when I get back. Have you heard from anyone about our friend Roger?'

'There's not been any word yet.'

'OK. We should be back in about forty minutes.'

28

Sophie had returned to her room after breakfast in the Castle dining room. She was thinking about the chain of events since the shot was fired at her in her own kitchen. She had been spending too much time at the Castle Inn. DS Jackie Joynton had provided her with whatever she needed to ensure she stayed out of the public view. The news of the shooting had not been given to the press and the police had been keeping Sophie hidden for her own safety. Unused to being confined to her room day in, day out, she was now experiencing the onset of cabin fever. She had to get out, to see other people.

Her problem was that she was instantly recognisable as a television personality. On the day of the attempt on her life, she'd been wearing very casual clothes, hair tied back, no make-up, yet DI Trussell had guessed her identity. Only her married name given in her 999 call had confused him momentarily.

Still, she had to get out, get some air, and see real people. There was no point in doing the celebrity thing, hiding behind a pair of designer sunglasses and pretending she was someone else. Indecisively, she twisted the two rings on the third finger of her right hand, something she found herself doing more and more in stressful moments. She decided to risk it, despite police advice. After all, she had never avoided risks before in the course of her work.

She put on a pair of casual trousers, an anonymous top, dragged her hair back into a single bunch with a cheap plastic clip to hold it in place, found a pair of old, battered but comfortable trainers, picked up a shopping bag left by Jackie, and with her sunglasses perched on top of her head, cautiously opened the door of her room. No sign of life in the corridor outside.

Leaving the hotel by a side door, trying to appear nonchalant, bag in hand, just another harassed mum trying to fit in the shopping after dropping the kids off to school, she set off down the High Street. She was nervous, discreetly glancing around, catching reflections in the shop windows. Was anyone following her? No sign of any silver Mercedes 4 x 4. This was a new Sophie - a complete contrast to the self-assured and glamorous image presented to the television cameras and her public. For the first time, she felt vulnerable - alone, as never before. She felt as though everyone was staring at her, waiting for someone to recognise her. a shout of 'That's Sophie Breckton.' But it never came.

Window shopping was new to her, but she wanted to be in the open, mingling with people, another member of the public going about her business. She wandered from one shop window to another, without really noticing what was in them. She found herself outside the local branch of W H Smith, and on a whim, ducked inside to buy a newspaper. She picked up a copy of *The Daily Enquirer*. The self-service machine accepted her money. She collected her receipt and walked out. The girl at the till was too busy serving other customers to notice her.

Emboldened by her new sense of apparent anonymity, she walked into the nearby coffee shop and ordered a Latte and a pastry. The barista, overrun with orders, paid her little attention. Sophie was just another customer. She took her tray to a corner table where she could see everything, a throwback to her investigative journalism days. Other customers were either chatting in groups or had their heads buried in their newspapers. She felt unnoticed. Maybe things were not as dangerous as Jim Trussell had suggested.

She peered around, looking over her newspaper: no one seemed to be taking any notice of her. She glanced at the paper, not really concentrating on what she read. Finishing the pastry, she drained the last of her coffee, folded the paper, tucking it inside her shopping bag and got up to leave. When she opened the door and stepped into the street, it was much busier than before. There were people everywhere. She joined the crowd, wandering slowly along the High Street, casually glancing in shop windows as she passed them. She had a nagging feeling she was being watched. Was it intuition born out of her job, or just paranoia?

Sophie suddenly felt a nudge in the back. Something hard. Like a gun barrel. Surely it wasn't?

A quiet voice said 'Sophie Breckton, just keep walking. I knew I'd find you sooner or later. Don't turn around and do nothing to attract attention. Just listen to my instructions. I'm right behind you.'

Her heart missed a beat and she fought down the urge to run. Perhaps there really was a gun. She carried on walking and reached the local Marks and Spencer's branch.

'Go into the store and start looking at the clothes on the left. Show an interest in what you pick up. I am still right behind you. I'm wearing a grey hoodie and jeans.'

She did as she was told.

A man in his early twenties appeared next to her among the clothes racks, dressed exactly as he had said. To her relief he discreetly produced a warrant card. 'DC Tim Beach, Miss Breckton,' he said quietly. 'Sorry about the approach, but I didn't want to cause a stir by stopping you in the middle of the High Street. DI Trussell asked me to collect you from the Castle, but you'd left. How did you manage to slip out without me seeing you? We're now certain the Castle is being watched. We need to walk to the station. Don't hurry - just stroll and talk to me. Try to look as though we're friends out shopping together.'

When they arrived at Woodchester police station, Jim Trussell looked relieved that Beach had managed to find Sophie.

'I don't want to labour the point, Sophie, but we would really appreciate you remaining at the Castle. We have enough going on without putting you under permanent surveillance. We just don't have the manpower or the time. Mind you there's always protective custody.' He laughed. 'But I think you wouldn't find our rooms downstairs as comfortable as the Castle.'

'I just felt I had to get out of that room for a while and mix with other people.'

'I understand. Anyway, we do, at least, have some good news for you. The whistle-blower in the Brownlowe-Jenkinson case has been found alive and well, living in the West Country.'

'Does it mean you can rule Roger out, now?'

'Not completely, but I'm beginning to think so.'

29

Sophie was sitting in her hotel room, sipping a cup of coffee while she watched the television, when her phone rang. She glanced at it. The caller's number on the screen was unfamiliar.

'Hullo,' she answered hesitantly.

An unrecognised voice said, 'Sophie Breckton, are you interested in some proof that Terry Burtonlee has been passing brown envelopes around to certain councillors?'

The voice was obviously disguised. Was that a hint of an accent?

'Who is this?'

'Names aren't important. Do you want the information or not?'

'How do I know this is a genuine offer?'

'Do you want it or not? There are other people who will be prepared to talk to me. Like Charles Stroud at *The Daily Monitor*, for starters.'

'OK. How do I see this proof, and what's in it for you?'

'It's a gift. It's personal. You don't need to know the reason. I just want to see Burtonlee get what he deserves. That will be enough for me. I came to you first because you are already chasing him in the press and on your television programme.'

'So where do I meet you?'

'Do you know Warminster Grove in Leverton? There are some lockup garages at the end of the street. I'll be waiting for you there. I'll meet you at the back of the block at ten o'clock. Leave your car near the Golden Lion pub and walk to the lockups. You won't be able to park any closer. It's about a hundred yards. Come alone. I shall be watching. Don't be late.'

Sophie was in a quandary. She desperately wanted that final piece of evidence which would put an end to Burtonlee's games, but there was a niggling doubt in her mind. She tried to dismiss it - she had been in this situation before, following up stories, and no harm had come to her. On the other hand, no one had tried to kill her before, and now there had already been several attempts on her life. Should she phone Jackie? There was no guarantee she'd be able to get there in time.

In the end, her need for some hard evidence against Burtonlee overcame her better judgement, and she decided to go. She was normally quite measured in everything she did. In her haste, she had overlooked one important question. How did the caller know she could get to the meeting in less than thirty minutes? She could have been anywhere in the county, or even in London.

Again, in defiance of police advice, she put on a jacket, picked up her bag, grabbed her car keys, and left the room.

She climbed into her car, switched on the satnav and put Warminster Grove and the postcode in. It was a twenty minute journey. She should just about make it in time.

The route was unfamiliar, but she got there at five to ten, saw the Golden Lion pub, and found a parking space a few yards away. The pub looked a bit rough, to say the least. Peeling paintwork, old brown tiled exterior, walls covered in graffiti in places. Just generally run down. It certainly looked part of the area.

Outside the pool of light from the pub, the street was eerily dark. The street lights seemed to have failed. The road was heavily parked on both sides. She set off carefully along the pavement in the direction she had been given in the phone call. Realising the lockups were on the other side of the road, she stepped between two parked cars to cross the quiet street.

There was a sudden blaze of headlamps, and the sound of a vehicle accelerating rapidly towards her. It swerved to her side of the road, and she just managed to step back, but a glancing blow from a wing mirror and the draught of the passing vehicle slammed her against the bonnet of one of the parked cars. Winded, and clutching her side, she managed to get back onto the pavement into the pool of light from the pub. She leant against the wall by the door, trying to get her breath back.

Nothing broken, but I'll have some nasty bruises there tomorrow. It hasn't done my jacket any good either.

Sophie looked around. Not a single person on the street. Very convenient, she thought. No witnesses.

She found her phone, called Jackie and told her what had happened.

'You'll be safer in the pub,' Jackie said. 'Even the Golden Lion. I'll meet you there. It'll take me about fifteen minutes to get there. I'll tell Jim Trussell.'

The pub didn't look very welcoming to a stranger. She opened the door and peered inside. It was definitely a lads' pub. The place was full of young men, clustered around the pool table, standing at the bar drinking or sitting at the few tables scattered around. The first thing that struck Sophie was that she had never seen so many shaven heads and tattoos in one place at the same time. Apart from the pool table, the lighting was very dim. It was both gloomy and threatening. An unpleasant atmosphere. As she stepped inside, everything stopped and she was greeted by a chorus of wolf whistles and ribald comments.

She walked up to the bar. The barmaid, a chubby bottle blonde with matching tattoos and facial piercings, looked at Sophie as if she had stepped off another planet.

'Lost, are we? What's 'appened to yer clothes? Waddya want?'

'I just tripped over outside. The pavements aren't very well lit here. I'm waiting for a friend to collect me. Can I have a brandy, please?'

The barmaid stuck a glass under the optic, filled it and banged it down on the bar.

'That's three quid to you.'

Sophie put three pound coins on the bar and picked up the glass, ignoring the stares. Novelty over, the regulars went back to their pool and conversations. No one paid her any more attention. She glanced at her watch. Ten minutes had passed.

'No sign of yer friend, then,' said the barmaid as she pulled a couple of pints of lager for one of the regulars.

Sophie ignored the comment and stared at the rows of wine and spirit bottles on the shelves behind the bar, trying to occupy her mind, pass the time.

The door opened, and there was another outbreak of whistles.

'Bloody 'ell. There's two of 'em,' said one of the Neanderthals, as Jackie walked in. But the comments stopped when they saw Jim Trussell following her through the door.

'Watch out, Jimbo, it's the Old Bill,' said a voice from the back of the bar. Sophie noticed one of the customers trying to leave discreetly by the back door,

The two detectives walked straight up to Sophie.

'Are you OK, Sophie?' asked Jim.

'Just a bit shaken,' she said. 'I'll probably feel it tomorrow when the bruises start to come out. The car I bounced off was rather hard.'

'Certainly made a mess of your jacket,' said Jackie, pointing to a large tear where the car's offside wing mirror had caught her.

'Finish your drink and we'll talk in the car.'

As they left the bar, there was silence until the door closed behind them. Then the conversations resumed.

They walked to Jim's car and got in.

'Now, tell us what happened. You should never have ventured down here on your own, particularly at this time of night. This is a bit of a no go area. People say that if you see a cat with two ears round here, then it must be a lost tourist. Start at the beginning with the phone call. What do you remember about it?'

'The voice was obviously disguised and his English a bit too correct, but I thought I detected a trace of an American accent in there somewhere.'

'Have you had any professional dealings with any Americans? Have any of your stories included anyone from that part of the world?'

'The short answer is no. He was rather persuasive. He led me to believe if I chose to ignore it, he'd approach another well-known journalist, Charles Stroud at the Monitor. The caller knew I wouldn't want the last piece of evidence to be handed to a competitor, after I had, publicly, done all of the spade work. So I decided to follow it up. I couldn't pass up the chance to get some real evidence against Burtonlee. The caller was counting on that.'

'Weren't you suspicious?' asked Jackie.

'I've had to meet some pretty dodgy people in the past following up some of my stories, without any real problems. You get a sort of feel for it. Now of course I've got some unanswered questions. How did the caller know I could just about get to this location in half an hour? Anyway I decided to risk it. Of course, with the benefit of hindsight, I should have called you first. When I got here, the street was deserted and the lights didn't seem to be working. I must have made a perfect target, silhouetted against the pub lights. The car appeared from nowhere and drove straight at me. I was just able to step back, but it must have brushed against me because I was thrown against one of the parked cars.'

'Were you able to see the car?'

'Not really. It happened so fast. It was a large car. Light coloured.'

Jackie turned to Jim. 'Could have been our old friend, the Silver Mercedes.'

Jim glanced at Sophie. He gave her a quizzical look.

'I couldn't be sure. It's possible. It all happened so quickly.'

'No CCTV round here unfortunately. The locals would never stand for it. It would interfere with their usual daily activities. If any cameras were put up, they would disappear again pretty quickly.

'Do you see any American connection, Jim? Is it too much of a stretch to think that someone has imported a hitman from the States to do this? Especially as the cartridge case found by the Crime Scene guys was American. That would point to someone fairly organised. Do you think we should be talking to the Serious Crimes people?"

'It's a possible line of enquiry. That would certainly move it to a corporate level. We'll see if they have any ideas.' He looked at Sophie. 'We'll need to get you back to the Castle. Jackie, will you ride with Sophie and I'll follow in my car. We'll discuss this in the morning. We can arrange to meet you at the Castle then.'

As they set off back to Woodchester, Jackie said, 'Jim was really worried when I phoned to tell him what had happened. He insisted on coming over with me.'

'Perhaps he didn't want me in this area on my own at this time of night. Or else he was worried that his case would be even harder to solve without the main witness.'

'No, I think there's more to it than that. I'm speaking as a woman rather than a detective. We've now seen four attempts on your life. It's getting a bit too regular. I believe he's very concerned for your welfare.'

Sophie looked at her in amazement.

'By the way, I seem to remember you told me your husband's first wife was killed in a hit and run accident that still hasn't been solved.'

'Surely, you don't believe there's any connection with Jenny? It's just a terrible coincidence.'

'We've reached the stage now with the sheer speed of events we cannot rule out anything now,' said Jackie. 'How do you feel now? Do you want me to take you to A & E for someone to look at your injury?'

'No. Thank you. I'm sure it will be OK. Just bruising, I expect. But I do appreciate the offer. If we can just go back to the Castle, I'll have a soak in the bath. I should feel better tomorrow.'

30

Sophie was sitting at the table in the small room she was still occupying at the hotel, busy on her laptop. The ongoing police investigation into the series of events that had overtaken her could not keep her from her work. There was too much at stake, The TV company was still providing further material for her to investigate and follow up.

Her phone rang. It was a familiar number. Her producer was on the line. 'Good Morning, Derek.'

'Hey, Sophie.'

'Grow up Derek, that modern juvenile drivel doesn't suit you. Especially at your age! What can I do for you?'

'Sophie, there's a lot of new stuff on Burtonlee coming in. I'll need to courier it to you so you can look at it as soon as possible.'

'Fine, but I'm not at the cottage at the moment. I had to vacate the place temporarily while some work is being done. I'm staying at The Castle Inn on Woodchester High Street at the moment. I'll give you the postcode.'

'OK. What's Richard doing? Is he there as well?'

'No. He's using our flat at the Barbican at the moment. It's more convenient for the City.'

'Ok. I'll get it to you for Monday morning. Call me when you've had a chance to look through the papers.'

'I'll do that,' she said, finishing the call.

Concentrating again on what she was doing, she was interrupted by the sound of someone knocking loudly on the door. She got up and opened it slightly, only for someone to push it open and knock her out of the way. A young woman stormed into the room, eyes flashing. She was furious and it showed.

'Well, Mrs Blaxstone, or Breckton, or whatever your name is,' she shouted, 'I want you to leave my father alone.'

Sophie was dumbfounded. She had often encountered hostility on the street in the course of her investigations, and had never let it faze her. She thought back to the time when the wife of the disgraced MP, Henry Kilhampton, had similarly confronted her, to try to stop her publishing the information about her husband. Sophie's calm reminder that he was a traitor who had abused his position by passing sensitive

135

information to a foreign power had soon shut her up. But this girl was different.

Sophie studied her. Probably in her late teens or early twenties, Average height, slim, long brown hair. She was wearing a summer top and jeans. Did she look familiar? Sophie bit her lip, as she tried to focus her thoughts. She started twisting the rings on her right hand again. She tried to connect the girl with one of her investigations. Was she related to the missing white van man, sent to get Sophie off his back? Could she be related to Terry Burtonlee? Sophie knew he had a grown up family. She had seen two of his three children when she had attended the court to listen to his divorce proceedings. Maybe this was the third.

'I'm sorry. I've no idea what you're talking about. Please calm down. Would you care to explain? Who's your father?'

'Detective Inspector Jim Trussell,' said the girl.

Sophie stared at her, open mouthed. It took a lot to shock her these days, but this had completely caught her unawares.

'What do you mean?'

'I'm not in regular contact with my dad much these days while I'm at Uni, but when I call him, all he talks about is his current investigation and how he wants to help you. You must have some sort of hold over him. What is it?'

'There's nothing to hide. Truth is, I probably spend more of my time with Detective Sergeant Joynton than your dad. I don't know what to say to you. I haven't given DI Trussell any encouragement at all. I've no idea why you should think like that. He's been trying to find out who wants to kill me. I just happen to think it's quite important. Well, at least it is to me. In fact, someone had another go last night. A vehicle tried to run me down in Leverton, but I doubt that would greatly concern you. Don't you think I've enough to worry about at the moment without getting caught up in your imaginary scandal?'

'I never thought someone would have turned his head that easily, after all these years. It must be the show business connection - he never had the slightest interest in the entertainment business before.'

'Well, I'm not in entertainment - I'm an investigative journalist. I just happen to do some of my work through television these days. My career up until my recent television work was spent entirely in Fleet Street, working for one of the national daily newspapers. I promise you, Liz, that is your name, isn't it? There's very little glitz and glamour chasing stories about the seedier side of life. Oh yes, that's where most of my time has been spent. It means lots of unsociable hours and very definitely unsociable places. Not to mention some very unsavoury and sometimes downright dangerous people. Then there are the threats, mainly on the internet. The trick is to avoid becoming like the people I've to deal with and write about.'

'How did you know my name? Dad must have told you.'

'Yes, he did. When we were talking about my work as a journalist, going through my old cases, he mentioned he had a daughter at university who wanted to write. I know he's very proud of you. I guess he was just trying to put me at ease after the problems I've been through. It's been a very difficult time for me, and both your father and DS Joynton have tried to ensure my safety while their investigation has been underway. I promise you, that has been the limit of my dealing with your father. He's been very professional throughout.'

'That's not the way I see it.'

'Look, Liz, please just sit down for a moment. Try to calm down and listen to me. There's nothing between myself and your father. I can understand why he might want to mention my case to you. I know about your family circumstances. I think your father needs some sort of safety valve, a way to ease the pressure he's being put under to solve this case. And you're it.'

'What do you mean?'

'This case has become very high profile - not just from my point of view, but in the higher ranks in the force. Jackie Joynton told me the Assistant Chief Constable's piling the pressure on your dad to find the guilty parties. Outside of his team, your dad has no one to talk to about it, which is why it comes up when you speak to him.'

'What has he told you about us?'

'Absolutely nothing. What little I know I've heard from other people. I can tell you his colleagues have tremendous respect for your father. I'm really sorry about your mother and can understand how you feel. In fact, I lost both my parents in an accident when I was only a little older than you. I know what it's like to be alone in the world.'

'I read your biography online and don't recall it being mentioned. I wanted to understand you before I came here.'

'How did you know my room number?'

'It was easy. I just mentioned to the woman at reception that Detective Sergeant Joynton had asked me to deliver an urgent message to you. Told her I was a trainee and had left my ID at the station. She didn't query it. Please don't say anything. I wouldn't want to get her into trouble.'

'Liz, I would rather we were friends. Why don't we go downstairs to the lobby - we can get some tea or coffee? We can talk there. I can't offer you anything in this room. '

'Alright. That's if you still want to talk to me.'

'It will look better for you if the woman at reception sees us together sharing a pot of something. It will make your earlier deception appear to have been legitimate. I have to admire your sense of invention on getting past the desk like that. Such a talent bodes well for your future as a journalist. You're obviously someone who'll do anything to get the story!'

'Thank you. I am sorry about the way I arrived in your room. I'm seriously concerned about dad.'

'Look, I don't want you to carry unnecessary ill feeling with you. It certainly won't help your dad at a time when he could probably do with some support. He would never even suggest it to you, though, I'm sure. Just try to be understanding if he mentions the case. Perhaps, even show some interest. After all, that's how good journalists learn their trade, by listening to other people. I've already said that your dad told me you wanted to write or be a journalist. He was just trying to put me at ease when I'd been seriously stressed because a bullet had just missed me. I would be happy to give you any career advice at any time, if you want. After all, I've spent almost twenty years in the business so I know a thing or two…'

They left the room and walked downstairs to the lobby. The woman at reception smiled at them.

'Can we get tea or coffee somewhere, please?' asked Sophie.

'Certainly, Mrs Blaxstone. Find a table in the lounge area and I'll send someone over.'

They walked through into the lounge and found the usual corner table. The room was deserted this morning. As promised, a waiter appeared and Sophie ordered coffee for them both. Five minutes later, it appeared.

The atmosphere had become almost congenial. They were chatting about Liz's first year at university and her aspirations when Sophie heard a familiar voice in the lobby.

'Hello, Trish. Can you give Mrs Blaxstone a call in her room, please?'

'Good morning, Detective Sergeant. No need. Mrs Blaxstone is in the lounge having coffee with a visitor.'

'Thanks, Trish. I know the way.'

Liz looked at Sophie, absolutely petrified. They had both heard the conversation.

'What can I do? I'll be in real trouble now. I've no business being here.'

'You can leave Jackie to me. I'll think of something.'

She opened her bag, produced a notebook, found a ballpoint pen and passed them to Liz.

'Quick. Write down your name, address and mobile number. The University contact details as well. Start listing your education, exams, subjects and so on. Write down what you're doing at Uni. Just make a start before Jackie gets here and then follow my lead.'

Liz took the notebook and started writing as if her life depended on it. Or at least as if her liberty might.

Jackie came into the lounge, spotted them, and walked towards their table. She was more casually dressed today in a tee-shirt and a pair of jeans. Her sunglasses were perched on top of her head. No sign of her trademark trouser suit today.

She looked sharply at Liz.

'Good morning Sophie. I thought I'd drop by to see if you would like some company, as Mike's working today. But I see you already have a visitor. I hope I'm not intruding.

'Of course not, Jackie. It's really kind of you.'

'What are you doing here, Liz?'

Sophie quickly took the initiative. 'I remembered you told me that DI Trussell's daughter had ambitions to become a journalist. So, I arranged for her to pop round as she was home for the weekend. I need some personal details from her as I am going to try to use my contacts to get her a work placement for the summer holidays.'

'That's nice of you,' said Jackie, looking hard at Liz.

'Given the state of your investigations, I would appreciate it if you pretend you haven't seen Liz here and didn't mention it to DI Trussell. I wouldn't want to cause any problems or embarrass him. I know it's probably a bit irregular but it seems the least I can do.'

'OK.'

'Please sit down, Jackie. I really appreciate you taking the trouble to come round. Liz and I are just about finished here,' she said, discreetly winking at Liz. 'Let me talk to a couple of my friends and I'll get back to you as soon as I can, Present circumstances permitting.' She smiled at Liz, indicating their discussions were finished.

Liz hastily drained the last of her coffee, handed Sophie her notebook and pen, pushed her chair back and stood up to leave. 'Thank you, Sophie; that's really kind. You can't imagine how much I appreciate it.'

With that, she left the lounge, heaving a huge sigh of relief.

'I thought I'd drop by so we can have an informal update on where we are,' said Jackie.

'Thank you,' said Sophie. 'I'll get us some more coffee.'

'We've ruled out Mr Kilhampton. Jim met him and is satisfied there is no connection there. The prison staff have confirmed he's had no contact with anyone inside, and the prison Chaplain, who spends a lot of time with him, has confirmed he doesn't harbour any grudges towards anyone linked with his case.'

'You're certain?'

'Yes. Now, we haven't made a great deal of progress with Mr Brownlow-Jameson, but we're in touch with the people looking into his affairs. Their best guess at the moment is that it's unlikely to be linked to him, because it would seriously jeopardise his chances of returning to the UK. However, Jim is not ruling him out at this stage and we're waiting to hear from the other Agencies involved. At least the Met have now updated us about the whistle-blower.'

'Any further progress with the incident last night at Leverton?' asked Sophie.

'Not at the moment. Jim still believes the silver Mercedes is involved, but we aren't much further forward with that line of enquiry. The local police have done a search today and spoken to the locals. You won't be surprised to hear that none of them saw anything. We've asked uniformed to check on silver Mercedes 4 x 4's with the DVLA, but I'm not hopeful – do you have any idea how many are registered in the country? Uniformed are also on the lookout for similar vehicles seen around Woodchester and surrounding villages. They've been told to note registration numbers, but a professional would probably have cloned the plate anyway. The forensic examination of the site where the shooting occurred didn't leave anything conclusive in the way of tyre tracks.'

'This mysterious Mercedes seems to come and go at will.'

'Yes but we'll find it. We have spoken to your friend, John Shalford, again, but he has been unable to add very much to his earlier statement. Forensic examination of the letter handed in at the Castle showed your fingerprints and some belonging to someone else. They don't appear on our data base.'

'So, we don't seem to have moved forward very much at this point in terms of the mysterious car, then?'

'The incident at Brandford was a positive step. We do have an idea who we're dealing with now.'

'I suppose you've eliminated our White Van Man from your enquiries now?'

'I don't believe we ever considered him a suspect in anyway. He was just someone to be eliminated from the list of possible culprits. DC Tim Beach has followed that one up and has tracked him down. Unsurprisingly, he can account for his movements at the time someone fired that shot at you. Tim has also spoken to the Council Trading Standards about it and dropped your name in there as the source of the enquiry, so it'll be a success for you when you start your programme. Tim will share the details with you and let you know where you can reach the man for your programme. I think he'll be happy to talk to you to put his side of the story, if he has one! I don't believe he enjoyed the experience of being chased down by the police. I think your earlier remark about him was right on the money – he's more frightened of you than anyone else.'

31

Sunday 30th June. 10.30 am.
Woodchester.

Trussell was at home, trying to catch up with his domestic chores. The washing machine was churning away in the background as he fought a losing battle with a shirt on the ironing board. He needed more for the week ahead.

His mobile rang. A welcome respite.

It was Jackie Joynton calling. 'Morning, Jim. Sorry to call you on your day off, but there's been another possible development.'

'What's happened now?'

'It might be relevant, so I thought that I'd better tell you as soon as possible. My other half, Mike, mentioned that there'd been a traffic accident on the outskirts of Foggenden yesterday.' She went on to recount what he had told her. 'An old 4 x 4, driven by an elderly man, failed to negotiate a bend on Furze Hill – that's a steep hill on the outskirts of Foggenden. A witness, following at a distance says that the vehicle's brake lights came on and flickered but the car failed to slow and just drove straight ahead through a hedge, finishing up on its side in the field. The emergency services took the driver, unconscious, to Woodchester Hospital. It's unclear at this stage whether the driver suffered some sort of medical emergency. I phoned the hospital to check on him, but he remains unconscious in intensive care.'

'Good of you to check on him, but why the interest, Jackie?' asked Trussell.

'Because the driver was John Shalford, from Sophie's action committee. It was he who took over the reins of the committee after Jack Finlay's death.'

'What was Mike's opinion about the accident? Did he think the driver had a health problem? It might be my suspicious mind but have they examined Shalford's vehicle? Could there have been a mechanical issue?

'He has an open mind at the moment, particularly as it involved an elderly driver. I believe they've recovered the car and it's been taken to the garage for checking over.'

'We'll need to know asap if there were any problems with the car. Ask Mike where they've taken it. We'll need to talk to whoever's dealing with it. Tell him we need to know urgently whether anyone tampered with it. In the meantime, we'll have to visit the hospital and talk to whoever is looking after Mr Shalford. Perhaps they'll be in a position now to tell us whether he had a heart attack or a stroke or something else that could have affected his driving.'

'OK, Jim. Do you want me to meet you at the hospital this morning?'

'I'll be there in about half an hour. We'll talk to the consultant.'

'OK. Do you think this is linked with the case?'

'It seems significant that the three main people leading the opposition to Burtonlee's planned development at Foggenden have all suffered in some way or other. It's the traditional way of dealing with a problem – take off the head and the beast is finished. Who else is left on the committee to carry on? We'd better contact Sophie as soon as we know more about Mr Shalford's condition.'

He heard her talking to Mike, asking the questions. He couldn't hear the conversation, just the sound of voices.

Her voice again.

'I've got the details. I'll share them with you at the hospital.

32

Trussell waited outside the main doors until Joynton arrived. Together they went in and approached the desk, showing their warrant cards.

'I understand a gentleman named John Shalford was brought here yesterday following a road traffic accident near Foggenden,' said Trussell. 'We'd like to speak to whoever's in charge of his case, please.'

The nurse behind the desk glanced at the warrant cards and then consulted her list. 'He's in the ITU at present. Just a moment and I'll phone the ward to find out for you.'

A quick call and she turned to them. 'The Registrar is on the ward at the moment, and he'll be down to talk to you in a couple of minutes, if you wouldn't mind waiting. Take a seat and I'll let you know when he gets here.'

They sat and contemplated the steady stream of people coming in with all sorts of injuries and problems. Trussell felt uncomfortable in the midst of so many emergency cases around them and thought that they both looked a bit conspicuous.

A doctor, wearing blue scrubs, appeared from a door by the desk and the nurse pointed to Trussell and Joynton.

'Good morning. My name's Michael Page. I understand that you want to know about Mr Shalford?'

Trussell showed his warrant card and introduced himself and Joynton. 'Is there somewhere quieter where we can talk?'

Page led them to a nearby office and closed the door behind them.

'Thank you for your time. How is Mr Shalford? Has he regained consciousness yet?'

'No. We're still monitoring him.'

'Are you been able to tell us whether his accident might have been due to some sort of medical emergency? Anything which might have impaired his ability to drive?'

'Nothing like that at all. His injuries were caused solely by the accident. We believe that he was OK until the moment of impact.'

'Mr Page, we have reason to believe John Shalford was the victim of a deliberate attempt on his life and that someone may have tampered with his car prior to the accident. The vehicle is currently being

144

examined so we can be absolutely certain. In the meantime, I think that we should arrange to have someone with him to ensure his safety.' Trussell turned to Joynton. 'Can you call the station, Jackie, and speak to the duty sergeant. Ask him to send someone from uniformed down here straight away. We'll wait here until someone turns up.'

He turned back to the doctor. 'I hope it won't inconvenience your staff, Mr Page. I believe that Mr Shalford could be in danger.'

'I understand.'

Trussell couldn't help wondering whether they should get the names of the remaining members of the committee and consider whether they all needed protection. That would seriously stretch police resources to the point of impossibility, even if he could persuade Watkins. It would depend on how many people were involved.

Sophie would have to be asked to provide their details.

33

Trussell sipped the coffee Sandcastle had put in front of him.

'Jackie, while we wait for information about Mr Shalford's car, I think today might be a good day to visit Burtonlee Homes and meet Mr Barlborough. We can't hold up the case.'

'Shall I get Greeno to phone him and tell them? Fix a time?'

'No. I think we might wing it. Turn up unannounced. Don't want to give him a chance to be out, make some excuse, or, even worse do a runner.'

'Do you want me to come with you?'

'Not this time. You keep an eye on things here. Can you check with the garage about Mr Shalford's car and call the hospital to see whether there's been any change in his condition? Chase up those other agencies involved with Mr Brownlowe-Jameson. I'll take Greeno with me. He's done the spadework on this part, so far.'

He drained his cup and called across. 'Greeno. Grab your jacket and the file on Burtonlee. We're going to talk to your favourite housebuilder in Maidstone. We'll take my car, but you'd better drive.'

'Is the arm still playing up, Jim?' asked Jackie.

'It's still uncomfortable. But it's improving, thanks.'

Trussell handed Mark Green the car keys. 'You know the way, Greeno?'

'Yes Guv. I located their offices as part of the research. I knew we'd have to visit them sooner or later. How do you intend to play it today? Are we just going to talk to Barlborough or will you try to see Burtonlee himself?'

'I don't plan to see him. Let's concentrate on Mr Barlborough.'

A forty minute drive from the office along the M20 and onto the A249 brought them into the county town.

'Almost there, Guv.' said Greeno, as he turned into the quiet road where the Burtonlee head office was located. There was a visitors' car park in front, so Greeno put the car as close as he could to the main entrance.

They got out and headed towards the building, a drab brick four storey building with anonymous windows betraying no sign of life inside them. They pushed open the double doors and walked into the lobby where the first thing they saw was a large photographic display of the many developments in which the company had been involved over the years. Terry Burtonlee's pictures featured prominently, beaming at prospective buyers.

They approached the reception desk.

'Good morning,' said Trussell to the girl behind the desk. 'We'd like to see Mr Barlborough.'

'Do you have an appointment?' asked the girl. 'He's a very busy man. I don't have any visitors listed for him today.'

'No. We don't have an appointment,' said Trussell, producing his warrant card. 'But I'm sure he'll see us. Perhaps you would tell him that Detective Inspector Trussell and Detective Constable Green of Kent Police would like a word with him?'

The girl was taken aback, but regained her composure.

'Certainly, Detective Inspector, just a minute. I'll check whether he can see you. He's very busy, you know.'

'Well, you have a choice,' said Trussell. 'Please call him now, or I'll be back again shortly with an arrest warrant. Take your choice.'

She immediately picked up the phone and spoke into it. 'Jonathan, there are two gentlemen here asking for you. I told them you're busy but they're insisting on seeing you. They're from the police.'

'He'll be down in just a moment, gentleman,' she said, her anxiety clearly showing.

Two minutes later he appeared. A slim man about five feet ten and looking pretty much the forty two years claimed by the birth certificate found by Greeno. His thinning black hair was neatly styled and he was wearing rimless glasses. His expensive mid grey suit, white shirt, striped tie and quality shoes completed the impression of a man used to the finer things in life.

He greeted them warily. 'Good morning. I'm not sure how I can help you. Perhaps you can enlighten me.'

'Good morning, Sir,' said Trussell. 'Is there somewhere we can talk?'

'Yes, of course. Please come this way.'

He led them across the lobby to a small interview room.

'Please sit down. May I offer you some tea or coffee?'

'No thank you, Sir. Like you, our time is limited.'

'Your visit's a bit unexpected, to say the least. Can you tell me what it's about?'

'We're looking into certain matters which seem to have a connection to your company's proposed development at Foggenden.'

'Yes. That's an enormous project for our company which will be hugely important and beneficial to the local people.'

'We aren't here to listen to your sales pitch, Mr Barlborough. Are you aware of the death of Jack Finlay, who was leading the opposition to the project? Or the death of Councillor Jeremiah Blackley, who, I understand, was one of your major supporters on Woodchester Council?'

'Yes. It was very sad. But what has that to do with Burtonlee Homes?'

'That is precisely what we're looking into at the moment. There's also a connection to other events which I'm not at liberty to divulge at this stage.'

'So, why have you come here to talk to me? I'm only an employee of the company. Shouldn't you be speaking to Mr Burtonlee himself? After all, he's the owner.'

Trussell turned to Greeno. 'Have you got the file?'

Green passed it over.

Trussell opened it and produced the birth certificate which had been sent to them from the Passport Office.

'Is this yours, Mr Barlborough?' he asked.

He gave the paper a cursory glance.

'Yes. Where did you get it?

'From the Passport Office. I believe you used it to obtain your passport.'

'Correct. What's the problem, then?'

'Would you mind telling us the names of your parents, where they live and when you last saw them?'

'I don't believe it's any of your business.'

'Unfortunately we've made it our business. We have reason to believe this birth certificate is not yours. Are you aware that using this document to obtain a passport or any other document, such as a driving licence, constitutes a criminal offence?'

'Where is this leading?'

'As I've already mentioned, we're looking at events connected with Burtonlee's plans for Foggenden.'

'You should speak to Terry Burtonlee,' he repeated. 'He owns the company.'

'We're aware of that but we believe you have effectively been in day to day control recently while he's been tied up in personal matters. We would like to invite you to accompany us to Woodchester police station to continue these enquiries.'

'And if I decline your request?'

'Then we shall arrest you now and take you with us. We've enough evidence to charge you.'

'It seems you leave me no alternative.'

'If there's anything you need to do, or anyone you need to tell, then I suggest you do it now. DC Green will accompany you to your office.'

They stepped out of the interview room, and Barlborough, looking somewhat shaken, disappeared through a swing door in the corner of the lobby accompanied by Mark Green.'

Trussell returned to the lobby, still holding the file.

The receptionist watched him warily. 'Is there anything I can get you, Detective Inspector?' she said.

'No thank you. Mr Barlborough will be leaving with us shortly, in case anyone needs him.'

'Will he be gone long?'

'It's difficult to say. No doubt he'll already have spoken to Mr Burtonlee.'

'I'm afraid he's not in the office today, Detective Inspector.'

'Where can he be contacted?'

'I'm not at liberty to discuss his whereabouts. More than my job is worth.'

'There's such a thing as obstructing the police, you know. Are you sure you don't want to leave your desk here and come to Woodchester with us?'

'If you put it like that, I'd better give you his home address and telephone number.'

'Does he not come into the office every day, then?'

'Not at the moment.'

'So, who's running the business?'

'Mr Barlborough, of course.'

'How long has he been with the Company?'

'He was here before I joined. So, it must be at least three years.'

Barlborough reappeared with DC Green. He looked over at the receptionist and told her, 'If there are any personal calls for me, then take a message, please. I'll deal with any matters when I get back. Otherwise, everything should be referred to the accounts manager.'

Mark Green looked at Trussell and raised his eyebrows slightly. His unspoken message to Trussell was, 'He'll be lucky. Not any time soon, sunshine!'

They went to Trussells's car and invited Barlborough to travel in the back. 'It's about a forty minute drive to Woodchester,' said Trussell. 'That should give you enough time to help you decide what you'd like to share with us. It will be easier for you in the long run. I've no doubt Mr Burtonlee will be very interested in what you've been up to in his absence. Abusing his trust, as a bare minimum.'

'I have nothing to say.'

'You realise we'll be taking your fingerprints as a part of the arrest process, Mr Barlborough? Are you certain you don't want to share your real identity with us? Your silence could be construed as an attempt to pervert the course of justice. It could also be the case our enquiries today will be overtaken by affairs at Burtonlee Homes, but I'm sure you know that better than me.'

Barlborough lapsed into a sullen silence. Had he realised the game was up?

They pulled into the Police station car park. Greeno opened the door to let him out.

As they walked into the building, Trussell said to Barlborough, 'You may care to contact a solicitor to be present when we discuss matters. If you don't have anyone in mind at this moment, then we can contact the duty solicitor and ask him to be present.'

'You mentioned you want to take my fingerprints? Surely, I have to consent to that. I'm not under arrest, am I?'

'You can offer to cooperate with us on a voluntary basis, or we can formally arrest you now. It's up to you.'

'I think I'll wait for a solicitor to be present. Perhaps you can arrange it?'

'We'll make the necessary arrangements,' said Trussell, opening the door to the interview room - the same room where the enquiry had begun with Sophie Blaxstone on the twenty-second of June.

'Stay with our guest, Greeno. Make sure he's comfortable.' said Trussell. 'I'll be back shortly. I'll get the desk sergeant to arrange for the duty solicitor to come in.'

Trussell then went in search of someone to take Barlborough's fingerprints. He agreed with Greeno's hunch about the man. If the suggestions were true, then what had happened to Burtonlee's money? Had he hired the hitman?

There were still plenty of questions to be answered.

34

'Barlborough's fingerprint information has come back already, Guv,' said Greeno. 'As I suspected, he's known. His name is John Ernest Whatesby, and he has quite a record. White collar fraud and forgery, of course.'

'I wonder how he managed to get into a position of trust with Terry Burtonlee?' asked Jackie. 'When you look at how his business grew so quickly, it does show a bit of awareness. I'm surprised he was taken in by Barlborough. There has to be more to it than a simple job offer. What about references?'

'As a fraudster and forger, that wouldn't have presented any problem for him,' said Jim. 'He would be able to write his own convincing references which would fool anyone.'

'The next question is, of course, what did he do with the money?' Jackie asked. 'I can't believe he hired a hitman to get rid of Sophie and paid the money over somehow without Burtonlee himself knowing about it. He would have had to know what was going on and sanction it. After all, it would have been to save his business. I can't believe Barlborough or Whatesby would have done it all on his own initiative. Yet I'm still not convinced that was the reason. I think it was all down to greed. After all, he has a lot of form in that direction.'

'Do you think all of this is part of a scheme to divert attention away from the real reason for the attempts on Sophie's life? Jackie asked. 'If so, it would certainly be a wonderfully constructed plan.'

'We haven't spoken to Richard Blaxstone yet,' said Jim. 'Maybe he can throw some light on the subject. Sophie seems adamant that no one would use her as a means of getting even with her husband, but I don't think we can rule it out. After all, she's told us there are mind blowing amounts of money at stake in the insurance market when business changes hands. It would be enough for people to be upset if they lose control of a client. Could there be competitors out there with serious personal grudges against Richard Blaxstone and his company?'

'Perhaps we should talk to him as soon as possible, Jim. We seem to be eliminating suspects rather too quickly in this case. We've trawled through most of Sophie's serious cases. We'll have to ask her whether we've missed anything. Maybe someone involved in one of her earlier cases has just come out of prison and is itching to get even. Or perhaps it's someone who's been nursing a grudge for a long time and has just acquired the resources to do something like this. I shouldn't think a professional hitman comes cheap at the best of times, and this chap seems to be premier league class. He's very resourceful and inventive.'

Jim turned to Greeno. 'I want you to dig into Whatesby's past. I want his complete record, including where he served his time and what for. It'll be interesting to know where he lived in between his enjoyment of Her Majesty's hospitality. Surely he must have a family? You'll have to go back to your hobby records on this one, Greeno. See whether there's anything in the press about him or his family over the years. It's a lot of work and we need the information in a hurry. Sandcastle can help you if necessary. Just let him know what you need. This has got to have top priority. I need it today. If Whatesby or Burtonlee have been paying someone to pursue Sophie, then we need to know and track him down as soon as possible.'

'Right, Guv, I'll get on it right away.'

35

Things were moving at quite a pace now in the Blaxstone case.

The report on John Shalford's accident had arrived and Trussell opened it. It was as he feared - confirmation that the brake pipe had been partially sawn through allowing the brakes to function normally when the car first moved off but progressively draining off hydraulic fluid each time the brake pedal was depressed. This resulted in a complete loss of braking at that crucial moment on Furze Hill.

They still needed a list of Shalford's fellow committee members from Sophie. If it became necessary to offer protection to them, it would put a huge strain on resources and that would lead to a very difficult conversation with Watkins. Trussell asked Mark Green to see Sophie and get the names and addresses.

Trussell felt it was now definitely time to confront Terry Burtonlee, the owner of Burtonlee Homes. His assistant, Jonathan Barlborough, was now under arrest on an initial charge of procuring official documents by fraudulent means - identity theft. He had used the details of a child who died soon after birth to create a new identity for himself, backed up by a birth certificate obtained from the Public Record Office. Their investigations had now uncovered the fact that he had diverted large sums of money from the company accounts whilst entrusted with the day to day running of the business during the owner's absence.

'Well, Jackie,' he said, 'let's go to see Burtonlee. We need to find out how much he knows about his own company finances.'

'How will you approach it, Jim?'

'We're going to have to wing it a bit. He'll probably already have been told we're holding Barlborough. The receptionist was very reluctant to give me Mr Burtonlee's contact details until I mentioned the little matter of obstructing the police. Our friend Terry seems to have created an atmosphere there. I'll let him know we have Barlborough on the identity theft charge and see what reaction it draws. If he's left the man in charge while he's been occupied with personal matters, then he may not be directly involved. We'll take my car, but you can drive.'

'Arm still troubling you?'

'Yes. It's OK for the short drive to the station, but it still seems to stiffen up. I'll know more when they take the stitches out.'

'What do we know about Mr Burtonlee himself?'

'Only what Sophie's told me. He came up the hard way. He left school at fifteen without any real education and went labouring on building sites. Somehow, he became a bricklayer and was apparently quite good at it. He met his wife when she was working in the office for one of the companies who employed him, and they eventually decided to set up on their own. He had the practical skills and a reputation as someone who could look after himself. He's a bit of a rough diamond, by all accounts. His wife had learned a lot about how the company operated, so they decided to risk it. They did well and were able to buy a piece of land to build a couple of houses. That was the beginning of Burtonlee Homes. The company grew rapidly and the champagne lifestyle followed but it seems our man Terry developed an interest in other women along the way and it eventually caught up with him. It resulted in an expensive divorce. His wife got the marital home and a fair chunk of change to go with it. Their kids sided with her.'

'So where does Mr Burtonlee live, then?'

'He occupies a rather more modest house now on one of his own estates in Maidstone. One of the benefits of being a homeless property developer, I guess. It should give him a chance first-hand to see the quality of what he's been serving up to those unlucky enough to have bought one of his houses. I think the word is Karma. It's on one of the estates a couple of miles away from his office. I'll just give him a quick call to make sure he's home and to warn him to stay there until we arrive.'

'You seem remarkably well informed, Jim.'

'Yes. Sophie attended the divorce court to listen to the details.'

Trussell picked up the phone, consulted the piece of paper given to him by Burtonlee's receptionist, and tapped in the number.

A rather gruff voice answered the phone.

'Yeah, what do you want?'

'Mr Burtonlee?'

'Yes? Who's that?'

'Detective Inspector Trussell, Kent Police speaking. I would like to call on you shortly with a colleague to discuss a matter we're investigating.'

'Oh yes? Are you the policeman who arrested my man, Jonathan Barlborough?'

'Correct. We'd like to talk to you about that and other matters.'

'Yes and what might they be?'

'I need to discuss them with you face to face, not on the phone. Shall we say in about an hour's time? That's ten-thirty.'

'Alright, if you feel you must. Not sure how I can help you. I've got enough on my plate without you adding to my problems.'

They set off in the direction of Maidstone. Jackie knew the area quite well so they arrived at the Burtonlee estate in good time.

'All we have to do now is find the actual house,' said Jackie, looking at the street names.

'Where do they dream up these names? Probably someone at the Council, for all we know.'

All the houses looked depressingly similar, with no pretence at style. Here and there were signs that people actually lived in them; curtains in windows, the odd parked car, but the place did not have a welcoming feel to it.

'We want Number 6. There it is, Jim.'

They walked up the short concrete path which showed signs of cracking. The small front lawn didn't look terribly level, and there were already weeds appearing on it. Cheap turf had obviously been put down, and badly.

Jackie pressed the doorbell, and a few seconds later the door was opened by Burtonlee. Jim recognised him from the pictures in the foyer of his company's building although he was not wearing his publicity smile today. He looked like a man who would command respect by his presence. His physique certainly reflected his early years on building sites; a man who could still take care of himself. A heavy-set man in his early sixties, about five feet nine, sporting an impressive tan. He was casually dressed in a designer tee-shirt and jeans and he had a pair of Hush Puppies on his feet. His carefully manicured hands could not hide years of hard manual work. His face betrayed the strains of recent weeks.

Trussell showed his warrant card and introduced himself and Jackie.

'You'd better come in,' Burtonlees said. 'Don't want the neighbours talking.'

He showed them into the small front room, as yet sparsely furnished. 'Now, what can I do for you? What's this all about? You've got my man, Jonathan?'

'Yes. Tell us, Mr Burtonlee, how much do you know about him? First I need to tell you that Barlborough's not his real name. He's actually John Ernest Whatesby, a convicted fraudster.'

Burtonlee staggered back and sat down heavily on the small sofa behind him. He looked astonished.

'So, while you've been otherwise engaged, you've left him to run your company. Have you looked at your bank accounts recently? How much authority have you given him?'

He made no response. He was still stunned.

'Have you been in touch with any of your other employees recently?'

'No. I've left it all to Jonathan. He's been my right hand man since he joined me about four years ago.'

'What about the adverse publicity your company's received in the last couple of years? How do you feel about that?'

'I don't know much about that. I've left Jonathan to deal with all the public relations stuff.'

'Are you aware of any individuals who've been complaining in the press and media about your company?'

'I had heard about some of it but I left it all to him to sort out.'

'Sort out? Precisely what did you tell him to do?'

'Just deal with the people who were complaining. Sort them out.'

'By violent means if necessary, Mr Burtonlee?'

'Good heavens, no. I don't operate like that. Stuff used to be sorted on the sites with the workers when I started. It was usually done by the foreman. But there's none of that sort of thing now. We try to get on with the workers. Talk anything through. Occasionally we have had to fire someone, but it doesn't happen so much these days. We wouldn't want to upset our customers. They are important to us. They buy houses.'

Jackie stood silently by, carefully making notes as the conversation proceeded. She smiled inwardly as she thought about the long list of unresolved problems that had been forwarded to Sophie's television programme.

'What about the media?' asked Trussell. 'How would you deal with someone who was making waves for your company?'

'I'd get Jonathan to talk to whoever it was. Schmooze them. Make them feel more comfortable. He's a pretty smooth character. He could charm the birds off a tree, if he put his mind to it.'

'Is he a violent man?'

157

'If he is then it's news to me. I've never had any complaints from anyone about him - staff or customers. What did you say his actual name is?'

'Whatesby.'

'That name rings a bell. Wait a minute. I need to think. I believe the Firm dealt with someone called Whatesby several years ago. It will come to me in a moment. It definitely sounds familiar. Not the sort of name that you'd forget.'

'What about Sophie Breckton? Have you had any dealings with her?'

'I know the name. Some bird on the telly, isn't she?'

'She's had quite a few complaints about your company to her programme, but apparently can't get past Mr Barlborough or Whatesby, to talk to you about it.'

'Well, he certainly hasn't shared that with me. As I've told you already, I've had to leave everything to him these days. My wife used to deal with a lot of this stuff until a couple of years ago but not anymore. I tried to look after the practical side of the business. Truth is, I only realised how much she did in the company after all our problems started.'

'What about the name Whatesby. Can you remember where you heard it? Was it a business connection or a client?'

Burtonlee was still somewhat crushed by Trussell's revelations. The full impact of this information on his company was beginning to strike home. He was fighting the urge to stop this conversation now and go straight to his office to see exactly what harm had been caused to his business, if he could get away from these two police officers.

What do they really want? He wondered. *I can't believe they came to visit me just to share the news about Jonathan. There has to be more to it than that. What's behind the Detective Inspector's friendly sharing of information?*

'Come along, Mr Burtonlee. Can you remember the Whatesby connection?'

'If my wife was still involved, she'd probably be able to tell you straight away, without looking into any records. I'll have to go to the office and look at the files. No good asking Jonathan, I suppose?'

'Hardly, Sir. I should think he'd be the last person who would want to tell you if it meant anything to him. May I suggest you do go to your office and find the information for me? I'll give you my card. You can contact me on either number, preferably the mobile as I'm likely to be out of the office. If you are going to your office now, would you please make my question your priority?'

'Certainly. I'll call you later this morning.'

'Thank you, Sir. I think that will be all for now. Thank you for your cooperation. I would appreciate your call later this morning. May I also ask you not to leave the area? We may need to speak to you again. No, please don't get up. We'll see ourselves out.'

With that parting comment, Trussell made for the door, followed by Jackie, tucking her notebook into her bag, leaving a somewhat confused and worried man slumped on his sofa.

'What do you think, Jim?' asked Jackie, as they got back into the car.

'I certainly don't think Burtonlee's behind any attempt on Sophie's life. You only have to look at him. He's been through the wringer on a messy divorce and now we've had to tell him, effectively, his business could be in serious trouble, thanks to a man he thought he could trust. I don't believe he's been in any fit state to orchestrate anything against Sophie. The whole process has moved too quickly.'

'What about Barlborough then?'

'If there had been any connection between Burtonlee Homes and Sophie's problems, then it could only have been Barlborough. Yet, I was interested in the way he reacted to the mention of his real name, Whatesby. We'll have to wait to see what he finds in his company records. I think this may be the key to Barlborough taking the money out of the company. I'm beginning to think Burtonlee Homes may not be the answer to Sophie's problems.'

'So, we're back to square one then?'

'It's certainly beginning to look that way. I wonder whether Sophie has turned up any much older cases where the individuals have been out of circulation and had a chance to think about how they might get revenge. Then there's the question of other people using Sophie as a means of getting their own back on someone else.'

'What about her husband's business, Jim? Could it be a disgruntled competitor looking for revenge? We've already talked about the huge sums of money in the insurance market. Surely that might be a possibility?'

'Well, Sophie ruled that out. But we can't be sure. Maybe it's time we spoke to Mr Blaxstone. We'll ask Sophie for his number.'

They had almost reached Woodchester when Trussell's mobile rang. It was Burtonlee.

'Detective Inspector Trussell? I'm back in the office. I told you the name Whatesby rang a bell. Well, I've found the connection. It goes back nearly seven years.'

'Tell me.'

'The company had a dispute with a Mr Whatesby over a house he bought from us. I wasn't involved personally, so I don't have any details as to what the problem was with him. All I know is it went through our legal department and eventually wound up in court. The complainant lost his case against us and copped all the costs. It all proved too much for him and I believe that unfortunately he killed himself soon afterwards.'

'Do you have the man's full name?'

'Yes. Just a minute.' There was a pause. 'Here it is. William James Whatesby.'

'When exactly did this happen?'

'It was six years ago when the poor guy died.'

'Thank you, Mr Burtonlee. That may prove useful information. I'll be in touch. Meanwhile, please stay in the area, as I asked earlier.'

He hung up to share the information with Jackie. 'I don't think we should delay this part of the enquiry,' he said and called Mark Green.

'Greeno, I've got an urgent job for your genealogical skills. We've just come from Terry Burtonlee. When I mentioned Barlborough's real identity to him, not only was he shocked, but thought the name Whatesby was familiar. He's just contacted me. He had a business dispute with a man named William James Whatesby six years ago that went to court. The complainant lost the case, was lumbered with the costs and then topped himself. Look into the case, and most importantly, see if there's any connection between the two Whatesbys. Get started on that now, please. We're almost back so you can share anything you find when we get back into the office.'

'OK, Guv. I'll get straight onto it.'

'If you need any extra help, ask Sandcastle to give you a hand.'

He turned to Jackie. 'How long before we get back?'

'About ten minutes. What do you plan to do next? You think Barlborough and Burtonlee are a side issue now, don't you?'

'That's right. We just need Greeno to corroborate what I'm thinking, and then we'll have to talk to Sophie.'

'So, what's your take on Burtonlee et al, Jim?'

'I suspect we shall find the two Whatesbys were related. Possibly they were brothers. If so, my guess is our Mr Whatesby deliberately got his job at Burtonlee's company with the sole aim of taking financial revenge on him. To recover the money lost by his family and make Burtonlee pay, personally, by ruining him. After all, he had the professional skills and motive to do it. He could never have known Mrs Burtonlee would get there first. I'm now convinced that neither of them has been directly involved in Sophie's problems.'

'We could always ask him, Jim. It would save a bit of time.'

'No, let Greeno produce the independent evidence. Then we can confront our friend Jonathan with the facts and perhaps we shan't need to even pass it to the Fraud Squad.'

Jackie parked the Skoda in Jim's allocated spot. She handed him the keys as they walked into the building.

Greeno looked up as they walked into the CID office.

'You were right about the other Mr Whatesby, Guv. I found them quite easily on the genealogy site where I've a subscription. He was the older brother of our friend in the cells. I'm just trying to find the details of the case. Sandcastle is checking the back numbers of the local papers, as his death occurred in Kent. I'm sure it must have made the front pages. We'll look for reports of the inquest. We've already established that John Ernest was inside doing four years when all this happened. He must have been very angry when he heard about it from the family.'

'I've found something, Guv,' called Sandcastle. 'There's an item on the funeral with a picture. It looks as though John Ernest was allowed out to attend. There's a photo of him, handcuffed to a prison officer, at the funeral'

'You were right then,' said Jackie.

'So now we have the motive for John Ernest's embezzlement. That certainly rules him out as a potential funder for a hitman and should make it easier to close his case. I doubt we shall have any protestations of innocence when we put the facts to him. All we'll need to know is exactly where he sent the money and how he managed it. It must have been over a period of time, rather than one withdrawal. I'm just surprised their accounts manager or their accountant didn't pick it up.'

'Is it too much of a stretch to think there was any sort of collusion between them? Was there a concerted attack by all of them to bring Burtonlee down? Could it have been due to sympathy for his wife, perhaps?'

'We'll have to find out how long these people have been there. How Burtonlee treated them as individuals? I'll need to talk to him again to find out more. I wonder whether he has any Human Resources department. They used to call it Personnel in my time. While these two are occupied, Jackie, we need to talk to Sophie. Can you get her on the phone and see if she can spare us a few minutes? We both know how busy she is at the moment, playing catch up for her television programme.'

Jim sat at his desk, reviewing the whole case in his mind while Jackie made the call. They had been presented with a whole load of possible suspects in the beginning, and frustratingly, they had made a very efficient job of investigating and eliminating them. What was left? What had they missed? Perhaps Sophie might have the answer without realising it.

'She's OK to see us now, Jim,' said Jackie, holding the phone as she looked at him.

'What do you want to do?'

'Say fifteen minutes. We'll leave in a moment.'

Jackie confirmed that and finished the call. 'She'll meet us in the lounge as usual.'

'Not sure how she'll react when we tell her we've run out of suspects and are looking to her again for ideas.' He rose from his desk. 'Right, Jackie. Off we go. We'll talk to Sophie again about her older cases and see if she can offer any fresh ideas or names. We'll have to arrange to talk to her husband and his partners to find out whether they have any thoughts about any past business transaction that might have led to this situation. That's about it for now.'

They walked down the High Street, past the shops, to the Castle Inn. It was becoming a well-trodden path for them these days. They found Sophie sitting in their usual corner table in the lounge, with a pot of coffee and three cups waiting. She looked up as they walked through the archway and smiled at them, although Jackie still had a nagging feeling the smile was mainly for Jim, despite her friendly relationship with Sophie.

'So, what's the news today?' Sophie asked, pouring the coffees as she spoke.

Jim looked at Jackie. 'Where do we begin?'

'What about Burtonlee? What happened there?'

'I can't tell you too much at the moment other than the fact that Jim had a very useful visit to their Head Office in Maidstone yesterday.'

'You're not going to tell me he managed to get past Jonathan Barlborough, surely?'

'Jim had an interesting chat with him. I won't say any more other than mentioning that Mr Barlborough is currently sharing his thoughts with us at Woodchester Police Station."

Sophie gasped. Even she hadn't expected that sort of development at this stage. 'I'd love to be a fly on the wall while that's going on. Do you believe he's implicated in this whole business?'

'I can't answer that at the moment. Jim suggests you back off Burtonlee for the time being, until our investigation has moved on a bit. Your intervention at this stage would undoubtedly be counter-productive. We'll let you know when the moment is right for you to speak to them. I can understand you might be rather frustrated about this after all the work you've put in, both on television and in the paper. My feeling is you'll be quite happy about what you'll be able to report when the moment arrives.'

Jim interrupted. 'The other development is that we've also been to see Mr Burtonlee this morning in his much reduced circumstances,' he said. 'He had to leave the marital home after his divorce settlement and he's living in a very modest house on one of his own estates. We don't believe now he was involved in your problems in any way. The divorce seems to have taken its toll on him and he's not been running his business on a day to day basis. He left Mr Barlborough, as we knew him, in charge of the firm.'

'What do you mean?' asked Sophie.

'We now have Mr Barlborough's correct identity. He's a convicted fraudster who's served several prison sentences. But here's the interesting part. We believe he's the brother of a man who lost a very expensive legal case against Burtonlee Homes about six years ago and subsequently killed himself. It seems Barlborough's been helping himself to Burtonlee's money as a way of getting his own back and passing it on to his family.'

'So Burtonlee hasn't been funding the man who has been hounding me, then?'

'That's what we now believe,' said Jackie.

'So, who is it? This isn't helping me. I don't believe I can feel safe anywhere now.'

'We have to start again, effectively. We seem to have exhausted all of our original lines of enquiry,' said Trussell.

'What's the next move, then?'

'I know we've spoken about this before, but we need you to think again, rack your brains. Were there any earlier cases where someone had been sent to prison and might, perhaps have been released recently? Someone who might have been nursing a real grievance over a long time? Think, Sophie.'

'I can look back through my files, but nobody immediately comes to mind.'

'We need to speak to your husband and his partners. I know you've discounted the idea of a competitor trying to get back at them by going after you but it's not as far-fetched as you think. Plus, you're someone who's very much in the public eye. It would make a statement, send out a signal.'

'I still believe it's highly unlikely,' said Sophie. 'I never heard of anything like that happening before.'

Jackie said, 'There's one other possibility, Sophie.'

'What's that?'

'I remember that first evening when we chatted about your life to date, I seem to remember you mentioning you'd helped your husband host some gatherings for his underwriting friends at his apartment in Docklands. You talked about wives, girlfriends and mistresses. Could there have been any expensive divorces amongst that circle? If the truth came out, might they blame your husband or you for some perceived indiscretion, even if neither of you were the source. Could it be enough to set someone on the trail for revenge? After all, it's only just over a year since you left that apartment.'

'I think it's unlikely, Jackie, but I'm prepared to believe anything at this point.'

'I'm going to ring Richard Blaxstone in the morning,' said Jim. 'I might ask that question as well. I'll make it plain I'm quite prepared to visit his firm and speak to the three partners, if necessary.'

'Well, something will have to happen pretty soon,' said Sophie. 'I can't spend the rest of my life cooped up in this place, hiding away. It's not my style, and it's hampering my preparations for my television series. That's not to mention the effect it's having on me.'

'We can understand your frustration, Sophie,' said Jackie. 'I fear that our lack of progress, so far, has caused you quite a few problems. We're conscious of the fact that in eliminating suspects, we're also reducing your options for your programme content. Mr Burtonlee will be a less interesting subject after the problems we've uncovered for him, the white van man's been found and the local council are on his case. Of your current crop of subjects, that just leaves Brandford, and I doubt you'll be too interested in going there again anytime soon.'

'Well, I'd be prepared to go there again. My informants have to be heard. But my cameraman Dennis is a bit reluctant to go back there at the moment without some sort of police escort. That would be counterproductive and would make the whole thing impossible. I certainly couldn't ask Jim to go there again, after the way he was injured. He saved my life that day.'

Jackie picked up on the way Sophie looked across at Jim when she spoke. Or was she reading too much into it?

'By the way, what will happen to Emile?' Sophie asked.

'Hard to say,' said Jim. 'It's up to the CPS. His information about the hitman was very useful to us. I've put in a word for him, but it's out of our hands now.'

'How is your arm today?' asked Sophie. 'It's been a week now. Is it still troubling you?'

'I'm more concerned with sorting this case out at the moment. It's worrying me more than my arm. I need suspects. There has to be someone out there with a reason to do you harm, and with the resources as well. This whole thing has been planned to throw us off the scent. It's very clever.'

36

Trussell knew it was time to talk to Richard Blaxstone and his partners to see if they could offer any ideas about competitors who might have a grudge against the firm and be prepared to use Sophie as a means of exacting revenge on them. He thought for a moment, and then took the plunge. He knew they were now scratching around for any sort of lead having eliminated all of the obvious ones. His famous intuition was letting him down. Where should he look next? There was something missing.

He took a deep breath and picked up his phone. He tapped in the number Sophie had given him and listened as it rang. It was picked up by a receptionist at the firm.

'Good Morning. Blaxstone Dalrymple Jagger. How may I help you?'

'I'd like to speak to Richard Blaxstone, please. My name is James Trussell.'

'Just one moment, Sir. I'll put you through to his personal assistant.'

'Richard Blaxstone's office,' said a female voice. 'Jo Curran speaking.'

'May I speak to him, please? My name is Trussell.'

'I'm sorry, Mr Trussell. You've just missed him. He had to go out. He left about ten minutes ago. He didn't tell me when he'd be back. Rather unlike him. May I take a message?'

'Please ask him to call me. I'll give you my number. Perhaps you could ask him to ring me as soon as he returns. It's rather urgent.'

'Certainly, Sir. I'll do that. Bye.'

So he was no further ahead. He just hoped Richard Blaxstone would quickly return his call. There was one thing that stuck in his mind. The words used by his personal assistant. *Rather unlike him.* Was something going on?

37

Sophie was in her room at the Castle, working on some background information for her forthcoming series, when her phone rang. It was Richard. He sounded troubled.

'Sophie, I need help. I have to see you now.'

'What's up, Richard? Where are you?'

'I'm in Woodchester. I took the train down this morning. I'm in the Weaver Street Car Park. Do you know it? It's the multi storey park at the end of the High Street. I'm on the eighth floor.'

'Whatever are you doing here? I thought you were in the City?'

'I had to get out of London. I'm in danger. You're the only one who can help me now. If you can't come immediately, then the situation is hopeless for me. I've only one way out. Please come now. Say you will. Please.'

Sophie had never heard Richard speak this way before. He was pleading. Sounding frightened. He had always been so self-confident in all his personal dealings.

Yet she was wary. He had made promises and extravagant threats in the past. What should she do? She thought for a moment, and then made a decision.

'Try to relax, Richard. I need to think. I'll call you back in just a moment. Just sit tight and do nothing.'

She cut off the call and immediately rang Jackie. She told her about the conversation.

'Jackie, there's something strange going on. Richard just called me. He's in Woodchester and says he needs to see me. That he's in trouble. I told him I'd call him back. I'll probably have to meet him. If I didn't know better, I'd say he sounded desperate. It surely can't be business pressure. He wants me to meet him on the eighth floor of the Weaver Street car park. What do you think?'

'Tell him you'll meet him in twenty minutes,' said Jackie. 'That will give us time to get there and discreetly keep an eye on things. I'll talk to Jim. I agree with you. There's something odd going on.'

Sophie ended the call and then tapped in Richard's number.

'OK, Richard. I've thought about it. My first instinct was to tell you the answer was a definite no, after the way you've treated me. But I still have a compassionate side. Even for you. It will take me about twenty minutes to get there. Where exactly are you?'

'I'm on the eighth floor, on the open side facing the church. You've got to help me. I've no one else to turn to, Please hurry. If you can't help me, then no one else can. Otherwise, I've only one way out.'

This was the Richard of old, still very persuasive. He knew how to influence Sophie. Or so he thought. But times had changed. She had been through enough over the last three weeks to question everything now.

Trussell and Joynton would have enough time to get to the car park. They could see it from the window in the CID suite.

'I've got a bad feeling about this too,' said Trussell. 'Why should Blaxstone travel all the way down from the City to a local car park? Does he mean to harm Sophie in some way? I think we should organise some back up.'

He stopped at the desk in the station lobby and spoke to the duty sergeant. 'Alan, I think we've got a problem brewing down the road in the multi storey car park. Can you get a couple of cars down there right away? Tell them to approach silently - no blue lights or sirens. The crew of one car should wait by the ground floor exit to stop anyone going in or leaving, and the other must park inside on floor six, again to stop anyone leaving the upper floors. Not sure who it will be at the moment. We're going there now. Something may well happen on floor eight in about fifteen minutes. Have you got a spare personal radio I can take? I'll need to keep in touch with the cars you send down there. I take full responsibility. Tell them I'm running this one and to wait for my instructions when they're in position.'

'OK, Jim. I can find two cars for you. It'll get the crews out of the canteen. Here's the radio,' he said, putting one on the counter.

The two CID officers quickly walked to the car park's pedestrian entrance and took the lift up to the top floor, which was the ninth, open to the elements as was part of the floor below. As they opened the door onto the parking area, Trussell glanced around and then touched Jackie's arm. 'Wait a moment, Jackie' he whispered. He pointed to the parked vehicles at the other end of the floor. 'Does that vehicle on the far corner look familiar?'

Jackie looked in the direction Trussell was indicating. To her horror, she saw a silver Mercedes 4 x 4 with darkened windows.

Trussell reached for his phone and rang the police station. He asked for the duty sergeant. 'Alan, it's Jim Trussell again. The situation is looking worse than I thought. We may need armed back up. Do you have any idea where the response team is at the moment?'

He waited, phone to his ear.

'They're in the station? How lucky is that? Send them down here now, please. Silent approach again. Tell them it has to be very low key. No time to go through channels on this one. Any delay might have very serious consequences. Tell the Chief Super, of course and say I take full responsibility. There's a situation here that could get out of hand very quickly. I think I may have spotted the vehicle used by the shooter who tried to kill Sophie Blaxstone last month. Tell them to park on floor six, be ready and wait there with their equipment. Tell them to be prepared. We'll be on the ninth floor when they arrive and I'll brief them over the radio.'

Trussell opened the door slightly and peered out. There was no movement at the other end of the floor. Using parked cars and a conveniently placed large white van as cover, they crept towards the parapet and looked down on the eighth floor below. They saw a dishevelled Richard Blaxstone, jacket open, pacing up and down, and repeatedly glancing at his watch. He kept running his hand through his hair. He looked agitated. He seemed to be muttering to himself, as if he was rehearsing what he wanted to say to Sophie? No sign of her yet. As they moved forwards, Trussell's foot touched an empty wine bottle left against the wall and tipped it over.

He glanced at Jackie.

'I see the winos still use this place, then,' he whispered, making a face, but standing the bottle up again.

The door accessing the lifts and stairs on the floor below opened, and Sophie appeared. She looked at the end of the floor, caught sight of Richard, still pacing up and down. He was obviously still in a highly nervous state. She walked cautiously in his direction.

'Thank goodness you've come, Sophie,' he said to her. 'I don't know what I'm going to do.'

'What's the problem, Richard?'

'Sophie, I owe some pretty difficult people an awful lot of money, and they're pressuring me to pay up. They've threatened to kill me if I don't. I know they're serious about it.'

'Whaat? However did that happen?'

'You remember I used to take Hank to the casinos when he came over?'

'Yes, and…?'

'Things have got out of hand. I've run up a bill I can't pay. Now they're leaning on me. They're really putting the pressure. They're making threats against my life.'

'Can't you go to the police?'

'No, they won't be interested. They'll say the debt is just a civil matter. Remember that they didn't take the threats against you seriously.'

'How much are we talking about?'

'They say I owe them a quarter of a million pounds.'

Sophie gasped. This was incredible. 'Be serious, Richard. You know I don't have the means to help you raise that sort of money.'

'What about the cottage and the flat?'

'I've already told you to forget that after the way you've treated me.'

'I've no one else to turn to now. It's gone too far. You're the only one who can help me.'

'How does that work? I remember you asked me to help you the day we had lunch at Luigi's. You told me some ridiculous story that the money was needed for the company. You lied to me, Richard. Why should I believe you now? The answer was no then, and it's still no.'

'I was desperate, Sophie. I couldn't tell you the truth, but I am now. If you won't help me then you leave me no choice.' He edged closer to the parapet, drawing her with him as he spoke. 'I'll end it all. Here and now. Is that what you want on your conscience?' He kept the pressure on. Pleading. 'It won't look good for you, will it? When the press learn that you just stood there while you watched your husband throw himself off the eighth floor. Imagine how it'll ruin your career. It will be all over the television news tonight. It will be on the same channel where you work. Your following will disappear overnight. You'll have nothing left. We both lose. That's why you've got to help me.'

All the time, he was moving closer to the edge. The two detectives watched as the scene played out.

'Jackie, look at his body language. He's trying to draw Sophie closer to the edge. I think he means to push her over and make it look like suicide. He's after her money and property. I should have seen this coming.'

'Just like his first wife? Reciprocal wills? Was her life insured for a substantial amount?

'Something we'll need to look at.'

'Hang on a minute, Jim. The Mercedes is on the move,' said Jackie, pointing to the other end of the floor.

It reversed out of the space, turned around and disappeared in the direction of the exit ramp. A minute later, it appeared on the eighth floor immediately below them, opposite Sophie and Richard. They turned towards the car. It stopped, and as Trussell and Jackie watched in disbelief, the driver's window rolled down and an arm appeared, extended, holding a silenced pistol.

Sophie, distracted, horrified, looked at the vehicle. The arm pointed towards Richard and there was an audible plop. A hole appeared in the middle of his forehead, and with a look of complete surprise on his face, his legs folded and he collapsed at Sophie's feet,

Trussell saw the arm and pistol swing towards Sophie.

'Nooooo!' he shouted and did the only thing he could. He picked up the wine bottle by his foot and threw it as hard as he could at the panoramic sunroof of the Mercedes, less than ten feet directly below him. It landed with a loud bang on the tinted glass roof, shattering both. The Mercedes jumped forward as the driver's foot slipped off the clutch and the shot went wide, hitting the front of another parked car. The driver's arm and pistol were withdrawn. The vehicle accelerated away towards the down ramp at the other end.

Trussell grabbed his radio.

'Attention, everyone. A silver Mercedes with darkened windows has just left the eighth floor. It's coming your way. The driver is armed and highly dangerous. He's already shot someone on this floor. He must be stopped somehow.'

With that, Trussell dashed for the stairs, followed by Jackie. When they reached the floor below, Sophie was standing, looking down at Richard in total disbelief. They ran up to her and Trussell asked Jackie, to move Sophie away. 'Take her into the stairwell. I'll check Blaxstone. I think he's probably beyond our help.'

Trussell knelt down next to Richard's body and felt for the carotid artery. There was no pulse. He still had a look of total surprise fixed on his face. There was very little blood around the small entry wound in the centre of his forehead, just above his eyes.

He brought the radio up to his mouth again. 'DI Trussell here. Richard Blaxstone has been shot. We need urgent assistance and a paramedic on the eighth floor. Send a couple of uniformed officers up here to keep people away from the body.'

Jackie meanwhile was steering Sophie away from the scene, an arm around her shoulder.

Suddenly they all heard an enormous bang, and a grinding of metal, followed by a continuous, pulsing car alarm. It came from somewhere below them.

Then a voice, shouting.

Two loud shots.

Trussell's radio crackled into life.

It was the armed response unit.

'Man down. Medical assistance needed.'

38

Two uniformed constables appeared in the doorway. Trussell pointed towards Richard's body.

'Stay here and keep everyone away. We'll need to tape this whole floor off. Get on your radios and organise it. No one is to try to move any vehicle from these floors. Tell everyone to leave by the stairs and go to street level. No one, repeat, no one is to use the ramps. I'll get you some help as soon as possible.'

He spoke into the radio. 'Trussell here. I'm on my way down from floor eight.' He raced for the stairs and took them two at a time. He pushed the door on the sixth floor open, making sure he was waving his warrant card above his head. He certainly didn't want any accidents.

The Mercedes was wedged against the outer wall of the car park, its alarm still pulsing. The noise was deafening because of the low ceiling of the concrete car park. The police car had heavy damage to the nearside wing and the front. A body lay on the floor by the open door of the Mercedes. The silenced pistol lay just beyond an outstretched hand. Two armed police officers stood over the body, their automatic rifles trained on it.

'We warned him as instructed, Guv, but he pointed the pistol at us and fired, so we shot him. He's still alive.'

The armed response officer pointed to the windscreen of the police car. It had a hole through it with cracks spreading in all directions.

Trussell looked down at the figure in leather jacket, jeans and fashionable trainers. He had a slightly olive skin and dark straight hair and was of Mediterranean appearance. Eyes closed, but still breathing. There was blood on his upper chest and shoulder. The bloody cuts on his face and in his hair were probably made by the bottle when it shattered the sunroof.

'I'm not surprised he used the pistol,' said Trussell. 'He's killed a man on the eighth floor and just missed the man's wife.' He didn't mention it was only his lightning reaction, throwing the bottle that had saved Sophie's life. 'What about ID? Is he carrying anything like a wallet or passport? Can't we turn that damn alarm off? We can't hear ourselves think.'

Turning the ignition off seemed to solve the problem.

'He has a US passport in the name of Javier Moreno. Complexion suggests he could be Hispanic - maybe Mexican or Puerto Rican origin.'

'We need to trace the car now we have a registration number. That is, unless the plates are false. I'll call it in to my team. They can start checking. Have you looked inside yet?'

'Not our business, Guv. You probably know every police shooting has to be investigated now by the Independent Office for Police Conduct, so they'll take over when they get here. Not sure exactly when that will be, though. We have to stand down. I've radioed our Super and he's calling it in. We shall expect them here shortly to take over, but in the meantime, the Super is sending more manpower down here to secure the car park. It won't be your immediate problem anymore. They'll deal with those people wanting to get their cars out of here. That will cause a real problem for workers wanting to go home, now.'

Donning a pair of rubber gloves from his pocket, Trussell carefully opened the boot of the Mercedes, an ML 300. There was a large bundle, about three feet long, lying there. He began to carefully unwrap it, to reveal a rifle, complete with telescopic sight. He called one of the firearms officers over.

'What do you make of this?'

He considered it, and said, 'I've seen one of those before, Guv. It's an American hunting rifle. A Ruger, I believe. Very nice piece of kit.' He called to his colleague. 'Jock, come and look at this rifle?'

The other firearms officer came over and glanced at it.

'That's very nice. American, isn't it? Don't see too many of those around. Certainly makes a change from the cheap hired out stuff and sawn off shotguns we normally seem to come across in our line of work. This guy's obviously a pro judging by this and the silenced pistol. You'd better leave everything to the investigators, Guv. I'll just move the pistol out of his reach in case he suddenly finds some extra energy from somewhere. The Super is sending someone qualified to make these two guns safe and remove them to the Station.'

'Wonder who he really is? No guarantee the name in the passport is right. It's an interesting puzzle for you, Detective Inspector.'

'The sooner the IOPC get here, the better. And we'll probably have to contact the FBI. Send them a copy of the passport. Take his picture, fingerprints and DNA to see if he's known to them. This thing's getting out of hand now. It seemed a relatively straightforward case when we all went to that address in Foggenden last month - the shot through the kitchen window. Since then, there have been several other attempts on Sophie Blaxstone's life; one of her neighbours has died under suspicious circumstances, a local councillor went over Beachy Head, and may not have jumped and another member of the committee was injured in a crash that looks non-accidental. To cap it all, now Mrs Blaxstone's husband has just been shot dead by this man a few minutes ago on the eighth floor.'

Mentioning Sophie reminded him. He stepped to one side and took his phone from his pocket. He tapped in Jackie's number.

She answered immediately. 'Are you OK, Jim?'

'Yes, I'm fine. The man responsible has been stopped by the armed response boys and immobilised. More complications now as the complaints people will be taking over. More importantly, how's Sophie?'

'She's still shaken but bearing up pretty well, under the circumstances.'

'Good. Well, you can just tell her I believe she's no longer in any danger. Spare her the details, but just tell her the man responsible is in custody now. Can you take her back to the Castle and get her some hot tea and a brandy to calm her down? Find a quiet corner and stay there with her. I'll get there as soon as I can.'

The paramedics had arrived and were attending to the gunman. Trussell showed his warrant card and asked them, 'What do you think? We need him alive. He has a lot of questions to answer.'

One of them said, 'Hard to tell at the moment. Touch and go. We need to get him to hospital as soon as possible. Luckily We're so close to the Woodchester, otherwise I'd be calling for the Air Ambulance. We've got him on oxygen and have the external bleeding under control, but we have no idea what's going on inside. He's best left to the experts.'

They had carefully placed him on the stretcher trolley and were preparing to take it down the ramps of the car park as it had proved impossible to get an ambulance inside the multi storey building and the lift was just too small to accommodate the trolley. A couple of the uniformed police officers helped them move the unconscious gunman down to the ground floor.

Trussell now called the station for more support to control the car park, as a number of drivers had returned for their cars and were not best pleased they couldn't move them. They were politely asked to leave the car park by the stairs. He had arranged for the whole building to be secured and closed to the public until the investigation was complete. The IOPC would now deal with that.

He had already called his two detective constables down to assist. When they arrived, Trussell issued his instructions. 'Greeno, I want you in the ambulance taking the gunman to hospital. Stay with him and be there when the doctors are dealing with him. Stress to them he's a murder suspect and highly dangerous. Arrange for him to be searched for any other weapons. If you find anything, bag it for Forensics. He was shot by the police armed response team in self-defence. If he survives the surgery we'll have to post someone on the door of his room and someone inside it. Armed, of course. We'll have to ask the Super to arrange it. No visitors. Keep me updated and I'll arrange for some relief for you as soon as possible. Now hurry down to the street. You mustn't miss that ambulance.'

He picked up the personal radio and spoke to the police by the carpark entrance. 'Trussell speaking. Is the ambulance ready to go? Tell them to wait just a moment. I'm sending one of the DCs down to travel with them.'

He turned to Tim Beach.

'Sandcastle, I want you up on the eighth floor. Uniformed should be there. Take charge until a senior officer arrives. Richard Blaxstone has been shot dead. I don't want anything disturbed until the investigators arrive. Tell them there were two shots fired by the killer. The first hit Blaxstone, and the second was meant for his wife, but went wide and hit the front of the silver Focus just behind them. It's important they look for the other bullet and the owner doesn't try to drive away when the cars are finally released. Watch out. There may be some broken glass lying on the ground. That will have to be cleared before anyone can eventually leave. We don't want any extra bills for damaged tyres. Clear that floor and the ninth. Make sure the public use the stairs and lifts only. No one must be allowed to walk down the ramps. Keep the public right away, even those trying to get to their cars. No one is permitted to go up there. Tell them it's a crime scene. Uniformed will tape it off, anyway.'

'OK, Guv.'

'A police doctor is on his way to certify death. A formality, I'm afraid. The body is not to be moved until the investigation is complete. The paramedics have dealt with the gunman first and he's on his way to hospital.'

39

Trussell's next, more difficult task was to inform his superior officer, Detective Chief Superintendent Watkins. He called the office and was put through immediately.

'What's going on, Trussell? Why wasn't I told in advance about this operation? I should have taken the decision to deploy an armed response unit. Weapons have been fired and the IOPC have been called in already, so they will have questions. You had better make damned sure you have the right answers. Your pension may depend on it. You've really stuck your neck out this time.'

Thank you for your support, Charlie, thought Trussell. 'I'm afraid we had virtually no warning and only realised the situation would escalate when we got there. I'll make a full report to you as soon as I can get back.'

'The Assistant Chief Constable is looking for someone's head over this, Trussell. It's going to be very uncomfortable for that someone. Be here in fifteen minutes. And make sure you look tidy.'

Just enough time for Charlie to polish his shoes, straighten his tie and smooth what's left of his hair, thought Trussell, as he headed for the stairs again and the ten minute walk back to the station. It would give him time to clear his head and gather his thoughts as well as phoning Jackie to tell her he'd spoken to Watkins.

'He wants me there now. Breathing fire and spitting feathers, as you can imagine. The ACC has been on his case already, and Charlie's looking for a scapegoat. They'll be calling a press conference later. They may need me, unless I can get out of it. Then I'll have to get back to the car park. I've to make sure everything is being sorted there. I'll be in touch as soon as possible. Are you OK with Sophie? How is she?'

'Still in a state of shock, Jim. Don't worry. I'll cope.'

Arriving at the station, he saw the duty sergeant at the desk and put the borrowed radio on the counter.

'Thanks again for your help, Alan. Dealing with the carnage and fallout up the road was child's play compared with my next job - explaining it all to Watkins, and probably the ACC. I've got to tell them exactly why I took the initiative and assumed full responsibility.'

'Good luck with that, Jim.'

He took the lift to the hallowed eighth floor and walked to Watkins' office. He knocked on the half open door.

'Come in!'

He gritted his teeth and pushed the door open. 'Afternoon, Sir.'

'Nice mess you've got us into, Trussell. You'd better have some good answers. The ACC is furious. The press are on our case already and we have nothing to tell them. Not good. You took all of this on your own responsibility. What've you got to say?'

'Well Sir,' said Trussell, 'we were faced with a situation that developed rapidly and got out of hand in the space of less than fifteen minutes. There was no time to go through proper channels on this one. I took it on my own responsibility. If we hadn't reacted in the way we did, then Sophie Blaxstone would have been murdered as well and the killer would have got clean away. One death is a tragedy, but it could have been much worse.'

Trussell recounted the chain of events, from Sophie's call from Richard to the moment the killer was shot by the response unit.

'In my view, Sir, everyone involved behaved in an exemplary manner. The ACC should be pleased. The last thing he would have wanted would have been the murder of a well-known television personality right on his doorstep because detailed procedures had to be followed. That was prevented by the efforts of all involved. It also means that, in my view, we're close to solving the entire Blaxstone case. I know the ACC and you've both been interested in it.'

'Quite so, Trussell. You'd better see the ACC with me. And smarten yourself up - hair all over the place, tie undone. He may want you at the press conference.'

Watkins picked up the phone and pressed the keys for the ACC.

'It's Watkins here, Sir. I've DI Trussell with me. We want to bring you up to speed on the shootings at the Weaver Street car park. We'll come right now, Sir.'

They walked to the other end of the floor to the ACC's office. Watkins was visibly nervous.

'Don't speak until you're spoken to, Trussell. Leave it to me.'

Get your defence in first, Charlie. Just dump me in it.

They were shown into the hallowed office. The ACC didn't look best pleased.

'Now tell me exactly what happened. I need to know before the IOPC get here and take over.'

'Well Sir,' began Watkins, 'No one knew anything about this…'

'I want to hear from Trussell. He was the man on the ground.'

Trussell went over the chain of events again, stressing Sophie's narrow escape and emphasised the bad publicity which would have followed if she'd been harmed. He repeated that this had now brought the whole Blaxstone case close to resolution. He mentioned the previous attempts on her life which had not been publicised, and talked about the efforts of his small team to bring the matter to a successful conclusion.

'I would also mention, Sir, that DS Joynton took Mrs Blaxstone away from the crime scene and has been looking after her at the Castle ever since. She'll probably need a break.'

'Seems to me, Trussell, that you took all the right decisions, given the circumstances. Normally doesn't do to skirt round the rules. We do have protocols, you know. The outcome, as you've said, could have been much worse. We need to talk about the press conference. It's scheduled for tomorrow morning. You'll need to brief DCS Watkins and our public relations people. You can expect to be interviewed by the IOPC over this.'

'I understand that, Sir. I just hope the official investigation over the shooting of the gunman doesn't hamper our own work. There are still people out there we need to track down and I don't want IOPC to slow us down. We need to say as little as possible at the moment at any Press conference. Promise more information later.'

'Why's that?'

'Well, Sir, I shall need to visit Blaxstone's partners at their offices in the City tomorrow morning. I intend to phone them the moment I leave here. I believe they should be told before they're approached by the media. They will have some valuable information which may help us wrap up our part of the case.'

'Our part? What do you mean?'

'Yes Sir. The gunman appears to be American. It's quite likely this may end up with the National Crime Agency, once the gunman's identified. I've every reason to believe this shooting may be linked to organised crime, both here and in the States. We can only go so far. The important thing is I believe we may have solved the trail of crimes linked to Blaxstone - the attempts on his wife's life, the suspicious death of one of their neighbours, the suicide of a local councillor which may have actually been murder. We'll have the answers when we've spoken to Mrs

Blaxstone. Her conversation with her husband before he was killed could hold the key to everything.'

'So why was Blaxstone killed?'

'I believe Mrs Blaxstone may be able to shed some light on that, Sir, when I speak to her shortly. She received a phone call from her husband earlier today, telling her he was in trouble and needed to see her urgently. He had travelled down to Woodchester by train. She told us he seemed distressed on the phone. She phoned us immediately for advice, and then told him they could meet in twenty minutes. That gave DS Joynton and me enough time to get there first to observe what was going on. It was only when we arrived, saw his body language and then noticed the Mercedes on our floor, that I realised things could escalate pretty quickly. I had no option but to call for support. No time to follow the usual rules.'

The ACC had listened with rapt attention.

'If we're able to speak to the gunman, should he survive, then that'll shed a lot of light on the case. If he talks. I believe it will be the point at which our case goes international and is taken out of our hands. However, we'll have solved all of the crimes on our doorstep.'

'Good effort, Trussell. That shows initiative. Make sure that you're available when the IOPC want to speak to you. You're lucky to have a man like this on your team, Charlie. It seems he gets results. Make sure you keep us posted.'

'If I might make one suggestion, Sir?' Trussell asked.' I believe we should avoid any mention of Mrs Blaxstone and all the other problems that led up to today's events. As far as the press are concerned, they only need to know that a City insurance broker was shot dead in the car park; the man suspected of the crime has been stopped by armed officers and is currently in hospital under guard. We can say further information will be released as soon as we have it, for operational reasons. That should buy us a bit of time to wrap it up. I see no reason to involve Mrs Blaxstone at this stage. Definitely no reference should be made to her maiden name. She needs to be kept out of public view. A much more pressing matter, in my view, is that more uniformed officers are needed right now to control the car park. The public have got to be kept out until the IOPC investigators have finished and the place has been cleared.'

'OK, Trussell. See to it, Charlie, will you. Keep me posted.' With that, he indicated the interview was over.

As they left the ACC's office, Trussell turned to Watkins. 'If it's all the same to you, Sir, I'd like to get back to the Castle. My DS has been looking after Mrs Blaxstone, and I think she should have a break. I also need to talk to Mrs Blaxstone to see what her husband said to her before he was shot. The case may hinge on that.'

'Do you want a WPC sent down there to assist DS Joynton?'

'That might be a help, Sir. But I think she should be in plain clothes. Don't want any uniforms around to tip the press off.'

'One other matter before I go, Sir. There's one more thing we'll need to do. We're dealing with a US citizen and, as you are aware, we're obliged to inform their embassy in London that we're holding him. They have the option of providing legal representation for him during any questioning. We also need to contact the FBI once we have his photo and fingerprints. I'm unsure of the procedure. I haven't come across this problem before.'

'I think you can leave it to me, Trussell,' said Watkins. 'The FBI has a contact in most of their embassies. They're usually called Legal Attachés. I did know their London man a while ago. Now, what was his name? Kelly? That's it, Jack Kelly. I'll contact the embassy and see if he's still there. If not, I'll speak to the new man. Either way, I know the drill. Anyway, they would expect to deal with someone senior on such a delicate matter.'

'That'll be useful, Sir. It will save me the bother of trying to find the right channel for dealing with the problem. Something I won't have to worry about with everything else going on.'

'Just give me the man's details, as far as you know them. You have his passport?'

'Yes, Sir. But I don't believe it's his real name. I'm just waiting for the hospital to give us the all clear, and then we'll take his picture, prints and DNA.'

'Soon as you can, then, Trussell. I'll make the initial contact with them straight away.'

If there's credit to be taken, you'll be at the head of the queue, Charlie, thought Trussell. 'Thank you, Sir. I'll phone you with his passport details and description as soon as I get back to my desk.'

'Quick as you can, Trussell. We must tell the Yanks we have one of their citizens as soon as possible. Don't want to cause a diplomatic incident. Off you go.'

As Trussell left the office, he saw Watkins reaching for his phone. He was obviously keen to get started.

He stopped at his office, sat at his desk and opened the file. Moreno's passport was inside. He picked up the phone and called Watkins.

'Sir, I've got the basic info you need to get started. The passport was issued in the name of Javier Moreno.' He spelt it out. 'His date of birth is given as eighth of January 1980. He's described as a US national born in Mexico. I'll let you know as soon as we have anything further. Perhaps you can tell me what the embassy wants to do about representation because we can't afford to wait on this one. There'll be other people involved and we don't want them skipping before we can get our hands on them. If necessary, we'll provide a local brief at this stage. The Americans may not be too happy about it now but I'm sure they'll OK in the long term.'

'Quite so, Trussell. I'll let you know what they have to say.'

40

Trussell left the building and raced back to the car park. There were now plenty of uniformed officers around to deal with the unhappy commuters unable to get access to their vehicles to go home.

Tim Beach was still helping to deal with keeping people away from the area where Richard Blaxstone's body was still lying on the ground. The police doctor had been to inspect the body to certify his death and they were waiting for a suitable vehicle to move it to the mortuary for post mortem as soon as the investigation team had finished their work.

The investigators had already turned up. Trussell identified himself, told them exactly what he had witnessed and then pointed out the silver Ford Focus which had been struck by the second bullet - the one which had narrowly missed Sophie.

'I'm not sure how you're going to find that one and dig it out. It will be a bit difficult to locate - could be anywhere inside the car if it missed the engine block. Either way, the owner of the car isn't going to be very pleased about it. He'll have to find another way of getting home.'

'We'll have to move the car to the garage and they can dig around for it there. It's really just a supplementary. We must assume the pathologist will recover the bullet from the deceased so Forensics can match it with the gun. We understand you have some witnesses?'

'Yes, you're looking at one of them. I watched the whole thing from up there,' he said, pointing to the ninth floor immediately above their heads. 'Nothing I could do to prevent it. Detective Sergeant Joynton was with me. She saw it all. The other witness was the deceased's wife, who nearly became the second victim.'

'At least there won't be any problem with the burden of proof. Difficult one for the accused's legal team to defend,' said the investigator.

The ACC was as good as his word. A senior uniformed officer had been dispatched to take over the car park to deal with the residual problems, pending the arrival of the IOPC, which would allow Trussell to leave and return to the Castle Inn.

41

Trussell was finally able to leave the car park. The Crime Scene investigation team had completed their work. Richard's body had been removed in one of the discreet dark windowless private ambulances and taken to the mortuary for the forensic post mortem, which would be carried out by a Home Office registered pathologist.

Trussell had left the investigators to arrange for the damaged Mercedes to be collected and taken away for further examination. It was out of his hands now. The weapons had been made safe and removed to the Police Station. The damaged police vehicle had also been removed after pictures had been taken. He left the uniformed officers with the unenviable task of dealing with the innocent, disgruntled car owners who had been unable to remove their vehicles from the car park all afternoon.

His next job would be a bit more difficult. He had to walk back to the Castle Inn and talk to Sophie. He needed to see whether she could shed any further light on the afternoon's events.

Ten minutes later, he walked up to the two steps at the main door, automatically straightening his tie. He crossed the lobby. The receptionist paid him no attention. He went through the arch into the lounge and peered into the dimly lit room. Jackie raised a hand discreetly from a quiet corner table. Sophie sat there with her, still looking pale and shaken.

'How are you?' he asked Sophie.

Jackie shook her head.

'I'm sorry, but I'll have to ask you a few questions while things are still clear in your mind. I realise how difficult it must be. I should also warn you there will be other investigators taking an interest in this as a result of the police shooting and you'll most likely have to speak to them.'

Sophie nodded. 'That's OK. I understand. You all have your jobs to do.'

'The first, obvious question is why was Richard shot first? Are you aware of any reason? Did he give you any hint or idea why he needed to see you? What was the pretext? What did he say to you?'

'He told me he was in fear of his life. I thought it was all a bit dramatic. He told me he needed money because he owed rather a lot to some very dangerous people - a quarter of a million, he said. Apparently he'd run up debts with a casino. He said if I couldn't help him, he would have to kill himself there and then. The people to whom he owed the money from gambling had finally run out of patience with him. If they had let Richard get away with it, then so would other clients. His continuing inability or unwillingness to pay had effectively signed his death warrant. *Pour encourager les autres*, as the French would say. He told me there was no other way. He kept moving closer to the parapet while he was talking.'

'We watched,' said Trussell. His body language suggested to us he was trying to lure you closer to the edge. We think his plan was to push you over. Did you have reciprocal wills? Leaving everything to him?

Sophie was visibly shaken by the suggestion. She looked at Jackie, who nodded in agreement.

'I knew he would occasionally visit casinos with one of his American clients when he came to London, but I had no idea he had any problems.'

'Do you know which ones?'

'No. I guess you'll have to ask his firm. They should know. The other two partners will have to be told about Richard. The three of them ran the firm.'

'If you can give me the firm's details and the names of the partners then I'll contact them by phone and tell them what's happened. We won't be able to keep this quiet for long. Too many people have seen what's gone down. There will be a press conference later. Obviously we wouldn't want the partners to see it on television first. I'll arrange to go and see them tomorrow morning. Obviously discretion is very important.'

Sophie opened her phone directory, and taking a piece of paper and a pen from her bag, wrote down the details for him. 'A number of things have begun to make sense to me now,' she said. 'From the moment I met Richard, he never seemed to have a lot of disposable money. I found it somewhat surprising, given his part ownership of the company. He always told me everything was tied up in investments. I had no idea he had a gambling habit. Do you think this is linked with the attempts on my life? Do you think these people were trying to lean on Richard by getting at me?'

'I'm keeping an open mind at the moment,' said Trussell, 'but I keep thinking about his first wife. We've looked at the file. She and Richard had reciprocal wills and he'd insured her life for a substantial sum. He was the only beneficiary.'

Sophie looked stunned. The remaining colour drained from her face. She began twisting the rings on her right hand, her left hand trembling. The realisation her husband might have been responsible ultimately for the attempts on her life had really struck home.

'Surely, you don't think he was involved in those other events? Jack Finlay's death? The councillor? His first wife, Jenny? What about John Shalford?'

'I think it's highly likely now we can look back on the whole train of events. I think it's imperative I speak to his partners now, before they hear the news from someone else. Please excuse me for a few minutes,' he said, rising from his chair.

He left the lounge to make the call. He didn't want Sophie to hear the conversation. He found a quiet area in the car park outside. Reception was good on his phone. He tapped in the office number given to him by Sophie. When it was answered, he said, 'Please may I speak to Gerard Dalrymple? It's urgent. This a personal call. My name is James Trussell.'

'Certainly, Mr Trussell. Please hold the line.'

A moment later, Gerard Dalrymple answered the phone.

'Dalrymple speaking. I don't think I recognise your name, Mr, er, Trussell?'

'Is this conversation private?'

'Yes.'

'Discretion is important at the moment. I'm Detective Inspector James Trussell of Kent Police. I can be contacted at Woodchester Police Station at this number,' he said, giving the central number, 'although I'm out of the office at the moment, using my mobile. I'll give you the number.'

'And what is the reason for this call?'

'I'm afraid I've some bad news for you. I wanted you to hear it first before the press got hold of it. Your partner, Richard Blaxstone, was shot dead in a car park in Woodchester today. I am making this call to you with the full agreement of Sophie Blaxstone, who gave me your number.'

There was a gasp. Then Dalrymple composed himself. 'Just a moment, Detective Inspector. I'll get my partner, Roy Jagger in here. He has to hear this as well.'

Trussell heard the phone put down and a distant shout. 'Roy, I need you in here right now.'

He heard the sound of footsteps.

'Close the door, Roy.'

The phone was picked up again.

'I'm putting you on the speaker, Detective Inspector. Roy Jagger is here. Please repeat what you've just told me.'

'Good afternoon, Mr Jagger. My name is James Trussell and I'm a Detective Inspector in Kent Police. I've to advise you that your colleague, Richard Blaxstone, was shot dead in a car park at Woodchester earlier today. His wife was there, but was unharmed. She gave me your details so I could relay the news to you rather than you hearing it via the press. I realise this is a terrible shock for you.'

A stunned Roy Jagger asked, 'Who's responsible? Do you have any idea?'

'Yes. The man is in custody. The news services will probably be running the story at the moment without naming names.'

There was a pause, and then he heard Roy Jagger say to his partner, 'He's right. It's on one of the newspaper websites already.'

'I would like to visit you tomorrow morning because I believe you'll have some vital information which will assist our enquiries. Say, ten o'clock. Would that be convenient?'

'Of course, Detective Inspector. We'll set aside as much time as you need. Are you in touch with Mrs Blaxstone? Should we call her? Or should we leave it until later? We'll need to speak to her.'

'She's aware I'm phoning you. She gave me the number. Shall I just pass on your condolences and say you'll be in touch shortly?'

'That would be very helpful, Detective Inspector. We shall obviously have to tell the staff here. Thank you very much for taking the trouble to call us. We'll see you tomorrow, then.'

They hung up.

Trussell went back into the Castle and returned to the lounge.

The two women looked up at him. Sophie, still subdued asked, 'Have you spoken to Gerry and Roy? What did they say?

'They were shocked, of course. They asked me to pass on their condolences. They both said they would be in touch with you shortly.

They have to tell the staff. It's already in the papers online, although no names have been mentioned yet. I've suggested to the Assistant Chief Constable and the Detective Chief Superintendent that the Press conference is limited to the basic facts. I've asked them to ensure there's no reference to you, particularly by your maiden name or any of the events that have led up to this. Obviously, it will all come out eventually. You won't need to be there.'

8.00 p.m. the same evening.

Trussell's phone rang. It was DC Mark Green at the Woodchester Hospital.

'The gunman has just come out of surgery, Guv. I've spoken to the consultant who carried out the operation. They have repaired the damage and are hopeful he will eventually recover, although the next twenty four hours are critical. He hasn't regained consciousness yet. I've told them he's to be isolated in his own room. An armed guard will be placed in the room and another outside. I'm waiting for them to turn up at the moment. I'll stay until that's organised. I also mentioned we'll need to take a picture of him and collect his fingerprints and DNA. They say not until he's out of danger.'

'Well done, Greeno. The ACC is happy now, so I don't think any extra manpower will be a problem. I'll be in touch as soon as I've some news for you. Meantime, don't let him out of your sight.'

'OK, Guv.'

42

Trussell walked briskly along Leadenhall Street through an unfamiliar towering City landscape, so much busier than he was used to in Woodchester. The pavements were full of people rushing to work, and he had to carefully avoid those who had their phones glued to their ears or were busy texting. A constant stream of buses, taxis and commercial vehicles produced a background traffic noise which was punctuated by the occasional sound of a siren, as the City police went about their daily business.

Looking around him, he found the office address and went into the lobby. Inside was a comparative haven of peace and quiet. A quick look at the board listing the building's tenants directed him to the third floor.

He took the lift for his 10 a.m. appointment and walked through the frosted double glass doors still bearing Richard's name along with those of his partners. It was quietly impressive and looked very professional without being showy.

He could sense the subdued atmosphere when he walked into the reception area. He identified himself to the receptionist and mentioned his appointment with the partners. Her eyes were red and swollen. She was dabbing at them with a tissue, but couldn't hide the tears staining her face.

She showed him into the boardroom. 'Mr Dalrymple and Mr Jagger will be with you shortly, Detective Inspector. Please take a seat. Would you like some tea or coffee?'

'No, thank you. I'll wait for the partners.'

Two minutes later, they walked in with sombre expressions on their faces. They were both wearing dark suits with black ties.

Trussell rose from the chair. He produced his warrant card. 'Detective Inspector James Trussell, Kent CID,' he said.

The taller one, looking even more serious, introduced himself, holding out a hand. 'Good morning, Inspector. My name is Gerard Dalrymple and this is Roy Jagger. Thank you, first of all, for phoning us yesterday before this dreadful news got out into the public domain. It was very considerate and I want you to know how much it was appreciated by both of us.'

Trussell raised his hand in wordless acknowledgement.

'As I am sure you can imagine, this has had a devastating effect on us all here. Not only on the business, but personally. Richard was a long standing friend and the three of us started this company together. He was very popular with the staff. This is still a relatively small operation compared with a lot of our competitors. The phones haven't stopped ringing this morning. People are already speculating this was a business deal that went wrong. That's a rumour we have to dispel as soon as possible because of its negative impact on the firm and the market. For now we've avoided making any public comments until we have the full facts.'

'Can we offer you some coffee?' asked Roy Jagger. 'Please sit down. Exactly why have you come up here this morning? We do appreciate your courtesy in doing so, but I'm sure there's more to it than that.'

'Correct,' said Trussell. 'I'm afraid you may not be entirely happy with what I've got to say. First, I must tell you I witnessed the whole affair but was powerless to stop it. Before I say any more, were you aware Mr Blaxstone had a serious gambling habit?'

Gerard turned to Roy. 'We'll have to tell him. It may help.'

They told Trussell about the meeting a couple of weeks ago in the boardroom when they had confronted Richard with the casino bills sent to the firm for settlement. It transpired he had got hooked and had started visiting the place regularly and passing his losses off as company expenses. 'We told him it had to stop immediately.'

'How did he react?'

'He tried to bluff it out at first. We asked him whether Sophie knew, and he claimed she'd thrown him out.'

'Well, what I am about to tell you,' said Trussell, 'may come as a surprise. Better you hear it from me now before you read it in the papers. I should be most grateful if you could keep it to yourselves until such time as the information is released into the public domain. Sophie Blaxstone did not know about her husband's gambling habit until he told her yesterday, just before he was killed. She didn't throw him out. He left her towards the end of May, telling her he'd met another woman.'

The two partners looked totally shocked.

'How much did Richard Blaxstone tell you about his life in Foggenden?

'Not very much at all, lately. He did mention Sophie had told him one of their local friends had died under mysterious circumstances. He didn't elaborate on it.'

'Had he been acting strangely recently?'

'He seemed to have been a bit preoccupied, but we put it down to business pressures. We've all been extremely busy over the last couple of months. We have some very demanding clients, Detective Inspector.'

'Perhaps we should ask his Personal Assistant, Jo, if she can add anything. She sees more of him than we do, day to day,' said Roy Jagger.

'We're now fairly certain Richard Blaxstone wanted his wife dead to be able to get his hands on her money and property. We don't yet know whether he'd insured her life separately, but that's something we have to check.'

'Oh my God,' said Roy, turning to Gerry. 'Jenny. She was his first wife, Detective Inspector. She died in a hit and run accident.'

'We're already aware of that, Sir,' said Trussell. 'Did Blaxstone ever talk about it to either of you?'

The two partners looked at one another in disbelief. The reputation of a long standing friend and partner was being shredded before their eyes.

'Of course, he did, Detective Inspector,' said Gerry. 'He seemed distraught for quite a while afterwards, as one would expect. He was obviously a very clever actor.'

'Yesterday,' said Trussell, 'I was watching from the floor above at the car park when the shooting took place. I was powerless to stop it. The gunman tried to shoot Mrs Blaxstone as well, but fortunately was distracted, missed and then tried to escape. He was detained at the scene. Blaxstone had asked his wife to meet him at the multi-storey car park to try to persuade her to help him raise money to pay his debts. She was, fortunately, suspicious of his motives and called us first before agreeing to go. So we were able to get there first and arrange for support. We then saw a suspect vehicle and were able to arrange backup, including the armed response unit. But the sheer speed of the sequence of events caught us all by surprise as well.'

'How can we help you, then, Detective Inspector?' asked Roy.

'I shall need full details of the casinos involved, the dates and amounts of money. A look at Mr Blaxstone's diary will be helpful, too.'

'Certainly,' said Dalrymple. 'Let's get John Swingle in here. Better ask Jo to bring Richard's diary in as well.'

'OK,' said Roy, picking up the phone. 'Jo is, or should I say, was, Richard's Personal Assistant. She's been with the firm since we started and has been Richard's PA for the last five years or so. She's very important to us and we wouldn't want to lose her.'

There was a rap on the door. Roy opened it. A studious looking man in his fifties walked into the room, carrying a bundle of files. He was of average height, had dark brown hair and was dressed conservatively in a dark grey suit and white shirt. His tie was as anonymous as its owner. He was wearing black framed glasses. He had accountant written all over him.

Roy made the introductions. 'John Swingle, the head of our accounts department. John, this is Detective Inspector Trussell of Kent Police.'

Another tap on the door and a girl in her mid-thirties walked in, tall, shoulder-length blond hair, smartly dressed in a mid-grey business suit. Elegant. She looked pale but seemed to have mastered her emotions. She was carrying Richard's desk diary.

'Jo, this is Detective Inspector Trussell of Kent Police.'

She smiled wanly. He could see it was an effort. She held out a hand. A firm handshake.

'Jo Curran is, sorry, was, Richard's personal assistant. She had charge of his personal diary and ran his office.'

'I understand how difficult this must be for all of you,' began Trussell, 'and I'm really sorry I have to be here today, but there are unanswered questions. I believe the information I need may be found in this office.'

'How can we help?'

'Richard Blaxstone had a serious gambling habit and had run up substantial debts. We believe this was the reason why he was killed. There are other ramifications of this case which need not concern you, so I will not go into them at this point. What I need today are the full details of any casinos or gaming establishments, bookmakers, or anywhere else he frequented and where he spent money, with details of the amounts. Dates, as far as you know them, and, the names of anyone from those establishments who might have phoned him at any time,' he said, looking at Jo as he spoke.

'That's a lot to take in,' said Gerry. 'Jo, what can you tell us before we start going through his diary?'

'I saw his expenses and the receipts, of course, and logged them in his diary. I believe he tended to go with one of our biggest American clients but I now know there were discrepancies, and the receipts did not always tally with Hank's visits.'

'What about phone calls? Are there any you can remember?'

'Yes. There were calls from time to time. The caller just mentioned a name. Antoine, I think it was. He had a slight accent. European, I think. He always refused to tell me the reason for the calls. Confidential, he said. Richard took them. He would usually swivel his chair so that he was facing the window. It was impossible to see or hear what was going on. Although, I did notice he often looked uncomfortable afterwards. He seemed almost rattled.'

'Can we trace the number?'

'If Jo can provide us with dates, then perhaps we can find it.'

'The last call was yesterday. Just after nine. When Richard put the phone down, he looked badly shaken. Not seen him like that before. He was always so self-confident. Then he seemed to compose himself, came out of his office and told me he had to go out, but didn't say where. It was the last time I saw him,' she said.

Then her composure went, and she broke down. Roy offered her a tissue from a box on the side table and pulled a chair out for her.

'I'm sorry,' she sobbed, looking embarrassed, as she sat down.

Gerry tried to divert attention away from her. 'John, have you managed to produce the list of dates, locations and amounts, as we discussed?'

'Certainly, Mr Dalrymple. I've got it here.' He produced it from his file and handed it to Gerry. He glanced at it, and then passed the whole file over to Trussell.

'Thank you. If I could take this with me, it will allow us to make some progress.'

Gerry nodded in agreement.

He turned to Jo, who had managed to regain her self-control. 'It would help tremendously if you could trace the number for this character, Antoine, and pass it on to me. We'll be able to see whether it's connected with one of the casinos. I would also like to know what you can tell us about Richard Blaxstone's behaviour over the last couple of months.'

'He's certainly seemed preoccupied lately. Almost detached from what was going on around him. I've managed to keep our clients at a distance as much as possible because I didn't think Richard was concentrating on what was going on.'

Rising from the chair, Trussell offered his cards to the partners and Jo.

'You can contact me on these numbers at any time. Thank you for seeing me at such short notice,' he said. 'I won't take up any more of your time this morning. I'll be in touch if I need anything more.'

They shook hands and Gerard accompanied him through the reception, opening the outer door for him.

'Thank you again, Detective Inspector. Please let us know if there's anything else we can do.'

Trussell nodded and headed for the stairs.

A lot of information to consider on the train back, he thought, looking at the file handed to him, as he walked back across the river to London Bridge station to catch the train back to Woodchester.

43

'The car registration is false, Guv,' said Tim Beach. 'It's been cloned from a similar vehicle. The registered keeper is in Hounslow. The gunman probably spotted it on his way from Heathrow. Some poor innocent chap is going to get a visit from his local police and he'll have to convince them where he's been on particular dates!'

'What about the VIN on the engine. That may help us track down the correct registration.'

'I'll get onto the garage where they took the car straight away, Guv.'

'Hounslow?' said Trussell. 'When you've sorted that, I've got another job for you, Sandcastle. We'll need to talk to the car rental companies with desks at Heathrow Airport. Find out if any of them have rented a silver Mercedes ML 300 to an American client, say, in the week leading up to the first shooting at Sophie's cottage. Eighteenth of June. It might make your job a little easier if you make a list of all the rental offices in and around the airport, then look on their websites to see which of them have Mercedes ML 300s. It's a premium car, so maybe only a few of the companies will offer it. We haven't got the correct registration number yet, but we do at least have a name. Javier Moreno. He's a US passport holder. Give them the details. Probably not his true identity but it's a starting point. It will be the name he used to enter the country and rent the car.'

He turned to Mark Green.

'Greeno. Get on to Immigration. See if they have a record of our gunman entering the country, say after the eleventh of June. Give them the name. Javier Moreno. Find out where he came in from. By the way, did the doctors give you any idea when we can photograph and fingerprint the gunman?'

'They seem to think it might be a day or two, Guv.'

'Give me the name of whoever's in charge of his case, Greeno. This is holding up our enquiry and may give anyone else involved the chance to abscond.'

'Here it is, Guv. Mr Leighton-Downes. He's the Senior Accident and Emergency Consultant. I've his direct dial number at the Woodchester.' He scribbled the details on a yellow post it note from his desk and passed it over.

Trussell picked up the phone, touched 9 for an outside line, and tapped in the hospital number. A secretary answered.

'Can I speak to Mr Leighton-Downes, please? My name is Detective Inspector Trussell of Kent Police. It's urgent.'

'You're in luck, Mr Trussell. He's just returned to his office. Hold the line a moment.'

A deeper voice. 'Leighton-Downes speaking. What can I do for you, Detective Inspector?'

'Good afternoon, Sir. I wanted to talk to you about the patient we sent you yesterday, suffering from gunshot wounds. The name we have at the moment is Javier Moreno.'

'Yes. I carried out the surgery myself yesterday early evening. Luckily it was relatively straightforward and I think he should make a full recovery, barring setbacks. It was very considerate of your colleagues not to inflict as much damage as we usually see in these cases. He's still under sedation at the moment.'

'When do you expect we'll be able to talk to him? More importantly, how soon before we can get a picture of him and take his fingerprints and DNA? We have a very good reason to believe Moreno is not his real name. We need to send his details off to the States to see if they can tell us who he really is. In the meantime, we'll need to caution him as he was involved in a murder at the Weaver Street car park yesterday. That must be done as soon as he's awake enough to understand his position.'

'I believe he should be aware of what's happening around him sometime later today.'

'Thank you. I'll arrange to come myself a little later. I should appreciate a moment of your time. Where will I find him?'

'On the fourth floor, in a side room attached to Canterbury Ward?'

'Thank you. There's just one other thing, Mr Leighton-Downes. I know it's something that makes us unpopular with the medical profession at times. The man will need to be handcuffed to his bed when he's formally arrested. He's extremely dangerous. We believe he's been responsible for one death, and possibly a second, depending on what the pathologists have to tell us when they've completed another post mortem. Thank you for your time. I'll look forward to meeting you later.'

He turned to Greeno. 'You probably heard that. I'm going to the hospital later. Can you organise someone to take the pictures and fingerprints? I'll let you know when I need them. I'll want to take them

196

just as soon as I get clearance from the doctors. I'll have to caution him. At some stage he'll be formally arrested, although he won't be going anywhere in the meantime.

'I'm on it, Guv. I'll call you when I've got the info'.'

44

Trussell arrived at Woodchester Hospital and found his way to the ward. He looked for the nurses' station and headed for it. The nurse, behind the desk, absorbed in a file, raised her head and looked at him.

'Can I help you?' she asked.

Trussell showed his warrant card.

'I'm here to see your guest in the side room, but first, I've arranged to see Mr Leighton-Downes. Please would you let him know I'm here?'

'Certainly, Officer,' she said reaching for the phone. 'Ah, Mr Leighton-Downes, there's a police officer here to see you…Thank you. I'll tell him.'

She looked up at Trussell. 'He'll be here in five minutes.'

'Thank you.'

On cue, the surgeon arrived. He was a tall man with only the merest hint of age in his dark brown hair. He had changed from his scrubs and was wearing a navy blue suit with a matching tie, ready for the weekend. He peered at Trussell through a pair of thick lenses.

Trussell showed his warrant card and they shook hands.

Thank you for sparing me a few minutes, Sir. I can't imagine how busy you must be. I'll be formally arresting your patient on one count of murder and one of attempted murder in the very near future. Other charges will certainly follow. The process will require me to secure him to the bed at that point. I realise it may create problems for your staff, but the man is highly dangerous.'

'I understand.'

'I also need to know how quickly we can safely photograph your guest and obtain his DNA and fingerprints, in view of his medical condition. We have reason to believe he's travelling under a false name and we need to do that as soon as possible and send everything off to the FBI. I should mention We're not obliged to seek his permission for the process. We're allowed to do whatever is necessary to get them.'

'He should be fit enough by the morning.'

'Thank you, Sir. I'll arrange the necessary then.'

'If there's nothing else, Detective Inspector, then please excuse me. I always look at my more serious cases before I leave the hospital.'

'Of course. Thank you for your assistance.'

With that, the surgeon left and Trussell walked to the side ward and showed his warrant card to the uniformed officer outside the door.

The figure in the bed looked at him, almost disinterestedly. He seemed oblivious of the other uniformed officer siting in the corner of the room. Trussell waved his warrant card in his direction. The man said nothing. Obviously the effects of the anaesthetic were still lingering. He had dressings on the wounds where the surgeon had operated. He had electrodes on his chest connected to a monitor above his head. A drip was attached to his left arm. He was still quite pale after the trauma of the shooting and the ensuing surgery.

'I'm Detective Inspector James Trussell, Kent Police,' he said.

'Well, bully for you,' came the reply in a hoarse whisper.' I guess this ain't a social call. I wasn't expectin' any visitors.'

'You're quite right. I understand from your doctor you've recovered sufficiently to understand me. Javier Moreno, I must tell you at some point soon, you'll be arrested for the murder of Richard Blaxstone at Woodchester on July the fourth, and for the attempted murder of Sophie Blaxstone on the same date.'

Moreno made no response. His eyes did not betray any emotion. They just stared back at Trussell.

'You'll be entitled to legal representation when we question you. In the meantime, I shall arrange for your photograph, fingerprints and DNA to be taken tomorrow for transmission to the FBI. Your doctor has agreed to this. I would urge you to cooperate and I must warn you we're entitled to do this, using whatever means are necessary. I would also mention we've advised the US Embassy of your situation. As a US citizen, you are entitled under our Code of Practice to have any request for assistance passed on to your embassy. That is your right.'

'I'm sure they'll be ready to help me...straight onto a plane back to the States,' he wheezed.

Was this a clue to his identity?

'I should also warn you there'll be a guard outside the door of this room as well as inside with you. Both are armed. There'll be no visitors. The medical staff will do exactly what is required to help your recovery. No more, no less. When you've been formally charged, we'll arrange for you to appear before magistrates so you can be remanded in custody, pending further legal process. This will probably take place by video link from this room, given your condition. Your medical condition will be monitored until you are deemed fit enough to be taken into custody. I shall return on Monday to question you. In the meantime, you'll be provided with a list of local solicitors who can assist you when we question you. Just tell the officer who brings the list which one you would like and we shall arrange it if your embassy hasn't provided legal assistance in the meantime.'

'Huh, I look forward to that,' the man masquerading as Moreno whispered sarcastically.

Trussell looked pointedly at him for a full minute. The man in the bed returned the stare for a few seconds and then closed his eyes. Without further comment, Trussell opened the door and then closed it behind him.

'Keep a careful watch on what goes on here,' he said to the uniformed officer outside. 'No visitors and make sure you keep an eye on the medical staff as they go in and out. I gather from the surgeon he's out of danger now, so there shouldn't be too much traffic in and out of his room.'

'OK, Guv.'

Trussell left the ward to return to the station. As soon as he had walked to the car park, he phoned Greeno.

'Yes, Guv?'

'I've just left the hospital, Greeno. I've seen the gunman and informed him as to the likely train of events. I've also spoken to the surgeon and he's cleared us to take fingerprints and photos tomorrow. I've warned our guest that non-cooperation with the process is not an option. Can you get that organised, please? I know it's the weekend, but this really can't wait. There's a distinct risk that whoever was behind the gunman might do a runner before we can get to him. The Chief Super is organising the contact with the FBI, so the prints and pictures will have to get to him as soon as possible. He's aware of the extreme urgency of this.'

'OK, Guv. I'll deal with it straight away.'

Trussell then called Watkins and brought him up to date.

'DC Green is organising the prints and photos tomorrow morning, Sir. The surgeon has okayed it. I'll be arresting Senor Moreno, or whatever his name is, on Monday morning. He's been made aware of his rights and of our contact with the US Embassy. I've warned him he'll be formally questioned on Monday and we'll organise a brief if the Yanks don't.'

'Good. Make sure your DC gets everything to me as soon as he's sorted it. I'll be in the office tomorrow specially. I've spoken to the embassy. My contact is still there, which has made my life a bit easier. He'll cooperate with us to identify the man as soon as possible, if he's known to them.'

Working on Saturday, Charlie? Trussell mused. *Missing your round of golf with the local politicians? There must be an opportunity for you to visit the embassy. Perhaps you're planning to take everything there tomorrow yourself. Who knows, there may even be a trip to the States in it for you if the man's important. Or am I just being cynical?*

He climbed into his car for the drive back to the station and his thoughts turned to Sophie.

I wonder how she is now. She had to watch her husband being killed yesterday and was in very real danger herself. Now she has no one to turn to. Should I call at the Castle to see how she is? I know Watkins has organised some support for her, and Jackie was with her as well. But it's still a terrible situation for her.

He realised his concern might be misinterpreted by others.

Dammit, I will stop by the Castle. Decision made. What the hell, he thought and a few minutes later was driving through the arch into the Castle Inn car park.

45

'Is there any news yet from the DCS, Jim?' asked Jackie.

'Greeno told me he got the photos, prints and DNA on Saturday morning and rushed back to hand everything over to Watkins.'

'It was like a relay race, Guv,' said Greeno. 'It was almost as if he was waiting for the baton to be passed over! As soon as I gave them to him, he was out of the door like a flash, rushing to London to take everything to the US Embassy.'

'Well, he knew we needed the information as soon as possible, so he was doing his bit, leading from the front,' said Trussell, pulling a face at Jackie.

'What do we do now, Jim? Just wait, I suppose.'

'That's all we can do. I'll be formally arresting Moreno this afternoon and I intend to question him immediately afterwards. Greeno, can you organise a brief for him, please. There's been no word from the US Embassy on that subject. He or she must meet us at the Hospital at two-thirty. You'd better warn the brief about the security on the ward. Jackie, you'd better come with me. Can you organise a recorder and fresh discs, please?'

'Not a problem. I already have them to hand.'

At that moment, Trussell's phone rang. He picked it up.

'Good morning, Sir…I'll come up straight away.'

He put the phone down.

'Right, Watkins has got the information from the American Embassy. He said he's never seen them move so quickly before. I've got to go up there for a quick briefing. Then we can get on with the case.'

He put his jacket back on. Jackie noticed him wince slightly. The arm was still causing him problems.

'Haven't those stitches got to come out, Jim?' she asked.

'A soon as I can find a moment.'

A couple of minutes later, he arrived outside Watkin's office on the eighth floor, tapped on the half open door and went in.

Watkins was sitting at his desk, looking very pleased with himself.

'Well, Trussell, you've certainly caught a tiger by the tail this time.'

'Pardon, Sir?'

'It's your man, Javier Moreno. His real name is Pedro Garcia and he's on the FBI's most wanted list. A professional hit man for one of the criminal organisations. He's committed at least ten murders they know about. They want him extradited as soon as possible and can't wait to get their hands on him.'

'I rather hope we can hang on to him, Sir. There are a lot of unanswered questions. I'm sure he's the key to the whole thing.'

'The Americans are really happy with us. We've achieved something they've been unable to do, track the man down and arrest him.'

We, Charlie? I only seem to remember you distancing yourself from the whole thing and trying to hang me out to dry with the ACC. Now you want to take the credit? Trussell was smiling inwardly at Watkins' attempt to take a slice of the credit for the success. Perhaps he shouldn't be surprised.

'Anyway, Trussell, my friend Jack Kelly is really pleased with us. He sent the file over to me first thing this morning. He phoned me quite early to say that it was coming. This should enable you to make some progress. Let me know directly you have some answers.'

'Thank you, Sir,' said Trussell, taking the file. 'If that's OK, I'll be on my way to make a start. I'll let you know as soon as there are any developments.'

'Keep me posted, Trussell.'

Trussell walked out of the office, carrying the paperwork and headed back down to the CID floor.

When he walked back into the office, his team looked at him expectantly.

'Right,' said Trussell. 'Give me a couple of minutes to glance through this and then we'll have a team briefing.'

46

Trussell and Joynton arrived at the entrance to the Hospital car park, taking a ticket at the barrier on the way through and Trussell found an empty space. His first step was to locate the Parking Company's porta-cabin and show his warrant card.

'I'm here on official business, and it may take a while. I don't expect to pay for any parking today. It's just an unnecessary complication.'

The man in the cabin took his ticket, made a note and gave him a pass.

'This should take care of it,' he said. 'It'll get you through the exit barrier OK.'

Trussell thanked him and they walked to the main entrance. Once inside, he followed the signs to the ward. On arrival, he was met by a uniformed officer, who indicated a side ward with one of his colleagues sitting inside the closed door. Trussell showed his warrant card.

'In there, Guv,' he said.

Trussell looked through the window at the figure in the bed.

'I'll just see whoever's in charge of the ward, first,' he said.

Leaving Jackie outside the room, chatting to the uniformed officer on guard, Trussell approached the desk where two nurses were deep in conversation, looking at some notes.

One looked up at him.

'Can I help you?'

Trussell showed his warrant card and asked to speak to Mr Leighton-Downes. 'He's expecting me. We're here to interview your guest in the private room over there, but I need to speak to the surgeon first.'

The nurse picked up the phone and spoke into it.

'He can be down in a couple of minutes.'

Thank you. I'll wait here, if I may.'

The nurse indicated a couple of empty chairs.

A few minutes later, the surgeon appeared, dressed in brightly coloured scrubs.

'Good afternoon, Sir,' said Trussell. 'Thanks for sparing me a few minutes. How's your patient?'

'He's progressing well now, Detective Inspector. Will it be absolutely necessary to handcuff him to the bed? It will make life very difficult for the nursing staff here looking after him. He isn't in any position to cause them any problems at the moment.'

'I understand that completely, Sir. As you know, we were able to take his picture and fingerprints and send them off to the States. We have heard back from the FBI now. He's on their most wanted list and is highly dangerous. I won't bore you with the details, but I fear we may face a real struggle to hang onto him here to deal with our outstanding matters. I believe an extradition request from the US government may well already be on its way to the Home Secretary's desk. So there can be no question of any relaxation in our security arrangements.'

'I see. Now, what about the nursing staff on the ward? How much should they be told?'

'Nothing beyond what they already know. That he's under arrest for a serious matter here. How long before we can remove him from the hospital?'

'At his current rate of progress, no more than a few days. I won't make a secret of the fact that the sooner he goes, the happier we'll be.'

'Thank you, Mr Leighton-Downes. Please let me know the moment he can be transferred and I'll organize it. I'll go in now and have a few words with him.'

Trussell watched the surgeon leave and then approached the door to the room. The uniformed police officer opened it for him.

The man looked up from his bed to study his visitors. He stared balefully at Trussell. 'Who are you? Waddya want?'

It was an attempt at bravado, but it came out as a hoarse whisper.

'I see you're as charming as ever, Senor Garcia. My name is Detective Inspector James Trussell. This is Detective Sergeant Joynton. You and I met last Friday evening but I doubt you'll remember. I'm currently investigating certain matters which involve you. We're here for a chat. You'll be free to discontinue this conversation at any time. Everything will be recorded.'

Jackie switched on the recorder.

'Record of a conversation on Monday July the eighth at 2.15 p.m. at Woodchester Hospital. Present…'

The two detectives identified themselves and Trussell turned to the man in the bed. 'Identify yourself for the record.'

'You've made a mistake. My name is Moreno, Javier Moreno,' was the response. 'I expect you've got my passport.'

'I'm afraid that doesn't work anymore. We sent your picture and prints to the FBI representative at the US Embassy. They sent everything off to the States and identified you rather quickly. It seems they're very anxious to get their hands on you. Our government is expecting an official extradition request any day now. It appears you're a very popular man, Pedro Garcia.'

'So, what happens now?'

'As a US citizen, you're entitled under our code of practice to have your request for assistance be passed on to your embassy. That is your right.'

'I guess the only help they're likely to give me is a plane ticket back to the States to face charges over there. If the Feds want me, then there's only one likely result. A trial followed by a quick transfer to the Federal facility in Terre Haute, Indiana. And I know what that means. A date with a gurney. The Federal Government ain't holdin' back with these things, not like some of the states. I know appeals can sometimes take years, but I ain't holding my breath. I guess they must want me quite badly now they know where I am.'

Trussell thought it would be unhelpful to his case to mention that the British Government's current stance was to avoid extradition of any foreign criminal where they might face a capital charge in that country. After all, it was only policy and not the law, and could change anytime to fit an individual, so Garcia didn't need to know that.

'It seems to me your best option is to cooperate fully with us and answer all of our questions.'

'And what's in it for me if I do agree to cooperate?'

'It would appear to offer you the chance to extend your life for quite a few years. After all, you seem to think the Federal system has surely already made their minds up about your future, from what you've said.'

'So, what's the deal then?'

'There are no deals. I just wanted to point out the reality of your situation.'

'Ok. What do you want to say?'

'You'll be formally arrested and, following questioning, then you'll be charged. You'll appear before magistrates, most probably by video link and then be remanded in custody. As soon as the doctors think you're fit enough to be moved, you'll be transferred to prison. In the meantime, we shall arrange a full interview to get the information we need.

'What if I can't afford an attorney'? The organisation ain't gonna pay me for this trip, now.'

'You'll be entitled to some sort of legal representation at that time which will cost you nothing. Your embassy doesn't seem too keen to help you in that respect, at the moment, but we're obliged by law to provide legal representation.'

'So what happens next?'

'We'll question you about a number of matters. You'll know what they are. If you decide not to share this information with us, then it'll be your decision. The matter will be out of our hands and the politicians will get involved. It may well be described as being in the interests of Anglo American relations, no doubt. It will be up to them whether they accede to the US Government's wishes and send you straight back. As I say it's your decision."

'You don't leave me too much choice.'

'That's about the size of it. I'll leave you to think about it. Now, Pedro Garcia, I'm arresting you for the murder of Richard Blaxstone at Woodchester on the fourth of July.' Trussell issued the formal caution and then, producing a pair of handcuffs, secured him to the bed by his left arm.

'Interview terminated at 2.45 p.m.' said Jackie, and switched off the recorder.

'I'll be back to talk to you tomorrow, and a lawyer will be provided for you. He'll be present at the interview. By the way, the nurses are aware of your identity and the risks you pose, so don't expect any favours from them, outside what is required of them in their normal working day. The guard on the door is armed.'

With those parting words, Trussell opened the door and they left the room. Outside he gave final instructions to the police officer on the door. 'Make sure that full security is maintained at all times. No one is to go in there apart from the nursing staff on duty. We have identified him as highly dangerous and he's wanted for multiple murders in the States. He's a man who needs watching. Ignore the fact he's recovering from surgery and stay alert.'

'Yes, Guv.'

'Good. I've now arrested him for murder and he's been handcuffed to the bed. That man is very important to us at the moment. He holds the key to solving several outstanding matters.'

47

Trussell, accompanied by Jackie Joynton, went straight to the room off the Canterbury Ward, where the American gunman was being held.

The armed police officer on guard outside the room acknowledged them and opened the door.

'Morning, Guv. The prisoner's brief has turned up. I checked his ID and searched him, just to make sure.'

'Thanks for the warning.'

A man was sitting in the chair next to the bed. He was about fifty, with glasses and wearing the increasingly ubiquitous dark grey suit and red tie of his profession. Trussell recognised him and thought for a moment. *What was his name? I've seen him before. Was it in court or at one of the police stations?*

Trussell couldn't recall his name, but Jackie saved him any embarrassment. 'Good morning, Mr Tyndale. I see you've been appointed to advise Mr Garcia.'

'Hello, Detective Sergeant. You're correct. I haven't had much time with him to take any instructions, yet.'

Jackie introduced Trussell as the DI in charge of the case.

'I doubt any instructions will be required from him,' said Trussell.

'That's a bit unusual, Detective Inspector.'

'Well, Mr Tyndale, we've already had a conversation with your client, properly recorded, about the future, He has decided it's in his best interests to cooperate fully with us. Let me share a few facts with you.'

'What facts, Detective Inspector?'

'Your client entered this country on a false passport which is an offence, for starters, but a minor one in the overall scheme of things. All sorts of other offences flow from that false passport, but he has committed a murder in front of three witnesses. That is beyond dispute. He's wanted by the US for at least ten murders and the Federal Authorities are very anxious to get their hands on him. He's also aware of that. It would be easy for our government to put aside what he's done here and just ship him straight back to the States to face a number of capital charges by the Federal Authorities. It would save the UK taxpayers a great deal of money and take some of the strain out of the legal system. It would be very tempting.'

'So, why are you continuing with your enquiries here, then?'

'Simply because there are other people involved whom we want to bring to justice here. Plus there are questions about some unexplained deaths in the South East, in which your client may be implicated.'

Tyndall looked over at his client. 'Have you already agreed to cooperate in exchange for what amounts to long prison sentences here?'

'Yes. What the Detective Inspector says is correct. I stay here - I live longer.'

'So what do you want to know, Detective Inspector?'

'We'll proceed on a formal basis, now, Mr Tyndale.'

Jackie produced the recorder and put a fresh disc in it.'

'Record of an interview at Woodchester Hospital on July the sixth at eleven a.m. Present are the accused, Pedro Garcia, a US national currently confined to bed following surgery and his solicitor, Mr Tyndale. We shall now introduce ourselves for purposes of record.

'Detective Inspector Trussell of Kent Police.'

'Detective Sergeant Jacqueline Joynton of Kent Police.'

'Robert Tyndale, Solicitor, appointed to advise the Accused.'

All three looked at Garcia who reluctantly, he identified himself. 'Pedro Garcia. US National.'

'Let's start at the beginning, Mr Garcia' said Trussell.

The solicitor, produced an A4 legal pad and began taking notes.

'How and where did you receive your instructions to come to the UK and from whom? You were in Mexico at the time?'

'Yeah, that's true. I was hiding out from the Feds. I always get my orders from one of my contacts in the organisation in New York. They arranged my travel, car rental and contacts over here. They also provided the identity and the passport.'

'Did you find it unusual that you would be asked to come over here to carry out a contract? Had you been here before? Wouldn't you expect a London client to have a choice of local talent for a job like this?'

'I was surprised, but the instructions came from the top. I didn't dare ignore them. I've been to London a few times before, so I know my way around here.'

Trussell and Joynton exchanged glances. Might he hold the key to other unsolved crimes? Maybe the cold case team might want to speak to him. Either way, his time behind bars would be unlikely to be solitary or boring. He would probably have plenty of official visitors.

'Were you surprised to find that you were working, in the first instance, for the very man you later killed in the car park at Woodchester?'

'Yeah. It was sure different. I understand he owed the casino a pile of dough and he could only pay if his wife died. He would get all of her property and money, and he told me he had a large life insurance to collect on her as well.'

'Did you meet Richard Blaxstone to arrange everything?'

'Yeah. He was one helluva devious bastard. The plan he worked out to hang it all on that construction guy, Burtonlee, was very clever. All of that to get his hands on his wife's money.'

'What about Jack Finlay who was found dead on the fields?'

'Blaxstone had it all worked out. He told me Finlay was leading the opposition to Burtonlee's plans. He said if something happened to Finlay it would really point the finger at the construction company. So, I called him at his home and arranged to meet him. I told him I had the dirt on Burtonlee. It was all part of Blaxstone's plan and he had given me all the background. I guess his wife told him everything about her work. Anyway, this old guy arranged to meet me. When he turned up, I told him I was from Burtonlee, and he'd been shooting his mouth off too much. I said it all had to end before he killed their business. I pulled out my gun, pointed it at him and cocked it. The idea was just to seriously frighten him so that word would get back to the police and drop Burtonlee even deeper in the crap. How the hell was I to know the old guy had a dodgy heart?'

'He didn't. The post mortem told us you literally frightened him to death. It's a well-documented medical condition. So there may well be another murder charge to follow on that one. Now tell me about the councillor, Jeremiah Blackley?'

'Well, it was kinda interesting. Blaxstone told me Blackley had been helping to push the development with the local council, but that was not enough. So we decided to start a few whispers. Suggested he was taking bribes. I got word to Sophie Blaxstone anonymously. We knew any rumours would embarrass Blackley, even if they were untrue. All of this was planned to stoke the Burtonlee connection. But, we had to go further. Work on his mind. Threaten to expose him, even though he hadn't really done anything at that time. He was kinda caught. His business was not doing as well as people thought.'

'So, what did you do? What happened to him at Beachy Head? Did you push him over the edge?'

'I called him at home and promised him some real proof that the committee opposing Burtonlee's development had cooked up these stories about him taking bribes so he could stop them once and for all. Sue them. Get some money from them. He jumped at the chance. He said the rumours were killing his business so he'd do anything to stop them. I arranged to meet him later that night at Beachy Head. Blaxstone had suggested the location. He said it was a popular spot for suicides and it would be easy to make it look like the guy had killed himself. It would add to the rumours that he was taking bribes. There wouldn't be any witnesses around at that time of night.'

'So you dangled the carrot to get him to Beachy Head?'

'Right. By the time he turned up, it was dark. He parked his car next to mine. When he got out, I went up to him, pulled out the gun, persuaded him to walk to the edge and pushed him over. It was just so easy. I thought I might have had to disable him somehow and throw him over the cliff, but he did the work for me. Softest contract job I've ever done. I left something incriminating in his car for the police to find after his body turned up the next day. Cash in an envelope. I locked the car and threw the keys away, then drove back. There were no witnesses and, as I said, it was dark by then.'

'What about John Shalford? Did you cut the hose on his car brakes?'

'Sure. The old guy was deaf. He never heard me outside, and there were no other houses around. No one to see me. It was real easy.'

Trussell was amazed by Garcia's matter of fact details of the crimes. Cold blooded wasn't in it. Having heard his confession, half of him wanted to ship the evil bastard off to the States on the next flight to let their legal system dealt with him. But the other half prevailed. He needed the rest of the information to nail the people at the casino who had ordered Richard Blaxstone's death. They needed to be taken off the streets permanently. When he had done that, he could turn the whole case over to the National Crime Agency.

'Right, let's talk about Sophie Blaxstone,' said Trussell. 'We know you tried to shoot her on the twenty-first of May at her house in Foggenden. You used the Ruger we found in the boot of the Mercedes.'

'It seemed a real shame. She was a good lookin' dame. But a job's a job. I still don't know how I missed her. Two hundred yards was an easy shot. She was right in the crosshairs when I squeezed the trigger. I've never missed one of those before.'

'Luckily for her, she dropped something she was holding and stooped to pick it up at that instant. Where did you get the information about her address?'

'My contacts in London had arranged the meeting with Blaxstone. He told me everything I needed to know.'

'Did you meet him at the casino?'

'Yes. Some guy called Antoine Lescalier arranged it. I believe he's the manager there. He's the contact with New York.'

'Now, what about the other attempts on Sophie Blaxstone's life?' Let's talk about Brandford. How did you know she was going to be there? I saw you talking by your car to the kid who tried to attack her with the knife.'

'Blaxstone again. He called me to tell me about Tuesday's trip, so I drove there on Monday, asked around and talked to that kid, Emile. He was ready for anything after I offered him some decent Spice and the promise of cash the next day. I took his phone number so I could call him once I knew the trip was on. I had staked out the hotel and I saw her standing outside waiting with some scruffy guy in a tee-shirt and cap.'

Jackie looked at Trussell and smiled at the description. His disguise had been better than he thought.

'When the blue panel truck turned up, I just followed them all the way to Brandford, called the kid and set him up with the knife.'

'That ties in with what we know. We're holding Emile now and he gave us a pretty good description of you. You scared him, but apparently not as much as I did when we interviewed him. He told us everything he knew. So did a witness at Foggenden, after you met Jack Finlay.'

'I don't remember seeing anyone there.'

'Seems you're getting careless, Senior Garcia. Losing your touch. I think we're doing you a favour, retiring you now, before someone better catches up with you and makes it permanent. Not to mention the Federal authorities.'

'Perhaps you're right.'

'Next day, you tried to push Sophie Blaxstone down the escalator at London Bridge tube station, and then tried to help her under the train on the platform. How did you know she was going to London? Her husband couldn't have known her exact travel arrangements?'

'He knew the day and guessed what time she would need to leave to make their meeting, I watched where she was staying, and when I saw her car leave, I called the hotel. The gal in reception was real helpful. Told me where she was headed. I followed Mrs Blaxstone to the station and got on the same train. It was easy because she didn't know me anyway.'

'What about that incident at Leverton. You tried to run Mrs Blaxstone down, didn't you?'

Trussell had no proof Garcia was involved. As far as the police were concerned, the file was still open. It was circumstantial. He thought it was worth asking the question to see what sort of reaction he got.

'Yep. That was me again. The goddam woman must have a charmed life. Just don't know how I lucked out that time.'

'You hit her alright and she had the bruises to show for it. Your wing mirror ruined her expensive jacket. I assume Richard Blaxstone gave you her mobile number?'

'Yes.'

'So that's how you managed to send her that threatening text on the day of the shooting?'

'Yep. I followed her to the hotel that evening.'

'You left the note in reception?'

'Uh-huh.'

'It's kind of you to confirm that minor detail. We already know anyway. We took your fingerprints so we were able to lift some from the note you pasted together.'

'It didn't work. She wasn't scared off.'

'So what about the car park at Woodchester? How did you know Blaxstone would be there?'

'Antoine called me that morning. He said he had just spoken to Blaxstone and told him their patience had run out. Said if he couldn't pay what he owed that day, they would not wait any longer but would make an example of him so any other clients who owed them would get the message and pay up. Antoine told me to deal with him. He said Blaxstone had told him on the phone that morning he was meeting his wife in the car park at Woodchester to have one more go at persuading her to part with the money so he could settle the debt. If not, he planned to push her off the parking garage. Antoine gave me instructions to watch, and if Blaxstone couldn't do it, then to take him out.'

214

'What about Mrs Blaxstone. Did they tell you to kill her as well?'

'I already had the contract to do that. I guess it was a matter of professional pride. She had escaped too many times. It was a kinda unique situation. Blaxstone had asked Antoine to arrange it for him and my fee was added to his debt. At least the organisation will save on that. They sure won't pay me now. It's only a matter of time before they catch up with me for spilling the beans on the whole deal. If you think I'll be safe in one of your jails, forget it. They've got a very long reach.'

'I've got a bit more confidence than you in our system, Mr Garcia. They will certainly look after you until your sentence is finished. Who knows, by then they may have abolished capital punishment in the States.'

'Mebbe, but the organisation has got a very long memory and can be pretty patient. I still can't work out what happened after I shot Blaxstone. I was just drawing a bead on his wife when the goddamn car roof exploded and covered me in broken glass. The cuts on my head still haven't healed up. I don't know what caused it?'

'I may as well tell you. One of the local winos left an empty bottle on the ground. Someone threw it at the top of your car from ten feet above to distract you.'

'I wondered what the hell had happened. Sure made a mess of my head.'

'I think we've heard enough for today,' said Trussell, nodding at Jackie.

'Interview terminated at twelve noon,' intoned Jackie, switching the recorder off.

The solicitor, Robert Tyndale, had sat there quietly throughout, listening to the story unfold. 'I can see why you inferred my presence here was superfluous, Detective Inspector,' he said.

'You know the law, Mr Tyndale. The accused has to have a legal representative present if he requests it. On this occasion, he hasn't asked his embassy to provide assistance. We'll transcribe the recording, and prepare statements for him to sign. I want him remanded in custody as soon as he can be moved. I am now going to formally charge him and he'll have to appear before the magistrates tomorrow morning, probably by video link from here. I'll organise it and let you know. You'll need to be present.'

'You'll give me a copy, of course, Detective Inspector?'

'If you're appointed to act on his behalf, then it'll be part of the paperwork to be handed over to the defence.'

Jackie picked up the recorder and the precious disc and put it back into its carrier bag.

Trussell thanked Mr Tyndale for his assistance, nodded at Garcia, and he and Jackie left the room.

He spoke to the uniformed officer on duty outside the door as he closed it behind them. 'Keep your eyes open. The brief should be OK when he leaves. We know him quite well. He's on the panel for legal aid. No one else is to go in there. Continue checking the nursing staff. They'll understand. I've spoken to the consultant and he knows the score. Under no circumstances are the handcuffs to be removed, OK?'

'Yes, Guv.'

They left to walk down the stairs to the ground floor and out.

From there it was a short journey back to the police station.

48

Jackie Joynton had been in touch with the Metropolitan Police, and after the appropriate warrants had been obtained from a magistrate, she travelled by train to London's West End with Jim Trussell to meet their CID counterparts. Their target was the casino identified in Richard Blaxstone's office records and phone calls. They would be accompanied by armed officers in view of the events so far. The object was to arrest Antoine Lescalier on an initial charge of conspiracy to murder. This in turn would give the Serious Crime Agency the opportunity to look at his international criminal connections.

They hailed a black cab outside Charing Cross station and told the driver where to take them.

'Even more experience for you, Sergeant,' said Trussell.' It will look good on your CV. Raiding West End clubs.'

'Are you trying to get rid of me, Jim?' she asked. 'I want to see this case through to conclusion. I think there are still quite a few ends to be tied up.'

'Oh yes. Mustn't forget the Burtonlee part,' he said. 'Have to resume that one when we get back. We now know they weren't involved in the Blaxstone case, but, from what we've found so far, I'm sure the Fraud Squad will want to look at the company and Barlborough's involvement. I think Sophie and the neighbours won't have to worry about a new town arriving on their doorsteps for quite a while to come. It will take Terry Burtonlee forever to get his business back on track after the damage Barlborough did to it. There'll undoubtedly be a few disappointed councillors in Woodchester but I'm sure Mr Blackley's unfortunate demise will have given them a bit of a wake-up call to listen to local residents a bit more closely in the future.'

Jackie said, 'And Sophie will have to find something more interesting for her programme now Burtonlee's been forced to catch up with the backlog of repairs for his customers. His new developments are on hold now. To add to her problems, Sandcastle ran the white van man to earth and the council are dealing with him now. What she needs is a holiday after all of this. I'm sure she could arrange time off with the television company if her investigations have gone quiet. Come to think of it, you

217

could do with some time off as well, Jim. Your arm still hasn't completely healed. A bit of R & R is what you need.'

'What are you suggesting, Sergeant? I think you'd better concentrate on today's events, rather than trying to arrange my diary for me.'

Jackie smiled. She had seen the way Sophie had looked at Jim recently. 'Observation's the sign of a good detective. Or so you're always telling me.'

The cab arrived deposited them outside the police station.

'Let's concentrate on today's events,' said Trussell, looking slightly embarrassed.

Inside Trussell produced his warrant card and asked the duty sergeant for DCI Proctor, the man leading the operation. The sergeant picked up the phone and dialled a number. 'Two visitors here from Kent CID for you, Boss.'

A couple of minutes later, a tall, smartly dressed man in his forties emerged from the door behind the counter. His brown hair was neatly combed and his dark blue striped suit was paired with a white shirt and plain blue tie. He had an air of authority about him.

'Ah, our friends from the sticks!' he smiled. 'Here come our country cousins, in town to bring us gifts. I'm Tony Proctor,' he said, offering each of them a handshake.

'DI Jim Trussell', said Jim. 'And this is DS Jackie Joynton.'

Proctor looked approvingly at Jackie who was wearing one of her trademark trouser suits.

'Nice to meet you both. Interesting case you've brought us. It's given us the opportunity to look at the casino, which we really appreciate. We can't just walk in there without a good reason.'

'How far away is it, Boss?' asked Trussell.

'There's the irony. We can walk there. The team will spread out and arrive from different directions and cover all exits. If we just march down there like some vigilante posse, they'll be tipped off.'

'Do you know the management there?' asked Jackie.

'Oh yes. Not well, but it's our business to keep an eye on these places. On the face of it, it's a legitimate operation, very popular with the gambling fraternity. We weren't aware of any real problems there day to day but not altogether surprised to find dodgy connections at the top.'

They left the police station and walked along the street, crossed over and cut through a narrow side-road with wall to wall clubs, cafes and bars. At the other end, their objective was located on the parallel street.

The club stood out, with its name, 59th Street Casino, in garish lights, very visible even at that time of day.

At the entrance, the doorman, a burly individual in a discreet dark suit stopped them. He had a shaven head and was wearing sunglasses. 'I'm sorry, folks,' he said in an affected American drawl. 'It's members only here.'

Proctor identified himself.

'You can't just come in here without a warrant. I know the law.'

'We have one. Where's the manager? What's his name? Is it Lescalier - something like that?'

'Yes. You'll find him inside,' said the doorman, stepping aside to let them through, his initial bravado and false accent both evaporating.

Inside, Trussell and Joynton had never seen anything like it. There were a large number of gaming tables and several croupiers were checking their equipment and setting up for the evening ahead. Proctor led the way to the bar. The best place to enquire.

'Is the manager in?' asked Proctor.

'Sure. He's de guy in de tux over there.' It was another affected accent to fit with the casino's American theme.

They approached the man pointed out by the barman. He was of Mediterranean appearance, average height with thinning dark hair, already wearing dinner jacket and black bow tie. He was discussing something with another member of his staff. He turned to them as they approached.

'Can I help you folks?' The accent was European - French, maybe.

'Are you the manager?'

'Yes, Antoine Lescalier at your service.'

'Good. You've saved us a bit of time and trouble,' said Proctor, producing his warrant card and identifying himself. 'Antoine Lescalier, we have a warrant for your arrest. Will you do the necessary, DI Trussell?'

'With pleasure, Sir.' He turned to Lescalier. 'Antoine Lescalier, I'm arresting you for conspiracy to murder Richard Blaxstone on July the fourth at Woodchester in Kent.' He cautioned Lescalier, produced a pair of handcuffs and secured both of his wrists in an easy, well-practised motion.

'What's going on? I don't know what you're talking about. Where's your evidence?'

'We have witnesses, dates, facts. You'll have an opportunity to talk about it. I have to warn you other charges will probably follow.'

'I need to talk to our lawyer. You'll get nothing from me until I see him'

'That can be arranged at the station.'

Proctor spoke into his radio and when they walked back onto the street, a police car was waiting to take them back. The decision would have to be made eventually whether to take him back to Woodchester for initial questioning, or to bring in the Serious Crimes Agency immediately. Either way, Lescalier would certainly be off the streets for a considerable time.

After seeing the man safely locked up, Proctor turned to his two visitors from Kent. 'I think this calls for a drink. You can tell me a bit more about the case. Quite a coup for you provincials, getting mixed up in international crime on this scale.'

Trussell took the ribbing in his stride but Jackie was finding it a bit patronising and irritating. 'You'd be surprised what we uncover in the sticks, Boss,' she said. 'That is, apart from the usual hay bale thefts and speeding tickets for tractors.'

'Touché,' said Proctor to Trussell. 'I like her style.'

He led the way into the nearest pub.

Over a couple of pints, Trussell shared the details of how the case had unfolded, from the shooting in Foggenden, to the other deaths, and the way a major house builder was implicated. Jackie was impressed by Jim's succinct and interesting summary of the chain of events, omitting mention of the trip to Brandford and the injury he sustained there. Jackie had heard rumours back in Woodchester that Jim had played it down and hadn't wanted any recognition for his actions. She still had a nagging suspicion at the back of her mind there might be a little more to his relationship with Sophie than a strictly professional one.

'Well, you do have your problems out there,' said Proctor. 'That must have taken some untangling.'

'Yes,' said Jim. 'We started with what seemed a relatively straightforward case of attempted murder, but the deeper we dug, the more complex it became. What we could never have known at the outset was that we were dealing with such a devious man, with, it now transpires, some previous form in this area. One thing we may never be able to do now, unfortunately, is to track down whoever killed his first wife in the hit and run. That occurred in London, so it's not really our problem although it would have been nice to have tied that loose end up as well. We have to assume Blaxstone arranged that too. Anyway he planned the whole thing meticulously, feeding the hit man with just enough information to get the job done each step of the way. The plot he wove to implicate Burtonlee Homes was impressive, but we had some payback there, because, coincidentally, we uncovered embezzlement in the company on a grand scale.'

'How did that come to light?' asked Proctor.

'Serendipity,' said Jim. 'One of my DC's has an interest in genealogy, and got hooked on the man's rather unusual name. He researched it, and found it was a case of stolen identity. That gave us the entrée into the company and the Fraud Squad will be taking that one on. There are large sums of money involved. It's nearly pushed a major housebuilder under.'

Jackie had stayed silent during the conversation, just sipping her second glass of Sauvignon Blanc as she listened. But she couldn't contain herself any longer. 'Jim always gives his team all the credit, but it's about time someone shared the facts around. When the journalist was about to be stabbed, whilst conducting interviews for her TV programme on a very dodgy estate, Jim stepped in the way to arrest the knife man, and got badly slashed in the process. And when the gunman shot Richard Blaxstone in the multi storey car park, and was about to shoot his wife, it was Jim who saved her life again. He chucked an empty wine bottle at the sun roof of the hit man's car just below us and made him miss his target.'

'It wasn't your empty bottle, was it, Detective Sergeant?' smiled Proctor, looking at Jackie's glass. 'I know how tedious those stake outs can be. Is that how you pass the time in the sticks? I understand you've got quite a few decent vineyards down there.'

'It was just a bottle of cheap red,' said Jackie. 'You wouldn't catch me drinking that rubbish.'

Jim looked a bit embarrassed and tried to change the subject. 'Anyway, we have a few loose ends to tie up and then the whole lot can go to the CPS. The local stuff will probably go to Crown Court at Maidstone. The gunman will plead guilty to three murders and five counts of attempted murder. The Fraud Squad will deal with the Burtonlee case, and that just leaves a decision on what happens with Lescalier. The gunman's testimony will be enough to sink him, but, of course, we don't know where Serious Crimes will want to take that one.

The conspiracy charge will be enough to nail him while they make up their minds.'

'I have to congratulate you both on a very thorough job,' said Proctor.

'Thank you,' said Jim. 'At least it's got the ACC off our backs now.' He glanced at his watch. 'It's time we were heading for the train back. Thanks for your assistance and hospitality today. I'll be in touch to let you know about Lescalier when I've spoken to the CPS. Hopefully it won't take too long. We appreciate you looking after him in the meantime.'

'The pleasure's all mine,' said Proctor. 'Keep those tractors under control.' He grinned at Jackie, looking unexpectedly boyish.

Trussell hailed a black cab outside the pub to take Jackie and himself back to Charing Cross Station. 'Well, Sergeant; how did you enjoy your trip to the big city? Do you see your future policing career amongst the bright lights? I was impressed by the way you put Proctor in his place over the tractors!'

'Do you know, Jim, I don't think that it's for me - at least not for the moment. I'm seeing enough career interest and excitement in Woodchester. You can't have seen too many cases like this?'

'It's been an interesting challenge. At least Sophie's come out of it safely. That had to be our number one priority. Whether her television career will ever be the same again for her is an interesting question. Her husband unwittingly removed most of her immediate programme content. Anyway, we'll have to bring her up to date when we get back. Perhaps you can text her now, Jackie, and ask if she'll be free around five.'

Jackie tapped in Sophie's number. Was there more to Jim's suggestion than a piece of official business? No, she was reading too much into it. They had both been too close to this case since that first day with the shooting at Foggenden, and yet? Her phone buzzed. She read the text message. 'Sophie will see us at five. No problem.'

At Charing Cross Trussell paid the cabbie and they walked into the station, searched the electronic indicator board and found their train and platform. The hour and a quarter journey was uneventful, and it was a relief to be back on home turf. They walked light-heartedly from the station to the Castle Inn to update Sophie on the morning's events. There was no doubt the arrest of the gunman had lifted a huge weight off her and their shoulders but now she would have to decide whether to vacate the Castle Inn in favour of a return to her cottage in Foggenden. Jim thought there might be too many memories associated with the place for her. As a widower himself, he could understand that only too well.

They walked into the lounge at the Castle, now so familiar to all three of them. Sophie was waiting with a pot of tea and three cups. Those piercing blue eyes had regained their sparkle. She smiled as they crossed the floor to her table and pulled up two chairs. 'Successful morning, then?' she asked.

'Yes. Mr Lescalier is safely locked up in the West End and we're ready for everything to go to the CPS. It will be out of our hands then, apart from the need to appear as witnesses at any of the court hearings. We're pretty sure Senor Garcia will plead guilty to all the charges, and the Crown lawyers will try to oppose any idea of credit or time off for doing so. Frankly, I think Garcia will be happy with as much time as he can get from a British court. He wants to put off any extradition to the States for as long as possible.'

'What about Lescalier?'

'We'll let the Serious Crimes Agency have him. They'll be very interested in working with the FBI in view of the links to organised crime, both here and in the States. I think the 59th Street Casino may well lose its licence and be shut down. So your husband's client, Mr Zarkowski, will have to find other means of entertainment when he comes to London.'

'Gerry and Roy spoke to him immediately after Richard's death, as a courtesy,' said Sophie. 'But there's been an interesting outcome. Wrongly, he blames himself for introducing Richard to the casino, and has felt a personal responsibility for his death. Nonsense, of course, but they can't change his mind. Anyway, unless the company does anything outrageously wrong, I believe they'll enjoy his business for a long time to come. As he's their single biggest client, that's good news for them.'

'So, Sophie, now you know you're safe, will you return to Foggenden?'

'I don't think so. Too many memories there. Not just the shooting, or Richard's death, but Jack Finlay, as well. I still feel for his wife Rose. Then there's John Shalford, as well. He's still in hospital.' The question brought back sharp memories of all the recent events at The Piggery, particularly of the day Richard walked out on her and then the bullet through the window.

'What will you do, then?' asked Jim.

'I have the flat in the Barbican, I suppose. But even that holds memories for me.'

Jackie was watching Jim while Sophie was speaking. Was that a quick flash of disappointment when the London flat was mentioned?

'Will you stay here at the Castle for the time being?' asked Jim.

Sophie considered the question. 'I think I may look for a flat to rent in Woodchester while all the outstanding matters get resolved. I need to talk to my producer to see where we go with the new series. I shan't be needed in London because we've not actually made the first programme yet, so we may have to put things on hold.'

'And then?'

'I'll look to sell the cottage when all the legal affairs are settled. There's a funeral to arrange when the coroner allows it and then there's Richard's estate to sort out. Somehow, I don't think the casino will be coming after me for anything Richard allegedly owed them. Then there's the question of his partnership in the firm. Under the terms of his will, I'll inherit his share. I'll have to make a decision about that. It's not something I can really delay forever. There are legal implications for the other two partners. On the other hand, I spent a great deal of my time with Richard, socialising with his clients and I've got to know some of them very well. Almost like friends. In some ways, I'll miss that.'

'You sound as if you're considering a career change, Sophie,' said Jackie.

'I haven't made up my mind yet, but it certainly beats being shot at or pushed down a London Underground escalator or under a train.'

'Of course, there's a chance you may have to appear as a witness at some point, Sophie,' said Jim. 'That is, unless the defence accepts the case as presented, with Garcia pleading guilty to all charges. That's what I hope will happen but...'

'What about Jonathan Barlborough, or whatever his name is? What will happen to him?'

'No idea. Not our problem. The Fraud Squad've got him and they'll deal with it. I don't think his problems will be linked in with all of ours, luckily.'

His sigh of relief was echoed around the table.

Epilogue

Sophie's phone rang. She checked the number before answering. It was Gerard Dalrymple.

'Hullo Gerry. How are you?'

'More importantly, Sophie, how're you getting on? We've been concerned about you. Life must have been very difficult over the last couple of weeks.'

'I'm fine now, thanks, Gerry. The biggest shock was discovering it was my husband who was trying to have me killed. Not some third party I'd upset in the past. Once I'd mentally processed that, the whole thing became a lot easier for me to handle.'

'I've held off calling you under the circumstances, but we must talk. There are some important issues to discuss following Richard's death. Would you feel up to visiting the office to talk to Roy and me?' There are some pressing legal matters to be resolved in connection with the company, and we need to talk about them urgently. You'll need to involve a lawyer at some stage, but, perhaps we can have a preliminary, informal chat first.'

'I have a pretty good idea what you want to talk about. When would you like me to come up?'

'As soon as possible, please, Sophie. Would tomorrow morning, say, ten-thirty, work for you?

'Fine. I'll be there.'

Tuesday 23ʳᵈ July
Woodchester 8.00 a.m.

Sophie left the Castle Inn for the drive to Headcorn, planning to catch an early train to give herself sufficient time. She had constantly glanced in her rear mirror whilst driving the ten miles to the station, still half afraid that a silver Mercedes 4 x 4 might be following her, but the journey was uneventful. Even the traffic was lighter than usual that morning.

She joined the other commuters on the platform, waiting for the train to London Bridge. She looked around at her fellow travellers and everything seemed as it should be. Her recent experiences travelling up to town were ingrained in her memory. She reasoned she no longer had

225

any cause for concern, but she was still being cautious, although the man responsible for her nervousness was now in police custody.

When the train arrived at London Bridge, she stepped onto the platform, and headed for the escalator down to the station concourse. She had already made the decision to walk over London Bridge, rather than risk another incident in the tube station, although logic told her she was no longer in danger.

At precisely ten-thirty, Sophie walked into the familiar reception area of the Blaxstone Jagger Dalrymple offices in Leadenhall Street. The receptionist, who knew her well, indicated the boardroom door on the other side of the lobby. 'Good morning Mrs Blaxstone. Mr Dalrymple and Mr Jagger are waiting for you.'

Sophie walked through the open door, to be greeted warmly by the two partners.

'Morning Gerry, Morning, Roy. Let's skip the platitudes and any expressions of sympathy you might be considering. The circumstances have forced a dramatic rethink of my personal life, and now I'm ready to face the world.'

Gerry pulled out a chair for Sophie at the boardroom table, and then closed the door. 'Coffee?'

She shook her head. 'No, let's get on with it. I'll hear you first before I share my thoughts with you.'

'Well,' said Roy. 'Richard's death has sent a bit of a shockwave through the company and there's obviously been a lot of comment in the market, not to mention the press, to put it mildly. But then you would know all about that, I'm sure.

Sophie nodded, but said nothing.

The three of us started the company, and we have been its embodiment, soul and ethos ever since. We've always pulled together, concentrated on a single aim and ambition, and it's really worked for us. Now we've lost one of the driving forces and we have to move quickly to restore confidence all round, within the company, in the market, but most importantly, with all our clients.'

'Putting it bluntly, Sophie,' said Gerry, 'we need to be seen to do something positive. I've already sounded out one or two people who might provide the necessary finance.'

'What for, Gerry?' asked Sophie. 'Is the company in financial trouble?'

'Not at all. In fact, things have never been better. Our results for last year have just exceeded any previous year.'

'Then, why's there a need for finance? Come on, Gerry stop tiptoeing around the edges. Say what you mean.'

'OK, Sophie. I need to ask you a question. Did Richard leave a will?'

'Of course. We wrote reciprocal wills when we were married, leaving everything to each other. As far as Richard was concerned, we're in a state of unintended consequences. It's clear now he aimed to grab everything I'd brought to the marriage, in terms of property and finance. But, unfortunately for him, the situation's been reversed. I've now inherited all of his property and investments, including the partnership in this company. He certainly couldn't have seen that coming.'

'That's what we'd expected, and that's why we've been discreetly talking to potential investors. We shall need to arrive at a fair valuation of Richard's share in the company, so that you can be properly compensated when we buy you out. That will require some legal involvement, so we can talk to the company's lawyers about it. You should have quite a windfall coming your way.'

'Wait a minute, Gerry. That presupposes I want to sell. You haven't even asked me the question. A bit quick off the blocks, aren't you?'

'We naturally assumed you would want to remove yourself from something which, with the best will in the world, you know very little about.'

'While it's true I've never worked in your industry, Richard and I did talk a very great deal about our respective careers and, in surprising detail. How else would he have been able to arrange such an intricate plot that enabled him to point the finger at Burtonlee Homes and to divert the police for so long?'

'Richard was always the innovative and imaginative one in the team,' said Roy, making a face. 'But, we never saw a Machiavellian side to him. We just thought he was clever and creative.'

'So, Sophie,' said Gerry, 'precisely what are you trying to tell us?'

'I spent a lot of time with Richard, wining and dining his clients. I got to know them very well. Their business was always discussed whenever we met. I listened and learned. I may not fully understand the intricacies of the market, but I know how it works and I've also got to know quite a few of his underwriting friends. When he still had the apartment in Docklands, it was quite a popular venue to invite them down for drinks, especially in the summer, on the balcony overlooking the river. They used to lap it up. I tried to be more than just a wife, there to entertain any wives, girlfriends or mistresses who turned up. So yes, I got to know quite a few secrets!'

'Where is this leading?' asked Roy.

'I don't intend to sell Richard's holding in the company. I intend to keep it and do what I can in any way to contribute to its continuing success. I shan't want to be paid at this stage. My share of the profits will suffice. That will free up Richard's salary to employ someone of the right ability to pick up the marketing and business development side. I'll be available to meet the clients I know well, and involve myself in their accounts, where it will help.'

Roy and Gerry looked at one another, stunned. This was not what they'd expected.

'It's not just a gravy train, Sophie. We have to work at it every day and there are risks, personal liabilities to consider.'

'I know all about that. Besides, there's only me now. I don't have to worry about liabilities. I've my television career and there's always journalism to fall back on. I was pretty good at it, you know.'

'Have you really thought this through? You already have a busy life.'

'It's all about challenges. I've had quite a few up to this point. Maybe I need something new.'

'OK,' said Roy. 'You seem to have made up your mind. Richard always said you were very determined. Let's talk about practicalities. Whether or not we proceed as you suggest, we still have to find someone from the market to take over Richard's share of the day to day work, for starters. We'll need to talk to a few underwriters to see what names are thrown out, likely candidates. I can think of one guy. Max Ledgerington. He works for a small outfit, Stoddart Shreeves. He took one of my accounts at the back end of last year, the cheeky sod! I think he's probably in his late twenties, maybe thirty, and he's been making a bit of a name for himself lately. He might well be a good fit here. He's young, ambitious and has an eye on the future. And he won't cost us as much as we have in the budget, if Sophie's declining Richard's salary.'

'There's one other thing, Gerry,' said Sophie. 'Richard's Personal Assistant, Jo – she's been very loyal, hardworking, and, most importantly, knows all our major clients. I'd want her job safeguarded. In fact, if I am going to take up Richard's partnership, perhaps she can work for me. She can run the office when I'm not in, keep in touch with Richard's clients and let me know what's going on.'

'Are you absolutely certain you really want a change of career?' asked Gerry. 'If so, there will still be a fair amount of legal paperwork to sort out. You'll need to make yourself available to sign anything the lawyers need.'

'That will be fine, as soon as I've finalised the probate. There's a lot going on, as you can imagine. I'm still waiting for the inquest, and for the coroner to release the body. It's just another thing I've got to deal with. Then there'll be the funeral. I don't intend any public outpouring of grief, under the circumstances, as I'm sure you'll understand. I just need to get it over quietly, no fuss.'

'Who've you got to help?'

'Effectively, there's no one. The Detective Inspector who worked on the case has been helpful, along with his Sergeant. She and I spent a lot of time together when all this started, and have come to know one another quite well. Her boss is a widower, so he knows his way around the probate system. I'm sure he'll be prepared to help me personally, now he's effectively no longer part of the enquiry. It's been passed elsewhere, to the authorities who deal with organised crime - the hitman was employed by them although Richard paid for his services. There's a huge amount of irony about that.'

'Well, if your mind is made up about the company, then there's nothing more to discuss today. Please let us know if there's anything we can do to help you. After all, we've known you a while now, and if you are to become one of the partners here, it's important we all have a good understanding. There's one last thing. If we're all agreed about the way forward, then I'd like to talk to Jo today. She deserves some sort of certainty about her future, and to be given the choice as to whether the new arrangement will suit her.'

'We agree. Let's call her in now and get it over. The fewer problems hanging around, the better it'll be.'

Roy picked up the phone behind him, dialled a number and then spoke. 'Jo, Roy Jagger here. Could you leave whatever you're doing and pop into the boardroom for a moment, please?'

He put the phone down.

'She's on her way.'

Richard's PA knocked and opened the door.

'Close the door and sit down, please.'

Jo looked at Sophie with surprise. 'Good morning, Mrs Blaxstone. I didn't know you were here.'

'Hello, Jo. It's nice to see you.'

Gerry looked at her, thought for a moment, and then said, 'Jo, what is about to be said in this room now is totally confidential at the moment because it involves certain legal issues yet to be resolved. We would expect that you, as Richard's PA, would particularly understand and respect that. We wanted to speak to you as it has implications for your future. Do we have your agreement that what is said today remains in here until such time as the partners decide otherwise?'

'Of course, Mr Dalrymple.'

'We realise life has been particularly difficult for you as Mr Blaxstone's personal assistant since his untimely death, apart from the obvious ramifications for the firm. We want you to know your job here is safe for as long as you want it. Mrs Blaxstone plans to assume her late husband's share in the partnership, and will be joining us, mainly in a consultative and client service role. We would like you to work for her, and run her office, maintaining client contacts, when her other business commitments require her involvement elsewhere. Is that a role that appeals to you? I should tell you this is Mrs Blaxstone's own idea and wish.'

Jo looked astonished. Open mouthed, she looked at each of the partners in turn.

Roy looked at his watch. 'I've got to make a couple of quick phone calls, Gerry. Why don't we leave Jo to talk it over with Mrs Blaxstone, and we'll pop back in a quarter of an hour. The business doesn't stop, you know.'

The two partners left the boardroom, closing the door behind them.

'Mrs Blaxstone, I haven't had a chance to tell you how sorry I am…'

'Jo thanks, but don't even go there. We need to talk about the future. Would you be interested in what Roy and Gerry have proposed? I'm determined to stay in this partnership and make a positive contribution, but I'm going to need a lot of help. I know already how incredibly loyal and supportive you were to Richard. It did you tremendous credit. But, he's no longer here, and the world moves on. Can we work together? I would really like that.'

Jo looked slightly dazed by this sudden turn of events.

'I know how deeply you were involved in the day to day business of the company, and your loyalty to Richard was never questioned. I know how much he appreciated it. But, as you'll realise, we have to move forward. Think of our employees, for example. I believe some of them have been with the company since the beginning. We owe it to them to restore everyone's confidence in us. Do you need some time to think about things? I realise this has been dropped on you without any warning, but we all think this is something that needs to be resolved.'

Jo looked straight at Sophie, thought for a moment, and said 'Mrs Blaxstone, I would be very pleased to carry on, continuing what's been built up. Before you ask the question, I would promise you the same total loyalty I gave your husband. You may rely on my discretion at all times.'

'Good, that's settled then. It starts now, with one important change. Please call me Sophie. We're going to be working closely together from now on and there will be no time for formality. It's exactly how I work in my other career. By the way, that's another issue. There will be a lot of crossing over of interests in the next few weeks and it's just possible you may receive calls from people in my other life, If so, please, tell them you'll pass their messages on to me, I'll try to minimise that, but should it occur, your discretion would be appreciated. In turn, I'll look to you to keep me up to speed with anything from our clients, particularly the ones I've met and know well. If anyone asks any difficult questions, then refer them to Roy or Gerry. What we have discussed here today remains between us until there's an official announcement and press release. If anyone in the office questions why you were called into the boardroom just tell them I asked to see you to talk about some of Richard's outstanding matters. There's a lot of legal stuff to be covered. You need to know we, that's to say, Roy, Gerry and I, will be looking for a younger broker to come in to join our team and eventually carry out Richard's marketing function. I shall lean heavily on Roy and Gerry in the beginning, which I'm sure you appreciate. Any questions from clients or the markets should be referred to Roy and Gerry for the moment. Do we have a deal?'

'Yes, of course. I shall really look forward to working for you... Sophie.' It was difficult for her to say Sophie's name. It felt strange.

'No, Jo, working with me. I assume you have my mobile number amongst Richard's records. You're going to need it, because I can't officially appear in the office until all of the legal paperwork is done, hence the need for absolute discretion in terms of my involvement. There are mountains of paperwork to deal with! Just let me know what's going on, by phone or text. We can talk if necessary so, if you're happy, then we can tell Roy and Gerry, and life can carry on. I've to get back to my other day job now. You can imagine this whole business has had an enormous impact on my life.'

The door opened and Roy and Gerry walked back in.

'All settled, ladies? Good. Now we can all move on to the next phase.'

Sophie said, 'I've explained my situation to Jo, and she will refer everything to you two, but keep me very much in the loop on Richard's clients, particularly the ones I knew personally. I won't take up any more of your time today. I believe we all understand the situation now and are moving forwards. Please keep me up to date with the legal matters. In the meantime, I'll spend some time looking through Richard's office for any personal stuff left there. It will all need to be cleared out. Jo will be able to help me.'

'That's good. We'll leave you to deal with those things and then we'll wait on you so we can progress the legal side,' said Gerry. 'Obviously, we can't make any public announcement until you've dealt with the probate part and have officially acquired Richard's share of the business. The sooner it's resolved, the better, but we all know you can't hurry the legal profession.'

An hour later, having searched through Richard's office and found little of any personal nature, which surprised her, Sophie left the building, clutching a carrier bag containing those pitifully few items and headed for London Bridge on the return journey to Headcorn and the Castle Inn.

Back in her hotel room, she sat on the bed and thought for a moment. She had always been a logical rather than an emotional thinker, but on this occasion, her head and heart had arrived at the same destination. She made her decision and picked up the phone. She scrolled down the directory, selected a number and hit the call button. It rang and was answered immediately.

'Hello, Jim. It's Sophie. I've just got back from my meeting in the City. Are you free later? Yes? Would you like to meet me in the lounge at the Castle? I've made some very important decisions today and I need to share them with you as they'll affect our futures….Good. I'll see you, about six, then?'

CRIME FICTION FROM APS BOOKS
(www.andrewsparke.com)

Fenella Bass: *Hornbeams*
Fenella Bass:: *Shadows*
Fenella Bass: *Darkness*
HR Beasley: *Nothing Left To Hide*
TF Byrne *Damage Limitation*
J.W.Darcy *Looking For Luca*
J.W.Darcy: *Ladybird*
J.W.Darcy: *Legacy Of Lies*
Milton Godfrey: *The Danger Lies In Fear*
Chris Grayling: *A Week Is…A Long Time*
Tony Rowland: *Traitor Lodger German Spy*
Andrew Sparke: *Abuse Cocaine & Soft Furnishings*
Andrew Sparke: *Copper Trance & Motorways*

Lightning Source UK Ltd.
Milton Keynes UK
UKHW021323130123
415302UK00022B/645